BLURB

Since the Slaughterhouse Rout, Daniel has nursed his abilities, but the decision he faces will change his life and those of everyone around him.
Whether the change is positive or not remains to be seen.
Cressida fears that history will repeat itself. Once before she lost everything she held dear, but after centuries of hiding she must face her past in order to forge a new future.
Has she waited too long and pushed Daniel away too well?

The darkness draws closer... How will it end?

<u>**The Blood Secrets Series**</u>

The Blood Bride - October 2020
The Illuminated Witch - November 2020
The Sorcerer's Touch - December 2020

THE SORCERER'S TOUCH

Blood Secrets Book 3

Imogene Nix

Many years have now passed since I wrote this story. It feels like I've waited forever for the rights to revert back to me. I first requested them back in 2017, and it does seem like forever!

Of course, 2020 has been such a strange year, that everything feels like it's been a lifetime. I hope you've stayed well during this time.

Back to the matter at hand, though. Here we are, releasing the new version and I have to say, I feel that it's a better and brighter story for the change in edits and the tweaking that's gone on.

As always, I must thank my supporters, who have stood by me, patiently waited for this title to re-release. Naming them all individually would be impossible, so I'll simply say:

Edits : Sassie Lewis

Cover Art: Tara from Fantasia Frog

My team of readers, friends and family.

The journey ends here
Among tears and sleepless nights
The shadow of failure and success on a knife edge
Ever present
My companion at all times
But in the darkness comes a truth
Where we can only do our best

Thank you for joining me on this journey.

Imogene Nix
2020

ONE

The crackle of firelight played over the features of the three women. They were so different—one small and dark-haired, perched in the high-back armchair she preferred. The redhead favored a boudoir chair; her legs crossed at her ankles and a book resting on her lap.

The third woman chose to reclined in a new armchair after insisting it sit in the center of the room. She'd raised the footrest and pushed the back to recline so it cradled her body, as she twined her blonde strands idly.

Now that the nights were cooling, they had gathered in their chairs gazing at the fire, seeking warmth.

"You know, I never expected it to get to this point." Jemima, the youngest, rubbed her eyes. "That we'd have to...*interfere* so much!"

"They don't seem to be the most...organized group of people. But the prophecy is quite clear." Selena settled more deeply into her seat. Around her, the other two women groaned. She glanced at her sisters and gave a slight smile. "The prophecy has been the only thing that has given us hope over the years, sisters. Do not discount it."

"We aren't, but to be honest, after all these centuries and false starts, how can we be sure that *this time* it will work? I mean, we've found *some* who could be the ones to end the curse, but never have there been all six with strong enough skills at the right time. Together."

"I know that, sister." Selena rested her hand on Jemima's arm. "But we must be strong a little longer. This time I'm sure—"

"Like before?" Selena smiled at Danicka's prickly comment. Danicka was always tense when she needed to recharge herself.

"Previously we couldn't move quickly. Most humans didn't believe in vampires, or at least they considered them demons. It was imperative that we stayed hidden or we would have ended up like the women in Salem. We all know how badly that went." Nods around the room indicated agreement. "This time... It's nothing like before. I feel it in my bones."

"You're sure?" Jemima sounded uncertain, and Selena itched to bring forth a vision of how it would be. If only she could, but there were limitations to her powers.

"I remember last time we sat around the fire like this, and we each decided who our charges were. I knew back then." Silence met her words, and Selena was sure they considered her words. Looking for anything that seemed wrong. Seeking problems. *Let them do so. That will only make our work stronger. Give us a greater chance of success.*

"Let's hope you're right, Selena. Because Danicka and I have done all we can. Now it is in your hands." Jemima's voice shook and Selena understood her fears. She too carried them, but if she let her worries take ascendency now, the battle would be lost before it could be won.

"Take heart, my sisters. This time I feel the power that the three exude." And she did—it washed over her—filled her with light and hope.

"I just hope that we can find him." Jemima frowned, the creasing of her brow a stark contrast to her youthful features.

"Already done, my sisters." They gaped at her and she smiled.

"Why, Daniel is just about dripping with power. I'd never felt it before, but it occurs to me he needed something to help unlock it. That battle in the animal house...the meat house... What did they call it?"

Danicka grimaced. "Slaughterhouse."

"Yes. The explosion of magic coursed clear and strong after the skirmish. He's aware of it and wants to learn how to harness it." Selena tapped her finger against her pursed lips. "Now all we have to do is give his partner a push in the right direction."

"Whoever she may be," Danicka muttered.

"Yes, well, she's proving more than a little difficult."

Her sisters goggled. "You've seen...?"

The witch smiled widely. "Oh yes. I've foreseen them. Now if I could snap my fingers and make it so..."

Selena reclined into the soft padding of her chair. *If only I could make it so.* But the human and vampire had to come together of their own choice. They had to be the ones to decide. No amount of pushing or prodding would work. After all, Cressida was too strong a personality to accept gentle nudges.

Selena focused on the fire dancing in front of her, and as she did, her worries slipped away and sleep claimed her.

ATTAR'S SLAVES WERE GONE. IT HAD BEEN DAYS SINCE HIS flight from the place of his warriors' defeat. The trek through the wilderness had angered him and stole the last reserves of his energy.

A light glimmered, shining through the gloom ahead. He cocked his head, listened, and, hearing little in the way of humans, headed in its direction. Dawn drew near and he'd need shelter soon.

For the last few days he'd been a fugitive, slaking his thirst with the blood of animals. But animal blood wasn't sufficient to sustain him for long. He gagged, remembering the game like taste that had nauseated him. Not for the first time, he thought longingly of the cells, filled with humans, their veins pumping with life-sustaining and gloriously unspoiled blood. "There will be shelter ahead."

Where there was artificial light, he knew he'd find humans. Sounds of engines had kept him hiding far longer than he'd wanted, but in this confusing age, caution had ensured he was still alive.

At the end of the settlement, he stilled. The structure's walls were metallic and stank of age, human sweat and exertion. He hadn't lived for so long that he'd forgotten the most basic of cautions. Attar flattened himself against the wall, not for the first time cursing those who'd meddled with his plans.

A quick look within showed him there was only one person—one human. He smiled, inhaled deeply and let the slow pumping of the human's heart fill his senses.

He thanked the stars that this building, in the middle of nowhere, seemed otherwise deserted. He had a choice—slake his thirst and leave the carcass behind, or take enough to sustain him and change the human.

His eyes narrowed as he chanced another glance around the corner of the doorway. He seemed healthy enough. Young and strong. In that instant, the decision was made.

On silent feet Attar advanced, sneaking within the tiny ramshackle building.

The human never heard him.

The bite was quick. Efficient. The human struggled initially, then Attar felt his power surge, returning with a rush.

The final trembling heartbeat dragged his senses back. With a savage twist, he withdrew his fangs, then slashed his wrist.

Thrusting it to the human's lips, he chanted, "Drink now! Drink deep and be one with me."

The human, unable to ignore the demand, fastened his mouth over the weeping gash in Attar's arm. He latched on and drew hard, like a babe suckling at the breast.

The cycle began anew.

TWO

Daniel sighed as he slumped in the seat, cradling his head in his hand. His eyes ached from the hours of squinting at the figures on the table in front of him. They'd started swimming up and down in the last hour, but he was determined to push through. To complete the task he'd set himself.

"You should rest, Daniel. You're tired." He gazed up as his half-sister entered his office.

"I wish. There's just so much..." His tired shrug left her frowning.

"But you told Javed things were going well." Celina stepped farther into the room, the crackling firelight playing over her red hair.

"They are, but with the expansion of the nest... There's much to think of and plan for. Contingencies to put in place." Budgets, forward planning, reporting both to the Council and the government, the list ran through his head like a reel-to-reel tape. With no form of administrative assistance, the workload seemed never-ending. If only he had time to find an office and hire staff. Until recently, he'd argued against the extra expenses. Then things had shifted gears. Needs he'd thought able to wait until the future could no longer be avoided.

Each task had a looming due date, complicating matters no end.

Celina smiled, the wide corners of her mouth extending upward. She rounded the table and laid a gentle hand on his shoulder, kneading it for a moment before stepping away. "I have good news for you."

Daniel rolled his shoulders, hoping to release the tension that had taken up residence in muscles that were tightly bunched. "And what would that be?"

"We've decided you need a personal assistant. In fact, Javed says you need a team to work with you, so you don't have to do everything. We've found office space nearby and he's planning on joining you to inspect it tomorrow evening. It just won't be available for at least eight weeks, but it should be more than adequate." The triumph in her voice lifted his flagging spirits. "As for staff... I'm going to begin the process of recruitment tomorrow. Hopefully that will take some pressure off you."

"Really?" He ruthlessly chained the buoyant mood that rose inside him. Until a lease was signed and they'd moved into the new work area, he wouldn't celebrate—not yet, anyway. As for hiring others to assist him? The thought of it released a flood of endorphins. The nest was prospering after months of hard work and effort. The manufacturing plant was finally online and they'd begun to sort out distribution channels for the various blood-related products that would financially sustain the nest. Everything took time, and after months of working long days and nights, he could finally see a future for the House.

"Yes. Now, as the consort of the Master, I'm ordering you to finish up your work for the night. Besides which, I wanted to see you. It seems like we are always busy and don't get to sit down and just connect."

It was true. With the threat to the nests from Attar, their main roles were incompatible right now. While Celina trained to use her magic, and learned to fight, he'd been working on stabilizing their financial situation.

"I see the girls are doing well."

Celina beamed at him. "They are." Since the attack on the slaughterhouse, Celina and Javed had formed a strong bond with the girls they'd rescued. They'd grown so close that she and Javed had adopted them. "Lucy is doing really well with her magic studies. She has a lot more power than any of us suspected. Rachel and Marian are both showing an aptitude for math, though they don't seem to have an ounce of any otherworldly skills. Javed and I hope they will wish to learn about management. But we aren't going to push them into anything. They've had a hard start and we want them to explore the opportunities they now have."

He hesitated for a second as her gaze narrowed on him. He glanced away, to the photos of his adopted nieces. "They're great kids."

"Daniel?"

"I've been thinking about what the women—the witches—suggested after you were turned. They said the three. They meant you, Hope...and *me*."

"Or Hope, David and me." Celina studied him, as if looking for a hint of what he was thinking. "We really can't be sure of anything. I know they said—"

"They were so certain. Selena, Danicka and Jemima... They said you..."

"They could be wrong." Celina shook her head, as if dismissing his words.

He'd have to tread carefully here, otherwise she'd latch on to his plans.

"They're old, Daniel. Ancient. Like anyone, they're capable of mistakes. Probably more prone to them because of their age." She wiped her hand over her forehead.

The cold ball of fear in his stomach grew, while his mouth dried. "I-I need you to arrange for me to see a training witch." He wanted to shy away from her gaze, but even though his stomach wobbled a little, he met her stare.

Her face blanked and he squirmed further. "Why?"

"I need to see one." He held out a hand. In his mind, he commanded the well of magic that he'd hidden from her.

A tiny flicker of light appeared, dancing over his palm. He knew exactly what he was doing. The magic wanted to be used. To be shared and shaped. "I'm not a warlock. At least I don't think so. I don't have the problems you had. I can control what I have, it's just... I think it's been dormant. It's... The need to use it has grown since Attar's awakening. I've been making a point of accessing it. Using it. It's getting easier every day."

Her face paled. "Oh my God." She staggered to a chair and slumped into it. "Why didn't you ever say...?"

"Because I didn't know what I had. Just that I had this thing—power—inside me. Sometimes in the past, stuff would happen, but I never made the connection that it was magic. Since the slaughterhouse, it's been there, and I became aware slowly at first... I'm too old for traditional testing. I've been reading about it, but I remember how you had to learn control. I know how it built up inside you until it was nearly too late. I realized instead of ignoring it, I had to use it. I asked my father about those sorts of things, but he dismissed it. According to him, if I was going to show an aptitude, someone would have picked it up long ago." He shrugged. *How do I explain that I'd kept that knowledge hidden?* "I didn't tell anyone. Not until now."

"But if you're not a warlock, what the hell are you?" She stared at him and he grimaced.

"I have no idea. I mean, yes, I can control power and I'm male, which should make me a warlock. Yet what I do feels different from you and all the other witches and warlocks of my acquaintance because I don't need words. It's instinctual, I think."

"I also think if there's some ability in David, then he should be tested as well," Javed muttered.

Celina shook her head. "No. Hope and I discussed that. He's a null. He was tested at thirteen. There isn't an ounce of magic in him."

He grimaced. "And yet... I guess I'm it, Celina. The only one who can be the third."

THREE

Attar smiled as his latest creation woke from the change slumber. "You will call me master and I will teach you to embrace immortality."

The woman before him smiled, the points of her needle-sharp teeth flashing. "I thirst." Her eyes shone a muddy black in the half-light.

"I will feed you." He tore into his own wrist and waited as droplets of scarlet blood dribbled into her open mouth.

She arched up, seeking more, but he held it away so she had to hunt like a baby rooting for a nipple.

"Soon. First you must swear yourself to me, that you will be my warrior and serve me faithfully in all things." In his mind, the memory of Jelani, flashed. Jelani, his long-term servant of centuries, had failed him, as had all his previous servants. It mustn't happen again. This time he'd bind them to his will.

"I do." She crooned the words, searching for the blood, but he held his arm away from her reach.

"Swear it."

"I-I swear. Anything. I'll serve you."

"You'll serve me faithfully?" He impressed the words on the servant's mind, the magic that bound maker and servant thrumming through him.

The woman bared her shiny white fangs. "I will serve you faithfully." She moved, as if pain lanced her body. He knew then that she was bound to him irrevocably. Attar smiled with satisfaction before he gave in to her needs. With a quick move he slashed the newly sealed skin, sending forth a gush of red liquid, which he offered her.

She latched on and fed deeply as Attar sighed with pleasure, his body moving in the sexual rhythm he'd rediscovered. He would indulge his body. Arousal filled him, warmth flashing through his veins. He'd not felt such pleasure in centuries.

Attar stared down at his servant. She'd been chosen to meet his physical needs. The best of those he'd stolen from the small settlement. She was tall and willowy with long golden-blonde hair, reminding him of the woman he'd seen in the feeding facility when Jelani had been neutralized. The other woman had been tall and graced with firm, high breasts. He wondered dimly if he could somehow encourage her to join him, before the urgent reminder of his pleasure stole that thought.

FOUR

The words on the parchment, found before the slaughterhouse rescue, ebbed and flowed before her tired eyes. Cressida sighed and let her gaze drift back to the wooden desk. "There must be more. Javed, you said you and Celina scoured the ancient texts? You've found nothing so far?"

Javed slumped into a deep chair in front of her. The exhaustion that pulled at her was also clear on his face, in both pallor and his red, tired eyes. "We did. There were a few notations here and there, but nothing substantive. I'm not so sure that there's anything more for us here, not now that we know how long he's been around. All we found was a list of other vampires Attar courted. When we dug deeper and contacted their last known locations, most had died. The few who survived..." Javed gave a slow shake of his head. "Well, we didn't find any useful information. There is no one single location he frequented that works. No hidey-holes or contacts. An exhaustive search of nests on this continent also came up empty. We could try overseas, but that request needs to happen at your level."

Cressida cursed. She would need to contact her overlord, something she was wary of.

Instead, Cressida considered the small amount of information they had gleaned. Since the Slaughterhouse Rout, as it was now named, Attar had disappeared from view. No matter how hard they searched, they had been spectacularly unsuccessful in tracking his movements. If she didn't know better, she'd claim he'd used some kind of magical veil to hide his tracks. The sigh that rose in her chest was ruthlessly contained. They knew the one servant he'd relied on was dead. So how had he managed to evade them?

He teased them, every now and again leaving a body for them to discover. No doubt he found it amusing, watching them scurrying fifteen steps behind him. By the time they'd found his leavings, he'd moved on. The evidence of his movements, though, wasn't the total sum of murders they would attribute to him. That she could be sure of.

Cressida bit her lip. He'd accessed assistance, and clearly the humans Attar had tapped were highly connected economically, politically or socially. But who would choose to associate with him, and why? For that matter, had they done these things of their own free will? The questions plagued her day and night.

They already knew he'd harvested several from the upper echelons of the business world—there'd been a CEO of a major technology firm, a senator and several local elected members among the many. They'd found the remains. At least one socialite had joined his ranks, as she'd been detected helping him gain access to other, more powerful persons. Entrée wasn't an issue for him any longer. He now had powerful allies.

One of his latest victims was a politician from Australia, who'd disappeared from an official function just over a month ago in New York. They'd located the withered cadaver in the deserted downtown area, amid slums.

"We need to find his source of assistance." She stalked the length of the room.

"We could try to scry him again," Celina mumbled. But they'd tried that several times, quite unsuccessfully.

"No. At this point there wouldn't be any appreciable difference. Nothing has changed." She balled her fist, her nails biting into the flesh of her hand.

"I'm not so sure." Celina's words stopped Cressida in her tracks.

"Just what do you mean by that?" She swung fast, the heel of her boot catching in the loop of the carpet. If not for her speed, she would have toppled.

"Well, I was talking to Daniel today..."

Cressida narrowed her eyes on the new vampire, whom had bound her life to Javed. "And?"

Javed shrugged. "Celina tells me he's arranged a series of sessions with a training witch. She organized it for him. Someone who might be able to...to work out what powers he possesses."

"Powers?" The very word froze her bones to the marrow. "He doesn't have..." She breathed deeply. She'd never detected any powers in him, and if he had some, she would have felt it. *Wouldn't I?*

The uncharacteristic questioning of her abilities leaked through a chink in her personal defences. Was she losing her ability to lead? Was that the reason they'd not found Attar?

With difficulty, she shoved the negativity aside and focused on conjuring an image of Daniel. Tall and broad-shouldered, with red hair and piercing green eyes. He'd caught her attention so many times in the past, but she didn't dally with humans. If she did, well, he'd likely be the one she made an exception for.

He was also Celina's half-brother. The thought pulled her up sharply. "Tell me more."

"Since the rout in the slaughterhouse, he's had these urges, I guess you'd call them. *He has magic.* But"—Celina raised an unsteady hand—"it doesn't feel like mine. In fact, I don't read it at all." Celina shuddered. "I can sense everyone else's. Maybe not pinpoint what it is or how it works, but with Daniel I can't. It's like it's not there. Yet I've seen him work magic."

Cressida narrowed her eyes. "You're sure he has magic?

"He showed me. Conjured up a flame. Without any incantation." Celina shrugged, her eyes shadowed.

Cressida considered her words. Witches wrought magic using the power of words and will. It bent the powers to their needs. So how could this be? It defied everything they presently knew.

"One second it wasn't there, then it was. He made it dance, Cressida, right across his palm. Even so, I felt no change in the air." Clearly shaken by what she'd seen, Celina wiped her hand over her face in a slow and unsteady motion.

She leaned closer to the young witch mated to Javed. "You're sure he didn't say a word? Didn't invoke any god or goddess?" Her stomach trembled wildly. *Can this possibly be true? Is this some missing piece of the puzzle?*

"Not a sound. Why is that do you think?" Cressida grabbed the other woman's hand, then scanned the Celina's memories.

"If what you are saying and I'm seeing is right, there is something more happening here. I can't—" She broke off, unsure how to explain her concerns. If that was the case, they needed assistance. Guidance.

Their experiences with Hope and now Celina told her they'd need to find his partner. That his power could possibly grow... He'd be a target if Attar ever learned of his powers.

She shied away from that thought because if she faced it, she'd have to embrace the emotions she'd buried. Ones that made her question the decisions she'd taken. That wasn't an option.

FIVE

They were sitting in the office when the phone beeped.
"Yes?"

"Sir, the Master has requested that you turn on the screen."

Daniel frowned. He rarely received such summons, and they never came in the middle of the day.

He groped for the remote on his desk as the line disconnected.

"Reports of an incursion by the rogue vampire captain known only as Attar have been streaming in all night." On the screen, in the distance, he could see thick plumes of smoke rising over a city.

"Let's cross to our reporter on the scene for more information. James, what can you tell us of the attack?"

"Sally, this building is owned by one of the smaller nests in Brisbane..."

As Daniel watched, the burn inside his gut rose. He gripped the edge of the wooden desk tight.

"A spokeswoman from the nest has indicated that upward of one hundred and fifty people, including young children, lived here. The emergency personnel have so far declined to comment on the situation, but people around me..."

The screen changed to the serious-looking newsreader in the studio. Her studied look of concern felt to him at odds with the immaculate blonde hair and youthful looks. *"Is there any update on the inhabitants?"*

"Sally, the authorities hold grave fears for those who live in the building. The action that took place tonight was unbelievable. We're hearing unconfirmed reports of up to one hundred combatants involved in the attack. As you can see, what is left is a smoking hulk, and the cordon around the building extends for several blocks in all directions..."

What would Javed request of them in light of this unprovoked attack? People? Funds? Warriors?

"...There you have it, Sally. People here are concerned for their safety. This is exactly what we are finding worldwide, with people airing concerns that vampires are dangerous, bloodthirsty and evil. The move to control their population and segregate them continues to gather impetus. Whether it's right or wrong, though, remains to be decided by the people and the legislators. Back to you, Sally."

Daniel flicked off the television before the young reporter could respond. He lifted the receiver he'd replaced and dialed Javed directly at the house.

The question was immediate. "You watched it?"

"I did. It's disturbing that in the last twelve months we've gone from unknown solitude to this. Attar has a lot to answer for." He gripped the handset and waited out the prolonged silence.

"They need resources over there, but we must ensure that we don't leave ourselves financially stretched. As yet, we don't have warriors or nestlings to spare. Run the numbers and let me know what we can do."

"I will, but, Javed, we should do more. Something tangible to dampen the growing concerns." He cleared his throat, wondering how to raise the next topic. "Did..." He paused, sucking in his breath. "Did Celina talk to you about—?"

"Finding you a training witch? She did. When we come home

tomorrow, we'll discuss it. Celina thought maybe we could talk to Lucy's teacher."

Daniel released the pent-up breath he'd not realized he'd been holding. "Good. That's fine then. Look, I'll get onto those figures now and—"

"Daniel?" Javed's question stopped him.

"Yes?"

"We've informed Cressida."

In his mind rose a vision of a blonde amazon of a woman. Tall and lithe, with golden hair shot with silver—a woman of both innate grace and immense power. He swallowed carefully, giving himself a moment to think before he spoke again. "What was her response?"

"It raises more questions than it answers, and I agree with her assessment. Come to my office when we arrive home. I'll be waiting for those figures." It took Daniel a moment to realize the buzzing sound in his ear was the disconnect signal.

Even as he carefully laid the receiver back in its cradle, his stomach churned.

Nothing would ever be the same again.

The gardens were calming, and Cressida desperately needed an interlude between the madness of a day without rest and the meeting that lay ahead. The Masters of all the nests, their *Yeux Secondes* and various advisors were sure to guarantee arguments before the meeting concluded.

The sound of tires on the gravel told her that another batch of representatives had arrived. If only the way forward was clear. But in the year since Attar had awoken, nothing had been easy and certainly anything that could have been construed as settled no longer existed.

She stilled, inhaling deeply, letting the scent of flowers in full bloom fill her. For just a moment she sought and found solitude and peace.

Searching for her inner balance as the head of the Council was a luxury, and now, in the middle of this war—for that was what she equated this to—the safety of the nests under her protection was her primary objective.

Soft footfalls dragged away the pretense of solitude. She refused to turn for an instant as her insides quivered and nerves jumped. On a visceral level, she *knew* who stood behind her.

"Yes?" She turned slowly and accepted the truth in what she'd divined. In front of her was Daniel. Javed's *Yeux Secondes*.

He gave a formal bow before cocking his head slightly to the side. "Master Javed requests that I let you know we are only awaiting the representatives from the Tudor House. Master Xavier and Hope have been delayed as their new *Yeux Secondes* arrived to take up his position, leaving the House representatives behind schedule. However, they have contacted us and should be here in about ten minutes."

"Ahh... I have a few more minutes." She gazed at the human in front of her, not for the first time questioning her decision never to consort with human males. "Walk with me, Daniel."

The disconcerted look on his face would have been comical if it hadn't hurt deep in her chest. "Of course, Councilor."

The steady thud of his heart sped up as he moved closer, and it was difficult to ignore the sound as it tugged at her senses. The primal connection between them fed her hunger, her gums aching with the need to bare her fangs. She ignored the urge, knowing that such a carnal act would only increase their difficulties. As it was, they treated each other with extreme care and caution.

For an instant, she wondered if he too felt the stirrings. She gave an agitated flick of her wrist, banishing the dangerous thoughts.

"Tell me how things are going at the nest. It's been a year since the investiture." Cressida received regular reports, but rarely was there an opportunity to talk to anyone about the growth prospects and financial stability. Right now, every moment was consumed with defeating Attar.

"We have made tremendous strides, Councilor—"

"Cressida." She stopped and turned to look at him. There was a mixture of confusion and something else she refused to name on his face.

"Councilor—"

A seed of emotion, almost devilry, invaded her. "My name is Cressida. *Say it, Daniel.*"

Turmoil churned in his gaze, but he nodded. "Very well, Cressida. We have made excellent progress and the production of the blood-based products has been successful. Thanks must go to the Council for the generous seed grant we received. We hope to turn a profit by the end of the financial year. As to the nest, I believe we should have repaid that loan well within the guidelines stipulated."

Cressida gave a small nod. She had expected nothing less since Daniel had taken over.

He was a dichotomy. Softly spoken, yet with a will of pure iron. He had taken on a new nest in trying circumstances. He'd guided Javed's decisions and led them into this position where their financial stability would soon be assured. In tough economic times, it was no mean feat.

She vacillated. There were other questions, other things she needed to know. "Magic. You have it, yet kept that secret." She avoided looking at him now.

"No. Yes. Not purposely."

She made a sound that was reminiscent of a growl, dismissing his half-truth. That would have to be dealt with later. "Show me."

He blinked at her order, then thrust out a hand. There in his palm lay a tiny rose. With a small bow, he held it out to her. The touch of his fingertips gently brushing her hand, had her senses leaping and energized her. She burned where they touched.

Her gaze wavered a little. Her heart beat a little faster in her chest and she wanted to... She snapped out of the cloud of introspection. "When did you know...?"

"After the slaughterhouse. I didn't know, had no concept that I could do something like this. After the rout it was there and I..." From the corner of her eye she saw him shrug. "I honestly don't know what to say. It wasn't until then and I needed to talk to Celina—"

"You should have made disclosure." He flushed and she turned in his direction, needing to read his face. "It isn't a secret you can keep, not now, when we need everything, every tool to defeat Attar."

"Cressida, I couldn't tell you because I didn't know..." He stepped forward, and his scent invaded her senses, heady and male.

"But you told Celina?" A small seed of hurt, the one she'd buried during Celina's briefing, raised its head. It made no sense, she was so far removed from day-to-day interaction with Daniel. Yet the pain remained.

"She's my sister."

In a quick move, Cressida turned her back to him. It wasn't quite a dismissal, she rationalized, but time marched on and the meeting was due to start soon. "We should go in now."

For a moment he remained still. The burn of his gaze cut through her and she wondered if he could read minds, then loosed a sigh.

This wasn't the time or the place, and Daniel wasn't—couldn't—be the man to change her ways now.

"Is that all you wanted to talk to me about?" His words came from her shoulder. Close... Too close for comfort.

"Of course it was." They remained still, while inside her the hunger she battled to bank roared to life.

"Fine."

Cressida waited as Daniel turned away, then tried to block out the sound of feet on gravel. She failed.

CRESSIDA HADN'T TOLD HIM EVERYTHING THAT SHE WAS thinking, he was sure of it. Over the years, he'd learned to read people's reactions. Right now that intuitive radar was buzzing off the scale. Of course, it could be because he found her intensely attractive. Her golden hair and wide, generous mouth, her sapphire eyes and cool demeanor intrigued him. He felt sure there was more to it than that, though.

Now, as she stalked into the room, her eyes held a frigid quality. Sometime between their brief discussion and this very moment, something had upset her. He wanted to soothe her and had to work hard to distract himself from the overwhelming emotion of cold fury. It was surprising and unsettling to realize that his *interest* in her delved to such deep levels.

Cressida took a moment to look over the attendees in the room, her presence commanding as she waited for silence to descend.

"Thank you for coming on such short notice. As you know, our Australian friends have been under attack, their nests facing annihilation and their human partners slaughtered. This morning I received a request for assistance through our Overlord, Gianna." As her eyes roamed the room once again, he could feel the cool wind of her glance. Those gathered in the house clearly found it unnerving, as more than one person flinched.

"Now, I understand the situation is difficult. I am aware of the financial constraints many of you face. I'm aware that giving such support to our brothers and sisters could leave us open to similar attacks. We must prepare, as we know this is not the first, nor is it likely to be the last, such attack. It is clear Attar has amassed a band of followers to wage war for him. My fear is that with the strength of his forces growing, we are going to be overrun."

Now Daniel looked at the vampires and their *Yeux Secondes* nods. They watched and waited, some whispering among themselves, but Daniel didn't detect any note of disagreement.

"Even so, we must help our brothers and sisters. The scourge of Attar must be checked." Javed spoke clearly and Daniel, seated to his left, watched heads swivel their way.

Cressida's eyes glittered in the low light. "Indeed we must. My concern is that we don't endanger our own nests while doing so."

Daniel surged up out of the seat he'd been filling during the meeting. "As much as this is of import, we also need to address the other issues, Councilor." When Cressida turned her gaze on him, he had to check the breathlessness that assailed him.

"And they would be?" Her tone was glacial and he grimaced.

"On the public relations front we've failed. It is imperative that we promote both vampires and nests as peaceful. Since we've been outed, the growth of ill feeling and outright anger against our lifestyle has increased, and I'm only talking in the last twelve months. Since the rout, businesses have actively avoided dealing with the nests and the humans who serve them. People refuse to acknowledge nestlings, and this has flowed through to schools, medical facilities and so much more. For those of us who serve, our very way of life as humans has been endangered just as much as that of our vampires."

An audible gasp spread through the room at his provocative words, but as much as some were professing shock, he spoke only what others had been thinking. He knew many of his peers had spoken quietly of these things. "Something must give."

"Indeed, Daniel. Then perhaps you have a plan to deal with this?"

He squirmed at Cressida's tone.

He had no idea what he'd done to deserve such derision from her, or how her attitude toward him had soured since they'd talked in the garden. "Not yet, Councilor, but with your permission, perhaps myself and my peers could construct some kind of campaign to address this?"

"Fine. Do so. Report back to me as soon as possible." His dismissal was clear, so he gave a sharp, deep bow and resumed his seat.

For the rest of the meeting, he watched and listened, but he refused to speak again.

SIX

Cressida detested contacting the witches' Conclave, but with the news of Daniel's powers there was no help for it.

Even as she reached for the phone, her stomach pitched. There was an unwritten rule that a vampire did not change a witch without the consent of the Conclave, yet Celina's turn had been the only thing that would save her life. Something the Matron—the woman who headed the Conclave—refused to accept with equanimity.

After the fiasco with Celina, and her change, there had been a distinct frostiness to the relationship between the head of the magical community known as the Conclave and the Council. In fact, it had taken a lot of promises and hard work to encourage them to continue their diplomatic collaboration.

There was a chance this encounter might make things worse—something she wished she could avoid.

The line rang several times before she heard the answering click.

"Councilor, to what do I owe this dubious pleasure? You are about to turn another of our kind? Or maybe you need our assistance with securing your nests?" The sickly sweet tones of the Matron set Cressida's teeth on edge.

Be calm, and above all, courteous.

"Matron, I am ringing you to make you aware of a member of one of our nests. He's a magic wielder, but I'm not sure—"

"Then he would be one of ours. We will require him to relocate —" The woman spoke in rapid-fire, and Cressida raised her hand to her already aching brow.

She'd hoped to be pleasant to the woman on the other side of the line. Obviously the Matron wasn't reading from the same song sheet. Every conversation she'd had with Elena, the new Matron, since their run-in had left her in the same state.

"Well, that's where the problem lies. You see—"

"No." The woman interrupted again and Cressida ground her teeth together. "I don't care what problem *you* might be imagining. The magical belong to the Conclave. You will surrender him immediately." The words were cold and demanding.

"He's not got normal magic. And he's a *Yeux Secondes*, so I cannot hand him over, as you are aware. That is why I am contacting you personally. One of your people, or you, Matron, will wish to come here and assess the situation."

For a second there was silence on the line, then it was broken by a hiss. She could almost see the woman glaring at her, eyes narrowed.

Another second ticked by and Cressida curled her hands into fists, ready to battle for the livelihood of the new nest if necessary. She knew, too, that she also battled for Daniel.

"Very well. However, Councilor, you will make preparations to surrender him to his peers with all due speed once I have undertaken his evaluation, and a replacement has been found. Expect me there tomorrow." With those words, the line cut off and Cressida raised her aching head, then pushed up from her seat.

Stalking from one side to the other of her office didn't dampen the anger that roiled inside her. A knock on the door stopped her and she spun to face it just as it opened.

Samra, her second and guard, entered the room. "So it's done?"

Cressida nodded without a word, knowing Samra would pick up

on her frustration. They'd been friends for a long time, and when Cressida had assumed her position on the Council, she'd requested that the female warrior join her.

"You know dealing with the Conclave is difficult, particularly when it relates to a *Yeux Secondes*. But that isn't the full explanation for why you're in here nearly burning with anger and have a splitting headache."

Cressida glared at Samra, who stood inside the door.

"Oh, for heaven's sake, Cressida. You've been watching him like a glass of fine blood wine since you met him. Why not take him as a lover? Get it over and done with."

"Do you honestly think I haven't considered that?" She rose, anger vibrating in her veins. "But I won't. I don't take human lovers."

"Then find a vampire who you can—"

"No." The thought soured her stomach and she turned away, unable to face even the thought of another touching her.

"Fine." Samra hissed and advanced into the room. Cressida sensed steps and moved to stand behind her desk, reinforcing that the discussion was complete.

"So when are they due to arrive?" Samra's voice carried an understanding that nearly tore the emotions from her chest.

"Tomorrow." She choked out the words and placed her fingers on the glass of the window before her. "Leave me."

For a moment there was only silence. Then, "As you wish." The door closed behind Samra. Cressida loneliness assailed her. *If only...*

DANIEL WATCHED THE GARDENS FLASH BY AS HE GAZED OUT OF the window. They'd arrived, the driver steering through the imposing gates before the car purred up the long drive while he'd been lost in thought.

The house before him glowed like a beacon in the night—one

he'd rather be passing by, he thought with frustration. Or visiting so he could come to terms with the enigma that was the Councilor.

Inside was Cressida. He'd dreamed of her the night before. All golden skin and luscious curves he'd run shaking hands over. The warmth he'd experienced suffused him again.

"Get your head in the game, Daniel." But, as with every other time he'd told himself that, it made no difference. He'd woken in the wee hours, aroused, his body bow-tight and aching.

He wanted her—and that wasn't nearly a strong enough worded description of the burn deep inside him. Every time she was near, since he'd first laid eyes on her, his reaction tore at him, demanding not just his attention but also his total concentration. His body reacted with more than an adrenaline surge every time she looked at him, but the hunger of his body and the way he felt this soul deep connection. Never before had he responded to a woman so totally. It wasn't just sexual. He felt a need to protect her too. And wasn't that plain crazy given she was a Mistress Vampire, both old and strong enough to break him?

He'd first met her in the house meet and greet, where he'd merely been a contender for the position of *Yeux Secondes* in Javed's house. A nestling without a future. Since then, he'd seen her on a regular basis. Each time the flame of need grew hotter and more demanding. If he didn't do something to quell his hunger soon, he was sure the conflagration would devour him.

The car pulled up outside the house and he inhaled deeply. He'd need all his wits for the interview that lay ahead with the Matron and the Councilor.

The door creaked as he opened it and stepped out. "Best done quickly, Daniel." He hastened toward the door, but before he could knock it opened to admit him.

"Come in, Master Daniel. Cressida is awaiting you in the Council Room." Samra, Cressida's second, indicated the large oak door ahead. Copper spikes stood proud and he smiled at the sight, as he always did. Only a vampire like Cressida would have a door impregnated with a metal that was poisonous to them.

He pushed through the entry and there she sat, regal and distant, her figure nearly swallowed by the deep ruby leather seat.

She looked cool and in control. Beside her sat a large blowsy woman—the Matron, David thought, swiftly noting the body language. Both women lounged, but where Cressida rested her hands lightly on the arms of the chair, this other appeared to be forcefully gripping her hands together. The Matron sported a beige pantsuit which highlighted her brassy red hair, making it seem tacky and altogether cheap. The overwhelming impression he got was that she couldn't compete with the composed but remotely lovely woman seated beside her.

"Is this him?" Without waiting for Cressida's answer, the woman rose, and Daniel stepped forward, as a frisson of power rippled through the air.

He inclined his head. "You must be the Matron. My name is Daniel and I am the *Yeux Secondes* of the house al bin Habbad." He bowed as appropriate to her status.

"Good." She hovered, gazing deeply into his eyes, as if all the secrets he carried were hidden in view. "Now show me what you can do."

Before he could open his mouth, she held up her hand. "Not yet. Just let me..." She walked a circle around him, making him feel like a bull on display.

She laid her fleshy fingers on his wrist and pressed. Her touch was cold and he tugged away, recoiling from the oily sensations that traveled through his nerves.

The Matron frowned. "I don't sense any vibrations of magic." The mutter was teamed with a shake of her head.

Daniel glanced to Cressida, who gave a tiny shake of her own head. He read the unspoken command. *Stay still.*

Daniel kept his counsel and watched as the Matron turned in Cressida's direction. "You *are* sure?"

Cressida's smile was thin. "Oh yes. He's demonstrated his powers, but they aren't like the normal warlock skills. Not as I've ever encountered, anyway."

He remained silent, given he had little to offer the discussion at this point.

"But surely…" The woman turned back in his direction. "Show me something you can do."

At Cressida's nod, he made a tight fist, clenching his fingers until the knuckles whitened. The Matron had watched the quick byplay and scowled. Daniel couldn't help the tiny hint of satisfaction that flared deep inside his gut.

With a flick, he opened his hand and imagined a tiny flame blazing. It burst to life on his palm.

The Matron stepped back. "How…? Have you learned a silent incantation?"

"No, Matron. I imagine it there, dancing on my palm, and it appears."

The Matron shook her head and Daniel chanced to look back to Cressida. She didn't smile, but the tight lines at her mouth had eased somewhat.

"No warlock or witch can do that. The use of magic must be conscious. It is the first of the Tenets of Wielding. Capturing and using it cannot be unconscious. It's never been found to be like that." Genuine surprise filled the Matron's utterance.

"For me, it isn't. I simply think and it happens."

The Matron's lips thinned, white pressure lines appearing at the corners of her mouth. "What else…? Do something different." She turned and pointed to a small wooden item on the desk. "Make that ruler fly."

Daniel bowed, then inhaled deeply and imagined it rising slowly, before setting it dancing and tumbling end over end around the table. After his slow circuit he made it slowly descend to the leather tabletop before removing his glasses and rubbing his eyes.

"So? Is he a warlock?" Cressida rose as he opened his eyes.

"I... *No*." Her tone was filled with frustration and anger. "For a witch or warlock to do such things, they need an incantation. It's clear he isn't using one. He... Our charter is only for witches and warlocks..." The Matron shrugged sharply.

He could tell she was at a loss as to what came next. A spurt of satisfaction bloomed before quickly dying away.

"If he isn't a warlock, *what is he*?" Cressida laid both hands on the arm of her seat and leaned forward.

"I-I would need to consult the Oracle. But he's a magic wielder, so he *should* be with us."

Cressida snorted, which he considered being highly unusual. "He doesn't fit your charter. That means he isn't one of yours."

"I never—"

Cressida surged from her seat and bowed to the woman. "I thank you for your time, Matron."

She shooed the woman toward the door as Daniel watched with a mix of dismay and amusement in equal parts. So, if he wasn't a warlock, then what was he? Some kind of aberration? An abomination? It was now clear that something odd ran in the family, with Hope's and Celina's skills lying somewhere outside the normal boundaries of magic too.

The door banged shut and the thud tugged him from his thoughts.

"Daniel... I'm sorry she reacted as she did." There was uncertainty in Cressida's voice. He ignored it. His gaze rested on her face.

He shrugged. Fury rose. He'd had to perform for the Matron, then Cressida had once again become the soft woman he'd met in the garden. The ups and downs of her reaction cracked open the seeds of anger.

"We need to work out what you are. To find out—"

Daniel raised a hand, stopping her from speaking. "I wish *I* knew what the hell I was. Then you might be able to—" He bit off the words.

See me as your equal. The words had been there, right on the tip of his tongue. One unguarded second was all it would have taken.

He knew better. She was a vampire. A *Councilor*. He was merely human and a *Yeux Secondes*.

It was all too much and he needed to escape before he betrayed himself and his fascination. Daniel refused to face that humiliation, so instead, he bowed deeply. "With your permission." It wasn't a question.

Cressida didn't speak, just gave a slight nod, and he retreated.

SEVEN

The pages in front of his face shimmered. Daniel raked his fingers through his hair. A glance at the corner of the computer screen told him it was five a.m. and long past time for him to have retired.

"Just one more thing…" The murmured words died away as his vision blurred and turned gray. The thud as his hand collided with the desk brought him around.

Daniel quickly tugged himself upright, cracking his jaw with a tremendous yawn. A last glance at the screen showed the final letter he'd tapped on the computer. The words ending with a single letter running along the screen. The results of his micro-sleep.

Daniel gave a snort of disgust and rose. "I'll take a nap and come back to it." The planning of the expansion was too important to leave for any longer than necessary, but exhaustion dragged at him.

The couch in the corner of his office beckoned and he headed in its direction, promising himself no more than an hour or two of rest, to be followed by a shower and change of clothes.

He pulled off his glasses and put them on the coffee table opposite the couch, then lay down with a sigh and closed his eyes.

Within seconds, consciousness fled.

*T*HE SCENE BEFORE HIM WAS UNFAMILIAR. SCENTS, THE ACRID TAINT
*of burning wood, lay heavy in the air as he looked around. The rough
room in the bar was populated by groups of men. Their hair hung in
greasy hanks and their clothing was stained while they bellowed to one
another and gulped down the liquids in their tankards. Clearly they
were employed in manual labor.*

*"I'm in a barroom? How the hell did I get here?" Disbelief
filtered through him.*

*A gentle touch on his shoulder caught his attention and he turned,
unsure what he'd see.*

*In front of him stood Cressida. A Cressida he'd never seen before.
Her hair was arranged in a halo-like single plait coiled around the top
of her head.*

*"How did you get here, Daniel?" Cressida's eyes narrowed and her
lush lips flattened.*

*"I honestly don't know. Where are we?" He glanced about the
room, the sounds swelling.*

*"This is my past. Or a part of it." Her face settled into the familiar
mask of acceptance—the one he knew she used to hide her feelings.
"Come with me."*

*Cressida gathered her cape closer. He noted the black velvet
fastened at her neck with an ornate silver clasp that shone in the dim
light.*

*"Where are we going?" His eyes darted here and there, watching
the hard gazes follow them as he left the bar.*

*Stepping through the door brought them into a drawing room. She
stopped and shook her head.*

*"That can't be right. It never used to lead here." Her soft words
were threaded with confusion.*

"Where are we, Cressida?"

She turned her gaze in his direction with a sad smile on her face. "This is my home. Or it was."

Daniel watched as she ran shaking fingers over the furnishings, as if reintroducing herself to them. "So long ago."

The sparseness of the clean and obviously well-cared-for room was clearly not of his time.

He waited until she turned back to look at him, and he was captured by the pain in her eyes. Not for the first time, Daniel wondered just how old Cressida really was.

A low sound of anguish ripped through her and, unable to help himself, Daniel strode forward and took her in his arms. She leaned in and he knew she was seeking his comfort. He meant only to kiss her cheek, but in that instant she turned her face.

As he settled his lips over hers, the inferno within him erupted. What should have been a simple peck grew. Exploded as their lips moved.

She opened her mouth on a moan and it kicked the desire that had been controlled up to a wildfire—a conflagration that spread through his entire body.

Tingles started at every point they touched while he caressed the dips and hollows of her body. The bite of her fingernails barely registered as he dropped his hands to her waist.

She tangled her fingers in the hair at the nape of his neck—a sting as she dragged him back from the precipice.

"Daniel, I..."

Her blue eyes shone in the low light. His heart pounded rapidly as he waited for her to tell him why this was wrong. The molten lava in the pit of his belly cooled and became a heavy weight.

"I shouldn't... God help me though, I want to." Her voice cracked as she swooped in, her kiss voracious and hungry.

His body ached with desire as he raised his shaking hand to her cheek—

. . .

THE SOUND OF A RINGING TELEPHONE WOKE HIM FROM THE dream which hadn't felt much like one. His body ached.

Even as Daniel reached for the receiver, he knew who the caller was. "Cressida?"

"What have you done to me?" The harsh whisper tore a jagged hole in his heart.

"I haven't..."

"Oh God!" She hung up.

He heard the disconnect signal and his immediate reaction was to hurl the telephone across the room as frustration warred with good sense. It took long seconds of internal struggle before he overcame the fury.

He placed the receiver very carefully on the cradle and rose, then snatched up his glasses and stalked to his desk.

Another day of planning while burying the hunger deep inside loomed—work might help to bank the emptiness that hollowed his belly.

Not for the first time, he wondered why he accepted the limitations of his status. He sighed and reached for a file.

CRESSIDA ACCEPTED THE FILES FROM SAMRA WITH A GRIMACE. All day and night she'd battled with herself. Ringing Daniel had been a major mistake. Potentially also a costly one.

Sleep hadn't come easily for her as her body had battled the tremendous surge of desire that thrummed through her veins.

It was the touch of Samra's hand on her shoulder that roused her.

"Cressida? Did you hear me?"

She raised her head to gaze at Samra.

Her second frowned. "You haven't heard a word I've said for the past few minutes." The warrior woman took the seat opposite her. "We've known each other for centuries and I've been your second for well over a decade."

Cressida winced at Samra's direct attack.

"Look, I know when something is screwing with your head, so you might as well tell me."

Cressida glanced away, knowing that action too was telling. "Dreams. I'm dreaming of— What am I doing here?"

"Oh no! Not you too!" Samra gaped at her, and Cressida couldn't disregard the concern and dismay on her second's face. "It's not the human, is it?"

She slumped in her seat. "I'm not even sure where to start. Samra, how do I deal with this?" Confusion rattled her. *I'm too damned old to be having to cope with these ridiculous emotions!* "He's barely even a baby, and I'm…I'm old enough that most of my peers are less than dust now. How the hell…"

Samra gave a sad shake of her head and clucked. "It happened to Xavier and Javed. I shouldn't really be surprised. It had to happen. But the timing sucks, Cressida."

She snapped out of the cloud of self-pity at Samra's words. "You're right, of course. Too much is at stake for me to wallow in this well of self-indulgence. Tell me again what you've learned."

"Only if you promise to listen this time."

She winced at the reprimand. "Of course." Cressida settled both hands on the wooden tabletop and gave her undivided attention to the woman on the other side of the desk.

Samra settled back, glanced at Cressida as if to check if she was listening—something Cressida found quite unnerving—then began. "We know it was Attar's soldiers who attacked the nest in Brisbane. They seem to rely on their overwhelming numbers and the element of surprise rather than any formal training and actual strength. But…" Samra's face clouded.

"But what?"

"Indications are they had a force of maybe three hundred warriors."

That stole the breath from Cressida's lungs. *Three hundred warriors? That means...* Shaking her head didn't help to clear the shock from her brain. "You're sure that is the number?"

"That's the estimation. Cressida, we both know that is a number we haven't seen in...*centuries!*"

Samra was right. For him to have amassed that number of warriors in so short a time was unnerving and placed most of the nests in danger. An average nest might boast thirty to forty warriors on site. Perhaps even the same number billeted elsewhere. Not enough to fend off a massed attack. "Do you have any positive intelligence?" Her lips were dry and it took a great deal of effort to force the words out.

"Maybe. I think...to have those kinds of numbers, I believe his warriors would have to be turning others." Samra braced her hands on the desk. "And we all know how dangerous that can be."

"No. Surely even Attar wouldn't make that kind of mistake. Past experience has shown—"

"If the situation is what we think, it must be something to do with Attar himself being able to strengthen them. Cressida, this is a significant and worrisome discovery."

"If it's right." Cressida raised a shaking hand to her brow. "We need to see the witches. Only they can clarify..." Her mind spun in circles. *How the hell can mere warriors be changing others?* Over the years, they'd seen young vampires attempt changes. They were never successful, leaving only hollow zombie-like creatures devoid of their minds. They were little more than killing machines. In the past it had been kinder to exterminate those who'd been turned before they could escape. Before humanity had discovered them.

Over the centuries, she'd cleaned up more than enough ill-conceived changes to misunderstand what was at stake.

She'd participated in the biggest cleansing, which had taken place in Spain under the guise of the inquisition. Finding the remains of their victims had turned her stomach, and the memory still had the power to horrify her.

"There were no instances of..." She looked over at Samra.

"The walking undead? No. Not from what we've found, but, as you know, it's sometimes hard to tell, after we find what's left..." Samra stopped, her words hanging in the air.

"We have to find their nest. Find Attar." A mixture of fear and anger rose, almost choking her. That Attar would bring them to this point was beyond bearing.

"Cressida, we're doing our best, but... We need help. The witches? Will they help us find Attar?"

"I'll contact them." She stood, needing to move, while turning over in her mind the reality that the witches might not be disposed to assist. Not after the contretemps with Daniel.

"Call a meeting of the nests for tomorrow night. We need *Yeux Secondes*, Masters and Seconds. Warn them they'll need security plans and ideas. We have to ensure the safety of our nests before we can consider engaging in any other kind of assistance now." She knew her voice sounded harsh, but at times like this, the weight of her responsibilities hung like a millstone around her neck.

"Yes, Cressida. Can I also suggest..."

She swung back in Samra's direction. "What?"

"Since the investiture I've been working with other Seconds. Given what the witches said at Javed's—" She stopped, and for a moment Cressida was sure she didn't want to hear what would come next.

"What?"

"If Daniel is the key, we need—"

"*No!*" The word was torn from her. Knowledge of what Samra hadn't said pierced her. She would shield him if she could. *It isn't right that he be asked to sacrifice himself and his future.* Cressida couldn't voice the argument that had played inside her brain since the idea had first been raised. Instead she ignored the thread of sanity that told her he was already a pivotal member of their forces. "That will not—"

"It may not be a matter of *options*, Cressida. We may yet need..." As if she understood the battle Cressida waged with herself, she stopped without finishing the words, then bowed deeply.

The jittery sensation in Cressida's belly rose. She could pluck the thoughts from Samra's mind if she wished to, but she *knew* what her Second thought. That using Daniel might yet be their only option.

But in order to defeat Attar, the texts they'd managed to decode had made it clear he'd need to make the ultimate sacrifice and undergo the change. She couldn't do that to him, if there were any other options. She'd exhaust them first. "No."

"If that is your wish." Samra retreated, leaving Cressida scowling.

EIGHT

He didn't want to be here. His head ached, his eyes stung and exhaustion, now his constant companion, was a palpable thing. It dragged at what remained of his wits and left him wilted.

The most powerful members of all the nests had been summoned to Cressida's. So he followed Javed and Kharisma—Javed's second— up the stairs and into Cressida's house.

The hubbub of voices hit him like a wall as they stepped into the foyer. Quick steps led them to the meeting room, where rows of chairs squeezed up against one another.

He looked around, seeking a quiet corner where he might regain his equilibrium, but the corners were already occupied. He edged to the side of the room where David, his cousin, stood propped against the wall.

"Do you know anything about...?" He waved his arm and Daniel shook his head, taking in the sight before him.

David clamped his arms on his shoulder, squeezing and lending support. Clearly he wasn't the only one dealing with heavy issues, he thought as he noted David's pallor.

"Are you okay?"

"I don't... I'm resigning my commission and plan to seek a place in a new House."

Daniel frowned. "Today?"

"No. When the mess with Attar is done. I've hung in only because... It was Hope that kept me together once I came to terms with what had been done. I treated her badly and so did my parents. I feel dirty because I believed everything I was told. Now, it's hard to stay after..." David shrugged and Daniel understood that David truly regretted everything that had gone before.

"But if Hope forgives you, surely the situation can be resolved?"

"No, Daniel. Everyone knows what I did. What *we* did. How we took her—Alexa's—side and left Hope to suffer the consequences of the lies. It just...it doesn't feel right, you know? She's built something good and true. I can't muddy it any longer than necessary. She needs to be able to rebuild her life free of that taint."

David's wife, Alexa, had betrayed their nest, hiding her real identity in order to cause panic and to cut off Hope. She'd known of Hope's special abilities and used them to her own ends. They now knew it had been an offshoot of Attar's original plot.

Daniel could only guess how hard that knowledge was for David to bear. "If you need to move, you would be more than welcome with me. I can talk to Javed..."

"No. But thank you." David shook his head. "When it's done... Once Attar is defeated, I'm thinking of going somewhere else. Somewhere far from here." Sucking in a deep breath, he stepped back, around Daniel, and wandered to the other side of the room.

Daniel watched his cousin before following and looking for his spot next to Kharisma and Javed. As he sat down, Kharisma turned to him. "Everything all right?"

"I'll explain later."

He turned his gaze to where Cressida stood still like a statue. He wondered if anyone else noted the tremor in her hands as she spoke, welcoming them. "As you know, our Australian nests have faced the terror of Attar's attacks. We have sent several of our best tacticians down there to assist them in securing the nests. We have also provided financial assistance, but now we must look to our own security. We believe they may have in excess of three hundred warriors available to them."

Gasps and words of dissent rippled through the room. "How do we know this?" one of the masters from another nest called out and Cressida's eyes narrowed.

"We have CCTV footage and eyewitness accounts."

Daniel watched while she fielded question after question. She didn't stop moving, like a caged tiger he'd seen at the zoo as a child. It forcibly reminded him that she was an alpha of the night. A predator. Her every action cautioned him. He had to remember that she was a warrior looking for a way to protect her territory. It didn't stop the constant need he felt to be with her, though.

He had to pull himself together. Blaming exhaustion for the wandering of his wits was inexcusable. It took extra effort, but he forced himself to concentrate, and before too long he'd immersed himself in the twisting conversation. The discussion turned to ways they could protect the nests, including early warning systems and internal safe rooms, which could be erected in the human offices and houses in case of attacks.

He noted they avoided the discussion of public sentiment, and he couldn't fault them for that.

However, as much as he could understand the situation, he still felt it was unwise to ignore the long-term ramifications.

As the meeting broke up, Cressida called him and Javed.

Kharisma caught his eye, then Javed's, before shrugging. "I'll wait outside."

The room emptied until finally there was only Javed, Daniel and the councilors.

A fraught silence twanged at his brain. He could see them looking at one another, and several exuded surprise and anger.

He wondered at the communication, what it meant. *It doesn't bode well*, he thought.

Cressida gave a silent nod, and as one the councilors rose and left the room, leaving him with Javed and Cressida. The door reopened and admitted three ancient witches who exuded unmistakable power.

"Councilor? How may we assist you?" Javed spoke smoothly, but he took position in front of Daniel.

His ire rose, though he knew it was an automatic action from his master.

"The witches are here to meet with Daniel. They...we believe that they alone can determine what...what skills Daniel possesses."

He waited quietly as the women stepped closer. He'd forgotten how beautiful they all were. While he gazed on them Javed moved aside.

"Come, boy. Step forward, so we can read you," the one he knew as Jemima called imperiously.

He moved in her direction but stopped as if some invisible force field existed. With his mind he tested it, letting his senses roam, looking for a chink. When he found one he gave a mental push and watched in amazement as the witch laughed. "Well done. You use your senses as if you were used to the wielding of magic." She nodded and took a seat.

The second, a red-haired woman, grinned as she raised her hand. A flash of pain slid through his skull and he sought to shield himself, and the pain fizzled away, though it left a greasy smear of nausea.

"Now *that* was impressive." She laughed before she too moved to a seat and slid down into the leather cushions.

So you have magic. Strong magic. Magic that you can use without the need for spells and potions. Your magic comes naturally to you. The voice echoed in his mind.

How can you do that? What is it you are doing to me?

The last witch tapped a finger against her lips and watched him. *I am merely communicating telepathically, Daniel. But you already know that.* She grinned. "I can tell you what he is. He's exactly what you need. He's a sorcerer, and I would guess a strong one, though his skills are... Well, they aren't polished, but that can be rectified."

He found himself gaping. *A sorcerer?* What the hell was that? "There's no such..."

The blonde pierced him with her sharp, blue gaze. "Oh, there are sorcerers. Not many, I'll concede. In my experience, most don't have such a strong grasp of what they can do. Your powers are instinctive. They're strong for all you are untrained, but with instinct comes the ability to learn quickly. You'll do perfectly."

His heart thudded in his chest at her words. "But I don't..."

The dark-haired witch leaned forward and held out her hand toward him. A sense of understanding welled in his mind. "You wouldn't. That's not how these powers work. But you, my boy, you are the last of the trio. Your powers will complement those of Hope and Celina. Once we've refined your skills, the three of you will be more than capable of winning in the battle to come."

The air felt as if it were being sucked from his lungs and he looked around the room, seeking something... Javed seemed as shocked as he was at the witches' pronouncement. Most, but not all. Cressida's eyes betrayed the fact that she'd had a suspicion of what they had just told him.

He became aware of a frisson of power winding closer around him. The ribbon of energy moved back and forth between the two vampires and the witches. The knowledge slammed into him. They were discussing him telepathically!

Caustic anger welled, and no matter how hard he tried to tamp it down, he couldn't control it. "I'm not a guinea pig. Talk to *me*, dammit!" The rage spewed over, burning him. The power fizzled away and everyone turned to him.

In Cressida's eyes he read a deep emotion that she couldn't mask. Fear was there, in buckets, but it was more than that. In her eyes, he saw a shimmer of regret.

"Please," she entreated the witches, "don't ask this of me." Her tone clawed at his insides, but he'd had enough.

"I'm leaving." He turned on his heel, but as he reached the door, a force stilled him with his hand on the knob.

Wait, there is yet more. The witch who'd communicated with him before commanded.

He pushed against the pressure that surrounded his mind, gripping the handle.

"Daniel? There is one more thing." As Javed spoke Daniel turned. "Someone... We think someone is leaking information...to Attar. He knows what we are planning before... We need to find out who this person is, without letting them know we're searching. You're the only one, we think, who can help us."

Javed's words forced him to still, even though his heart pounded in his chest and his mind commanded he leave the room and the machinations.

He closed his eyes as his duty to the nest warred with self-protection.

The truth was inescapable, though.

"What do you need?"

NINE

The councilors waited for her in the foyer, but she needed to finish this, then she could approach them. Tell them a percentage of what had been discussed. Even through the layers of wall and door, she sensed the waves of dissent pulsing against her mind. They were like a battering tide, pushing against her consciousness. They'd been angered by her insistence that they leave the room, but given the circumstances, she couldn't have them there. *What if one of them is the mole?* They might inadvertently let on the only possible option they had to fight Attar.

For an instant, she'd almost given in to the tide of anger, but the anxiety gnawing at her had regained ascendancy. She'd caught a flash of an unusual emotion, but with so many minds—and thoughts—to sift through, and so much interference from high emotions, she hadn't been able to pin down where it was coming from. It was clear that one of the participants had exhibited *fear*.

"Daniel, Javed is right. We think someone is passing on knowledge of our actions before we can act. We need to find a way to beat Attar, but the options are few. We need you trained as soon as possible, otherwise this battle will be over before we can even turn up to fight it."

She had one more request, and she tried desperately to avoid it. *How I hate asking this of him.*

She studied the human man in front of her. He wasn't muscular like many of the human nest guards, but he was toned and carried himself with an innate grace. Like a trained warrior and yet not. Cressida bit her lip. "You work out?" With careful steps, she circled him. "Have you been trained for combat?"

He gave a short, jerky nod.

Cressida turned to Javed. "What skills does he have?"

"Councilor?" Javed attempted to hide his surprise, but the final sound betrayed his astonishment. She smiled.

"What self-defense and combat skills does this man possess?" She indicated to Daniel, ensuring they only saw a surface reaction of disinterest. It wouldn't do for them to realize there was a huge dose of uncertainty mixed up there. She didn't want to see him injured, or even worse, dead. For a moment her breath caught at that thought. It made her stomach tip and yaw, while the burn of bile rose in her throat.

Clearly unwilling to let Javed answer for him, Daniel straightened to his impressive six-foot-plus height. "I am versed in karate and boxing and I have some experience with a sword."

"Hmm..." So he had some rudimentary skills. Not enough to preserve his life against a vampire, but it was a start. *We can build on that.*

"Javed? I want him trained further. Get someone to cover his work, I don't care who you get or where they come from at this point. Offer whatever you must. He will also work with—"

Daniel interjected. "Councilor—"

She heard the anger, ignored it as she thrust out her hand, stopping his remonstration.

"I'll be the one to train him in the use of magic." Selena, the blonde-haired woman, stood. "Master Javed, if you would be kind enough to arrange lodgings for myself and my sisters in your nest, we would prefer to be on hand so we can take advantage of opportunities whenever they arise."

Cressida glanced at Javed, who nodded. Taking another deep lungful of air helped her to clear her mind. "Good then. Now go, I have other things to attend to."

The door slid open and Samra entered. On the other side of the wall she could hear the councilors as they waited impatiently. Javed, Daniel and the women left quietly and Samra slid the wooden closure across the opening. "So?"

Cressida turned, unwilling to give away all her secrets. "So what?"

"Are things as bad as you think?"

Cressida absorbed her words. "Why do you ask that?"

"Because you are avoiding direct questions that involve your thoughts. You also have a deeper plan."

For a moment Cressida swayed. "Who else has—?"

"I don't think many have worked it out. At least, not yet. So?" Samra pressed closer and Cressida sighed.

"Maybe. I think there is someone here who has. Someone with connections to Attar is what I honestly think. They are feeding him information." She grimaced as she spoke. "But I can't prove it. I need proof so I can take it to the Council, and deal with whoever is sharing the intelligence. I can't do that yet because right now it's only a gut feeling."

Samra frowned as she listened. "So what do we do about that? How can we combat the situation?"

Cressida wanted to grin as she watched Samra's hand curl over the hilt of her ceremonial sword. Samra had been born in France during the reign of Louis IX. To her, it was imperative to watch her back and always be armed.

Until recently, the inability to go in public armed with her sword had caused Samra great consternation. That had changed since the vampires had announced their presence, and once more, the scabbard and sword were an extension of her clothing, like many women wore jewelry.

Cressida gave a tiny smile before it melted away. She shrugged, settling her gaze to a spot over her Second's shoulder as she weighed the question. *Exactly how?* Subterfuge and planning were both options. But preparation was only going to get them so far. Maybe they could lure Attar...? But she'd been down that path before. She turned and observed the outcomes of the plan over and over again in her mind. There could only be one way they'd all survive.

"I need to think on it."

Samra nodded at her words, although Cressida could see the frustration building in the woman's eyes. "Hmm. Okay. What about the Daniel situation?"

"The Daniel situation? What situation would that be?" She tensed again, wrapping her fingers around the goblet of blood wine that had been sitting on her desk.

"Oh, come on. Be honest with me and yourself. I can see how much you're trying to avoid looking at him, how he watches you. The air between you practically sizzles with lust, and you're turning your back on that? Cressida, you aren't a stupid woman—"

"And therein lies the rub. I'm not. I'm a *vampire.*"

"He could be too..." *Ahh and there lies the single thing that I must avoid at all costs.* The price she might have to pay was far too large for her to consider. The possible pain too deep to recover from.

"Not now, Samra. I need to contact Gianna."

Samra's eyes grew wide, as if she finally understood Cressida's fears. Samra bowed before leaving Cressida to her thoughts.

DROPLETS OF SWEAT DRIPPED DOWN HIS ARMS. "WHAT NOW?" His voice showed the strain as it wobbled.

"Keep it up. Think of it flying, feel the air underneath you as you soar. Visualize the flight." His mentor—or tormentor—Selena, smiled slightly as she walked around the cavernous room the witches had commandeered.

Damn it, I've been doing that for the last hour. The large metal cooking pot wavered, and he refocused his mind to the task before it careened to the ground.

"Tell me about Cressida."

"What?" His concentration splintered and the cauldron fell to the floor with a reverberating thud. With his mind—and hands—free of the task, he swiped at the perspiration that stung his eyes.

"Yes. She is your weakness." The woman's smile ebbed away as she studied him.

He wanted to snarl. Nights of endless erotic dreams and days of fighting and magic tutoring were messing with his head. "I don't want..."

The witch's eyes glazed. "She is your future. You want her and she wants you, but you both fight it." There was puzzlement in her voice and Daniel closed his eyes, shuddering as he *saw* the two of them entwined—as he had the night before in his dreams. "Why?"

"I'm not talking about Cressida." The words were little more than a snarl.

The woman cocked her head to one side. "Why is that? It's not fear..." She frowned. "I don't understand what you gain by ignoring the connection between you." She moved closer, placing her hand against his biceps. "You hunger for her, and for what could be. You know it. Do you not want her as your lover?"

"It's private." He muttered the words, hoping she would back away and change the subject. His gut churned wildly as he fought for control of the frustration that clawed at him day and night.

"Humph. Tell me how your replacement is working out." The change of topic gave Daniel a moment to control his anger. One breath, then another, deep down into his lungs as his mind cleared.

"David is doing okay. He's used to a more formal nest. He's

adjusting as the majority of the nestlings came from other areas. They don't know all the gory details of his past. I think that makes it easier for him to cope. Apart from that, he'll be fine in time. I check in on him daily..." He hefted the cauldron, making it rise slowly.

"Will he stay?"

"What?" Daniel was startled by the change of discussion and the cauldron once more clanged to the floor. "Why would he?"

"When you and Cressida..." Her eyes glowed in the half light.

The anger surged again. These days it was near the surface most of the time. He advanced toward the witch, as if hoping to make his point, his strides long and determined. "I told you—" She simply smiled at him and he stilled.

"Nonsense. You need to face the truth. In order to beat Attar, you must come to an understanding. Embrace what is before you so that you, together, will be stronger."

"She doesn't want me!" He roared with the anger that rippled under his skin.

Light pulsed and the recessed globes in the ceiling flared brightly, but that quickly petered out as he regained control of his emotions.

"So... What will *you* do about it?"

For the first time since the discussion had begun, he felt surprised. The wrath he'd carried melted away, and it confused him. "*Why?* Why do you care so much?"

The look she slanted at him was full of understanding. "We have always cared, Daniel. We chose to give up our future in order to care-take the future of humans, but sometimes when you give up everything you find the greatest pleasure."

Her words confused him further. Daniel waited, sure she'd explain.

"Attar must be stopped. You are fortunate, Daniel. What you humans have is love. What Attar exudes is hate and he excels at that, but love is a strong magic of its own, one which will strengthen you all, if you will only accept it. Hope and Xavier have a bond so strong it couldn't be broken. Celina and Javed also possess it. That strength is rare and infinitely more powerful than anything Attar feels. It has few barriers and cannot be tamed or controlled."

"Cressida isn't human. So where does that fit?"

She held up a hand, stopping the questions that ricocheted around his mind from finding voice.

"You are rattled, and full of bad temper. The blinding flash you've just demonstrated is from your loss of control. You need to learn discipline. Of course, you are right, Cressida is a vampire. So were Javed and Xavier when they met Celina and Hope, but they retained their humanity. So does Cressida. That is a small part of the key." She nodded as if reminding herself of something.

"But—"

"But nothing. Because they—and Cressida—are no longer human, or should I say they are more than human, doesn't change the fact that they care, they love and experience deep emotion and loyalty to those they have protected for centuries. Cressida feels it even more deeply, as she does guilt."

Guilt? Why would Cressida suffer guilt? He wanted to ask but something held him back. It was an innate knowledge that he wanted her to be open with him, not to learn what made her unique from secondhand sources.

Her words flowed and the cadence of her voice soothed him, easing the ache that pulsed through every part of his body. She'd spoken of logic and loyalty, and it made sense. After months of tossing the issue over, though, he didn't want to make a step that would forever push her away. In his experience, each time he'd thought he was close to breaking through the icy wall she'd thrust between them, she skittered away. "She doesn't want me."

"Cressida fears emotion and love, Daniel. You must find out why and vanquish those fears before she will share all."

"How? How do I make her see...?" He turned away.

"You keep working with her, let her see what you have to offer. Soothe her fears and make her believe in your connection."

Daniel nodded, letting the information seep into his brain. He would reevaluate her words later, when he had time to consider them. "Maybe we should get back to work."

The witch grinned and nodded. "Maybe we should."

TEN

Cressida patted her blonde hair into place, then smoothed down her ice-blue suit. Everything must be perfect for their Overlord's arrival. With Gianna, any appearance brought drama, and in this instance it would come laden with danger.

The entire nest was on alert, prepared for the formal welcome she usually demanded.

A sense of losing control nearly overwhelming her as she watched the fleet of vehicles glide toward her.

"All will be fine," Samra leaned close and whispered.

"Nothing will be well until we beat Attar." There was no further time to talk as Gianna's car came to a smooth stop at the bottom of the steps.

One of the guards slid from the front seat and opened the door for her as Cressida reached the base.

"Liege, I welcome you formally on behalf of the nests."

Gianna emerged from the car. She was, as usual, a vision with her red-gold locks tamed into a perfect knot at the back of her head. With immaculate makeup, a black leather pantsuit teamed with a peach camisole, she could have just strutted off a catwalk.

"Cressida, I welcome the shelter of your house."

With the initial formalities complete, they looked at each other. "You are aware of why I'm here?"

Cressida nodded at Gianna's words. "I am. We have possibly located the third and ascertained what powers he has discovered. It's umm...Daniel. Of the House—"

Gianna eyed her, golden-green eyes stabbing her with their intensity. "Good. I wish to meet with him."

A glance at Samra and a telepathic message relayed the need for Daniel to present himself as quickly as possible. Her memory helpfully supplied images of the last time Gianna and Daniel had met. The questions she'd fielded. The interest she'd discerned. "You've seen him before."

A wide grin split the face of her Liege. It made the cold weight in Cressida's chest seem heavier. "He hasn't taken a partner yet?" Gianna's question put Cressida's teeth on edge.

"No. At this point he's busy taking instruction from Javed, Xavier and the witch, Selena."

"Excellent. I will assess how that is coming along. I'd also like him relocated to this household from today."

Cressida remembered all the other times Gianna had shown interest in nestlings, and how she'd used similar tactics before. They were memories that she wished to avoid. Endless nighttime strolls, moonlit picnics... A rush of jealousy seized her.

She wants him only as a warrior.

Cressida felt a flush of anger at Samra's unspoken message. She knew the woman attempted to reassure her. The loss of control was not acceptable in a Councilor, she reminded herself.

With slow and studied motions, Cressida preceded Gianna to the suite she'd had prepared for the overlord. "I have stocked the supply of blood wine you prefer as you requested."

"Excellent. I will arrange myself here until Daniel arrives." With that, Gianna dismissed her.

Cressida withdrew from the room with a deep bow, then turned to see Samra waiting at her elbow. "He's here?"

"He's due here soon. Cressida…"

The hint of Samra's fears lay just below the surface of her mind. Cressida didn't want to think about how she would feel if Gianna chose to act on her interest in Daniel. That would open too many old wounds. "Not now and not here."

Samra narrowed her gaze as Cressida turned and stalked down the hall and the stairs. Her office beckoned and she entered it, seeking sanctuary. The door banged after her and she gazed out over the night, hands braced on the glass as she tried to banish the emotions that welled.

Behind her there was movement, but she didn't look. No doubt it was Samra, come to gather files, or—

Hands settled on her shoulders and she gasped in surprise. They were warm, burning her cool skin, and instinctively she knew it was Daniel. The urge to cover his hand with her own was like a siren's call. She ignored it, curling her hands into hard fists.

"Cressida, we have to talk." His tone was earnest and she trembled, while the whisper of his breath sent ripples sliding over her skin.

"Gianna is here. She needs to see you." To her ears, her voice sounded hoarse.

"In a minute…" He curved his hands over her shoulders and she couldn't hold back her moan of pleasure.

"Please…" She held her breath, but his scent filled her, male and spicy. Her mind whirled. He pressed closer and she arched against him while she absorbed the feel of his hard body.

"Don't turn me away." With soft fingers he caressed her neck and she turned her head just enough to look into his eyes. He dipped his head.

The kiss was soft, a velvet touch, but the heat flared deep within her. Eyes closing, she leaned in, the drugged sensation making them heavy.

Heaven.

For a moment she let herself float in the haze of sensations, before tugging away. Her hand shook as she raised it flat to his chest. The need to touch him was urgent. "Daniel..."

His face was tight when he looked at her. "Dammit, Cressida..."

"No. We have a job to do. So we'll do it." She gave a tiny nod, hoping to present a focused front. It was a sham, as her mind whirled with the knowledge that she could only push him aside so many times before he stopped coming back.

With an expletive he jerked back, spinning on his heel, and left the room, the door banging loudly behind him.

IN THE FOYER, DANIEL STOPPED. HIS HEART THUDDED IN HIS chest. Why did Cressida have to make this harder than necessary? If the witch was right, they needed to settle this once and for all. "Bloody woman."

"And which woman would that be?" He looked up, seeing a woman at the top of the steps. The light illuminated her figure, picking up every lush curve to great effect, and he didn't doubt she knew that.

Gianna! Great. That's all I need. "Uh, Liege." He bowed low while she chuckled, the sound echoing off the high ceilings.

"Come, Daniel. You and I have much to discuss." He raised his head to see she'd made her way down the stairs and stood, watching him. "*Come.*" She extended her arm and he took it. "Show me the gardens while we talk." She tugged him in the direction of the door, and Cressida's guards bowed deeply as they made their way through the opening.

As they hurried down the steps, he shed the last of his anger. The night air soothed the heat of his body, leaving him slightly chilled. The vampire at his side clutched him close. "What do you...?"

She shook her head and Daniel breathed deep, accepting he was no longer in control of his destiny.

She towed him toward the rose garden and once there, in silence Gianna lowered herself onto the weathered marble bench, then patted the spot next to her. "Here, sit beside me. We have much to discuss."

Daniel couldn't possibly think what they had in common, or what she would feel the need to talk about with him, but she was the Overlord and he couldn't afford to alienate her. With great care, he settled himself beside her. "What do you wish to know, Gianna?"

She swiveled a little on the seat and smiled broadly. "Tell me about your skills."

He let his gaze settle on a rose. The reds had become almost black in the moonlight and he wondered where to even begin. "When the Matron came, she said I wasn't a warlock, because I don't use incantations. I'm fairly sure that surprised her." He remembered the look on her face when Cressida had dismissed her and he felt a glow of success, but that dimmed and melted away as he considered where things had gone since then. "The witch, Selena, has said I'm a sorcerer. Apparently my skills are innate, though, triggered by the events that happened—"

"Yes, I understand all that. Have you discovered your limits?"

He turned to the woman beside him, surprised at her question.

Limits? He and Selena were working on the basics at the moment and she wanted to know his limits? "I-I don't know."

"She has taught you levitation?"

He nodded, remembering the dented and cracked cauldron in their practice room.

"Warding?"

"Yes. I believe she will be working with me on merged powers next. She made me to understand that may be necessary..."

Gianna snorted. "That and much more." For a moment silence stretched between them, before she fished around in her pocket and withdrew something. "Now hold out your hand, Daniel. I have something for you."

In the moonlight she dropped a thin, discolored chain decorated with a tiny fairy into his hand. Gianna folded his fingers around it. "This was found at the slaughterhouse. I thought you might appreciate it."

His heart stuttered. *Could it be?* It looked so much like the one she—his mother—had been wearing that very last day. The tiny brooch he'd saved for and bought with his father.

"How did you...?" He glanced up at her, for the first time noting the lines at the side of her mouth.

"There was a familiar sort of aura about it. It's taken some time for me to work out why, though, otherwise I would have returned it to you before now. Each person—human—has a sort of signature or aura that they exude. Perhaps it's linked to the DNA. I really don't know why it drew me, but when I entered that stall, I felt an urgency to pick it up. Anyway, I did." She gave a tiny Gallic shrug.

"Aura? So you...?" He tried to understand what she was saying. She could read them by their auras?

"Daniel, I'm old. Only Attar is older than me, but he's somehow not retained or acquired any hint of what you might call humanity, whereas I..." She grimaced, and Daniel couldn't ignore the tiny pang of pity at the exhaustion that showed on her face. "My skills and abilities have had time to mature in ways I can't even begin to explain to you. I've been around so many people, tasted the essence of their blood or savored the vibrations they give off, that I've become wary. Jaded. Every action requires evaluation before I respond. Otherwise..." Her words died away.

"And this reminded you of me?"

Gianna curled her hand around his. "It did. I wanted to return it to you, but that wasn't all I came to talk to you about, and that can wait for the moment." Gianna nodded in the direction of the tiny necklace he held. "You gave it to your mother, didn't you?"

Visions filled him of that long-ago birthday when he'd presented the gift to her. He saw her, clear as day, and the ragged thumping of his heart sped up. She'd been hung over and dressed haphazardly, hair standing in untidy tufts. He'd made her breakfast, so pleased he'd done something for her, and she'd sat down. He'd forgotten that she rarely ate. In hindsight, he realized the hangover usually made her ill. On the plate in front of her, the bacon had sat untouched and congealing as she'd unwrapped the present, lying in the folds of blue tissue paper, tied with a cheery pink bow.

When she opened the lid her face had paled, but his mother had smiled and hugged him. He remembered the words she had spoken. *'Thank you, Daniel. It's the best gift ever'*. She'd kissed him, and he remembered the papery feel of her skin. His grip on the pendant released slightly, exposing the links to the light.

His hand shook as he closed it around the old tarnished item once more. The memory of the following day left him with a lump in his throat.

"I gave it to her on her birthday. The day before she disappeared."

"Ahh, I do apologize. It was not my intention to give you pain."

"No. It's..." Daniel had to clear his throat. "I'm glad you did. Now I have something to remember her by."

Gianna smiled, and for a moment he wished he experienced some kind of attraction to her. He was sure she wouldn't push him away as Cressida did. He jerked himself from the thought, knowing it was unworthy to feel such self-pity or to see Cressida's action in that light. He focused on his hand.

"I hope...?"

He glanced in her direction as she spoke again. "Thank you, Gianna, this means a lot to me."

She smiled and relaxed a little. "Good. Now I want to raise an idea with you."

"What?" He would do almost anything right now. She'd given him back a memory of his mother that he could cherish, and he owed her for that.

"I was thinking you should become a vampire."

He stilled, every part of his body solid with shock, then he choked. "What? I can't!" He stood and made to stride away, but she flung out a hand, stopping him.

"You must consider, in order to defeat Attar, you and those you fight will need to be equals. Consider the prophecy of three. It doesn't say two and one."

His blood froze as he weighed her words. Gianna stood and laid a light hand on his shoulder. "Consider it, Daniel. Now I think I'll go inside. I have much to discuss with Cressida."

The sound of her steps died away as he stood in the rose garden, clutching the pendant. He'd never wanted to be a vampire, but if she was right, if he embraced the future that seemed to stretch out before him...

Some distant but strident part of his brain wondered how Cressida would react? *Will she accept me then?* It was little more than a whisper in his mind. That would surely make them equals on one level. Both vampires. Was that what he needed to do, in order for them to achieve the future he was sure they deserved?

He growled and stalked back in the direction of the house.

ELEVEN

"He's *gone*, Cressida."

Cressida knew Samra was frustrated with her. Hell, she was frustrated enough with herself! For a moment, a sense of urgency grew before she shoved it away.

Right now she had bigger problems to focus on.

The cycle of kidnappings had begun again. This time in Hong Kong, with a newsreader and a well-known designer. The news agencies had caved to the Chinese government, keeping the situation quiet, and for once Cressida was pleased they'd intervened. But the news of the strengthening numbers in Attar's forces was beyond disturbing. Attar had become far more blatant, almost daring them to act.

"He's getting closer, Samra. The attacks on New Zealand and Australia were well-covered in the media. First, he attacks those of high profile, then he lets the hysteria bank before attacking a nest. A prominent one."

She stalked to the map on the wall where she pointed. "Here, then here, and finally here." Her eyes scanned the multicolored outline, looking to see where he might attack next.

"Perhaps he's goading us?" Samra made her way to stand beside Cressida.

For a moment Cressida wished she could snap her fingers and make things better. Fix the issues. If only it were that simple.

"No. There's more to it. I wish we knew what."

"Maybe there is no more. Maybe he wants to get even for—" Clearly lost for words, Samra loosed a short, guttural sound. "I don't know. I mean, if he's as clever as you say, he must realize that we have the third of the prophecy. Put that together with the knowledge that he and his people have failed once..."

"Maybe, Samra, but I wouldn't be so sure that he has come to the same conclusions as us. He's likely guessed we've found the third, but so far, he doesn't seem aware of who the third is, does he? Unless someone has told him."

They were missing a significant piece of the puzzle. The one that connected—

"Samra?" She whirled around to face her second.

"The latest attack... Was there anything that would make you think...?"

"*Faex!*"

Her eyebrows rose at Samra's outburst. "*Really?* Samra, I haven't heard you use that term in at least a century." Her mirth died away when she noted the pale visage of her second. "What?"

"The attack on the house? When Celina and Javed were in Egypt? That timing was odd. Then the battle at the slaughterhouse... How did Attar's people know to have their guards there? And we thought Attar had gone to ground, but he's come back better equipped and more knowledgeable of the time. How?" Samra's eyes glowed.

Everything Samra said was correct. Frighteningly so. Except it was clear Samra hadn't bought into her assertions that there was a mole. "Now you see it. Someone passing on information."

"It's not just that, though. Clearly someone helped him to work out who he should kidnap and gave him the funds he required. We need to let Gianna know."

The door opened. "I already know."

Cressida shot the Overlord a keen look, but she shrugged.

"Samra, you were thinking very loud. But yes, both Cressida and I have been aware of this for some time."

Cressida slumped into her chair. "So, Samra. What do you think?"

Samra's face was pale as she pondered the question. "I knew and kind of agreed with what you were saying, but the ramifications... I don't know what we should be doing. I mean, I guess you have a plan?"

Cressida shook her head. "No."

Gianna took the seat opposite, looking guileless, something Cressida was sure she practiced. "You catch the fly."

"What? I don't—" She bit her lip, hard. Felt the sting that settled the nerves that had been threatening to overwhelm her for weeks.

"Think about it. A fly buzzes around and touches everything. Ruining everything as they move along. They flit from one thing to another. But to catch them, you need to set a trap. Do it right and the fly lands exactly where you want them."

"And how do I achieve that?"

"You bait the trap, my dear." Gianna leaned in close and gave a tiny smile. "Oh, and Daniel is very cute. I think I might invite him to join my nest when this is all done."

Cressida fought for control of the jealousy that raged. Gianna was watching her and for some reason she was sure this was a test, not that it wiped away the hot well of anger that churned in her gut.

"I'm afraid, when this is done, there will need to be a lot of things to consider. That is but one."

Gianna smiled and rose. "Indeed, that is true. Or partly so. I think I'll retire now."

Once the room was silent again Samra placed a large goblet in front of Cressida. "You aren't really planning on letting her get her hooks into him, are you?"

"Oh, Samra, it may not be a case of what I want." She bit her lip and nearly looked away, but that would have smacked of cowardice.

"*Morologus es!* He wants you and you want him. That's the simple bit. But if you don't act soon—"

"Stop it, Samra! Whatever my feelings, he's a human and I'm not." The snort from across the desk jabbed at her emotions. With a huff, Samra left the office and Cressida stared at the wall, hoping no one could hear her. "And I already have enough regrets and guilt. I don't need more."

Walking into Javed's office was like stepping into a baptism of fire. Daniel's head whirled with the concept that Gianna believed he should change. Being a vampire wasn't something he really wanted, though there would be side benefits. The swirling thoughts were both terrifying and seductive, he concluded.

Concentrate, Daniel. He had to push these thoughts away if he hoped to make it through the interrogation that awaited him. The door slid open under his hand and he smiled, noting the way Javed and Celina both frowned.

Daniel took his time, settling himself without a word in the seat opposite Javed.

"So?" He almost laughed at the confusion on his half-sister's face. *She hates being kept waiting.* If the situation hadn't been so grave, he might have laughed.

"I met with Gianna." His blunt words filled the air and he waited for them to ask what about, or even to come to the natural conclusion, seeing as he was here to meet with them. They both eyed him with blank looks. Clearly his suspicion that Gianna would have spoken to Javed, given he was the head of the House, was wrong.

"She suggested..." Now that he was about to say the words, they lodged in his throat. It hadn't seemed that hard before arriving in the office. He'd expected them to guess what would come next.

"What?" Javed leaned forward, Daniel heard the creak and groan of the metal of the vampire masters chair. "Daniel, just tell us, so we can deal with whatever needs to be addressed."

Celina's hands curled and Daniel wondered, not for the first time, if she was aware of her actions. In the past months he'd come to know Celina well, and he'd learned the small things she did that gave away her concerns.

"She thinks..." His mouth dried and he had to swallow. "She suggested I should embrace the *change*."

Javed's face might as well have been carved marble, and Celina continued to look oddly unaware of what he was saying.

Celina moved in his direction. "She what?"

He cleared his throat. "She, and I, agree. In order to fight and hopefully defeat Attar, I should become a vampire."

Shock stole over Celina's face. "No!"

He winced, as did Javed. "Celina, let me—"

"No. Javed, tell him that's not what he wants." Her voice was hoarse, and not for the first time he saw a shadow of pain cross over Javed's face when she made such a comment. He knew Celina had been changed without her consent. It wasn't that she didn't want to be a vampire, but she'd been dying and there'd been no opportunity for her to make the decision herself. Javed had changed her in order to save her life. Daniel knew Javed struggled with guilt over that.

"Listen to me, Celina. The prophecy says..." He had to stop and regain his equilibrium as she kept shaking her head.

"Damn the bloody prophecy! You don't want that. Please, don't let them... Javed?" Now she gripped her mate and Daniel felt an odd sense of embarrassment, and to him it was like an invasion of their privacy.

The vampire on the other side of the desk scooped Celina into his embrace, holding her close. A spurt of envy almost overwhelmed Daniel. "Hush, Celina. Let's hear what he has to say first."

"But, Javed, you can't let them turn him into a monster!" Once again Javed's face blanked, but not before Daniel caught sight of the deep pain.

Daniel needed to act before the situation became worse. "Celina, I would do anything to stop Attar. When I took my oath to Javed, I swore whatever I could, I would help save the innocents. It's the same oath you took."

"But you'll never have children. You'll be condemned never to see the daylight again. You have to think rationally."

"I have. I am. Celina..." Daniel moved in her direction, reaching toward her. "I love you and know that you are worried for me. But this is my decision." He kissed her cold cheek. "A decision I've made. Javed?" He knew that the choice he made, the one both he and Gianna agreed on, was right. In order to beat this creature, he'd have to become one of them. Until he embraced his new future, he would remain fragile. Easily overcome. He needed the strength that came with the *curse* to fight.

Now that he'd accepted the truth, he felt free.

Perhaps it had been his destiny all along, or maybe it was his need to balance the scoresheet. Daniel just knew he'd made his decision, and he wasn't going to look too carefully at his reasons why. *Now I'll have to tell Father.*

Javed rubbed a hand across his chin as he stared at Daniel, as if searching for a hint of doubt. Daniel knew all he'd see was resolve. "You're sure?"

Celina gave a mewl of distress, and Javed wound an arm around his mate in comfort.

"Yeah. What do I need to do?"

"The next step is to petition the council for permission. We haven't received an allocation this year, however, I'm sure... Given the circumstances, I doubt they'll refuse." He shook his head, and Daniel could tell that Javed and Celina were communicating telepathically.

"Maybe, and this is merely a suggestion, talk to Cressida first.

Given the situation, she may have something to say about it."

"Of course." He inclined his head in agreement. "I'll make some inquiries and let you know." Thus dismissed, Daniel rose and headed across the room, the carpet eating up the sound of his footsteps.

At the door he stopped, but when he looked back, he noted the way Javed's arms encircled his sister and her head nestled into his shoulder. With a shrug, Daniel closed the door behind him.

"So, I'm sure your plans are sufficient for now, Cressida. But I've taken the liberty of talking to Daniel, too. I'm sure it was something that you were going to attend to in the near future."

Cressida froze at Gianna's words. *'I've spoken to Daniel'*. That could mean a million things. None of them anything she wanted to contemplate. "You mean...?"

"Oh, Daniel and I understand each other implicitly. I'm sure we both will see the benefits of our mutual decision."

The words slammed into Cressida's brain like spikes. *Their mutual decision.* "I see. And he'll be leaving with you...?"

Gianna's tinkling laugh echoed through the room and for an instant Cressida had the sense she was being toyed with. But how could that possibly be? Her stomach soured, though.

He'd professed to have feelings and affection for her, but he'd agreed to Gianna's overtures without any hesitation. The emotions of being unwanted—as if set aside—overwhelmed her.

You were the one who rebuffed his advances.

She stalked the length of the room. Standing in front of the massive glass panes overlooking the garden. *I need to approach this in a rational manner.* Her heart broke as she came to the realization. The pain didn't lessen, though.

"Of course, our plans can only go ahead if he meets the criteria."

Cressida tensed, muscles coiled, ready to spring. "Criteria?"

"Well, the human government is so focused on ensuring only the most suitable can undergo the change that—"

The change.

What have you done, Gianna?

She whirled around to see her Overlord smiling, only it didn't reach Gianna's eyes. "What had to be done, Cressida! In order to fulfill the prophecy, he must become a vampire. And he must find his mate."

"But he won't be human anymore! It's not for us to direct this." Deep inside her mind, a sliver of hope lit up the gloom. "You shouldn't have—"

Now Gianna's facial expression hardened. "You forget yourself, Cressida. It is my place. I am your Overlord and you will obey me."

The words boomed throughout the room, a palpable wave of pure power washing over her. Cressida shivered as the magically imbued command ricocheted around the room. Pain sparked briefly before it melted away, leaving Cressida exhausted.

"Of course, Liege. I would beg your forgiveness." Cressida dropped into a deep obeisance and when she raised her head, it was to note the smile that wreathed Gianna's face.

"Good. Now you will make the necessary arrangements. A word of advice? I will ensure this happens. It might be unwise to inform the council at this point."

Cressida nodded, unwilling to trust her voice.

"Good. I feel for now there isn't much else I can do. I'll be leaving tomorrow and heading for my next holding."

"Of course. I'll make the arrangements." But when Gianna left the room, all Cressida could do was slump to her seat. *Daniel, a vampire.*

Cressida? I'm on my way. Samra's tones reverberated in Cressida's brain.

Tears dribbled down Cressida's face as she sat with her elbows resting on the desk. Surely no one else could read the fear and misery in her mind.

Nope, Cressida. Just me, and that's because we've known each other for so long. So what does… Vae! *She wants to what?*

The door slammed open and Samra stood there. "Tell me she hasn't done that."

"Oh, she has." The words emerged as a wail and Samra strode forward to kneel beside Cressida.

"How could she do this to you? After everything you gave up?" Samra's voice vibrated with anger and Cressida gave an inelegant snort.

"Because she can. She's looking at the overall picture while I sit here and weep in my misery." Cressida reached into her pocket, pulled out a handkerchief and wiped her eyes. "It isn't that she doesn't realize, it's just that she's focused on the needs of the innocent. My pain is old and mine alone."

Cressida felt foolish and weak. They weren't exactly emotions that she allowed herself to experience regularly, and for that Cressida was pleased. She needed to be more like Gianna and think outside herself.

Samra tugged on her hand, making Cressida focus on her Second. "We have to get to Daniel, make him realize…"

Cressida shook her head, understanding exactly what Gianna didn't say or ask. A *ping* sounded throughout the room and she moaned. A new email.

Was this the one that would change so many things? "I'd say no matter what you did now, it's resolved, if that email header is anything to go by."

Both of their gazes settled on the screen while Cressida tapped the key. A message with the subject heading *Change Application—Daniel* opened. She didn't have to read it to know that Javed had granted consent to the request. They were at the point of no return.

"It wouldn't bother you so much if you didn't care. You're going to have to address that. And soon."

"I can't, Samra. You should understand that." She pulled free of

Samra's hold. Suddenly the tiny necklace weighed a ton and she had to work hard to refrain from pulling it away from her skin.

"I know what you gave up. I know how much it hurt you to try to change your husband. I know how much you lost personally. I'm aware of the child. But that was then. Times have changed, and if he's—"

A tiny wave of her hand stopped Samra. "I can't face this again. I can't lose the man I—" Cressida wanted to call back the words, but Samra's expression told her she understood exactly what she'd nearly said.

"You can't hide from life forever. You're going to have to deal with this mess, otherwise it'll be too late and you'll lose him anyway."

"I can't... I need to work. There are things that the council needs me to attend to. I have to concentrate on them." Cressida opened the top file on her desk and tried to focus on the sheet titled Budgetary Report, but the words swam in front of her. She knew Samra was watching her, but right now the memories of painful times were too much to bear. For so long she'd tried to hide her past by remaining cool and detached. *When did I change?*

"Think on what I've said. You can't hide from this forever." On that, Samra rose and left her.

TWELVE

Attar looked around. The building he'd chosen was perfect for his needs. The raised dais allowed him to look over his minions. They churned like a million ants as they struggled against one another.

"Master, you are enjoying the spectacle?" The woman beside him undulated, rubbing her naked form against his side.

Taking the girl had been the highlight of his latest raid. She'd cowered and bleated until he'd fed from her—or it could have been the beating. Not that he really cared one way or another.

One of his vampires went down and he grinned, watching the spectacle. Only the strongest and best would survive. That was what he needed. An army of warriors. Only those strong enough to defeat those who opposed him could be allowed to survive.

A spurt of blood splashed up onto the wood at his feet. For a moment his focus narrowed.

"You wish to feed, sire?"

The girl kneeled beside him, her naked flesh arrayed for him so that he could inspect every pulse point before deciding where he would take sustenance from today.

He grabbed at her with his clawed fingers and for an instant a flare of fear shone in her eyes. He smelled it and gloried in the arousal that hummed through his body.

Fear. Pain. Blood. Power.

He'd have it all.

She collapsed against his lap and his teeth extended. Glorious sustenance squirted into his mouth as he broke the skin at her neck.

It slid down, rich and heady, the liquid feeding and enhancing his need for the secondary release he'd soon experience. Anticipation filled him until the sound of footsteps intruded.

"Master? News."

He thrust the girl away and watched emotionlessly as she teetered on the edge of the dais. A hand rose to grab at her and for an instant Attar snarled as the chain in his hand tugged tight. He let go, watching as the girl fell into the pit.

"Get me another slave." The warrior at his side bowed deeply and hurried away while Attar opened the missive that had been shoved into his hand.

We have been summoned to an urgent meeting. I will report afterward.

Oh yes, his plans were starting to bear fruit. He steepled his fingers, but the roar from below was now an annoyance battering at his mind.

"Cease!" he bellowed and those nearest stilled, hearing the command of their master. Some still gyrated on the floor, fighting for survival. Clearly they'd not heeded him. Or heard him. Anger rose and he let it grow, welcoming the surge of power. "Get rid of them and return to your cells."

A series of sharp cries rent the air and the scent of spilled blood tantalized, but he'd already dismissed the scene before him. He closed his eyes. What could they be planning now?

Soon. Soon he would plot his ultimate revenge, then they would understand. He was a God.

Cressida's hand shook as she read the request.

I, Daniel, Yeux Secondes of the House of al bin Habbad,
request the privilege of The Change.
I am cognizant of the inherent dangers, but I feel that I am an
excellent candidate and will be able to offer the nests and
council my skills and abilities for the period of my life.
Whether natural or vampiric.
I hereby submit references from my Master, Javed, and his
partner, Celina, who attest that I do this for the benefit of all
and not for my own needs. Further references from Xavier,
Master of the House of Tudor, and his partner, Hope, bear out
my past service to the nests I've belonged to.
I promise to swear and pledge my life to the protection of inno-
cents and my nest, should my petition be successful.
Attached are the necessary clearances and I'm more than
happy to schedule any such evaluations as may be required...

The rest of the words on the page blurred.

Cressida's lips felt stiff as she opened her mouth. "He has submitted this of his own free will, Javed?" She might be outwardly calm, but inside she was screaming with denial. Since she'd met him, there had existed an invisible thread binding them together. A mixture of hunger and need that moved beyond blood lust. Fear of naming it had left her with evading the truth, an action so unlike her natural response.

It scared her.

He was human, so she'd told herself ignoring those emotions was *acceptable.* Human lovers died and left her kind alone, something she'd learned early on in her extended existence.

While pledging their love to her, each human who'd promised her love and affection had eventually abandoned her for a future that included love and children. In her experience, turning their back on *life* left them bitter and angry. Resentful.

In desperation, she'd taken the occasional vampiric lover, but that too left her feeling empty and somehow more shallow than before.

Many of her lovers had forgotten their humanity, an action she had viewed with regret. Unwilling to chance losing the small sliver of her soul, she'd chosen to embrace celibacy. It allowed her to focus on the humans who served her and the nests she'd headed.

But from within her mind came the cry, *I've been lonely for so long.*

"Cressida?" Javed's words brought her back to the matter before her.

If she allowed him—if the council allowed this—Daniel's humanity and, even more gut-wrenching, the man that he was, might be lost forever.

"He has, Cressida. If I may—"

"You may not." She choked on the words, realizing that Javed, so recently united with Celina, would happily accept the burden and guilt of this very final decision.

It wasn't his place. It wasn't his cross to bear. Gianna had long ago tasked her with the role of protecting their kind—though she'd shied away from accepting the position in the Council for a long time. Now, her knowledge of the task ahead—that of spearheading the hunt for Attar and neutralizing the threat he stood to their collective future—chilled her.

"You may leave us to deliberate, Javed."

She turned slowly and met his unwavering gaze.

Cressida slid the paperwork to Samra, who blinked slowly, accepting the sheaf, then bowed her head to read. Normally this would be a decision of the Council, but in consultation with Gianna, it had been decided that she and Samra would determine Daniel's eligibility. Of course, she already knew Gianna considered this the best option.

Dragging her gaze from Samra's studied interest, she looked to Javed, giving a pointed reminder that she'd dismissed him.

"As you request, Councilor." He bowed deeply, spun on his heel and left the chamber, the door clanging shut behind him.

"Cressida, if you change him..."

She acknowledged Samra's words with a nod.

How can I put my fears into the right words?

"Samra, if I change him, and I am by no means convinced this is our only option, we steal his future. He will be what we are. Creatures of the night."

"Indeed, but we save the innocent. That has been our role for centuries, Cressida. You've told us repeatedly, the protection of one must never outweigh the needs of the many who will suffer for our inaction."

The words hit hard and she had to stop herself from rearing away. "You are right, of course, but what about—"

"The councilors have noted your interest in Daniel, especially since his elevation, but you must put aside your emotions. You are our leader, second only to Gianna. If you cannot make this decision with the mind of a warrior, we are lost before the battle even begins."

Emotions were clouding her thoughts. Her needs and fears were bringing those involved to a point they couldn't afford to reach.

Samra was right.

"Then...then we must decide now."

Samra slid the papers back across the desk. "You already know my thoughts. If his powers will help us to defeat Attar, I feel there is no other option."

Cressida sighed, took up the ceremonial dagger that rested on her desk. The weight of it and all it represented was a heavy yoke. In her mind, the lifting of this blade to conclude the tradition seemed far more dangerous. Her hand shook as she made a tiny incision in her wrist, then handed the dagger to Samra, who did the same. "As is our custom, we bond our blood, as we bond our thoughts. Another will join with us as a result of our joint decision." There was a shimmer in the air as the magic of vampires rippled. The deed was completed, but even as the power died away, another portion of her soul withered.

Tap. Tap. Daniel raised his head. "Come in."

The door opened with a creak and Celina entered, her face grave. "You have your response." She handed him a letter, sealed with blood-red wax. He noted that her hands shook.

The letter, held so tightly, contained the decision on his future. What direction would it take him? His stomach curdled a little as his mind weighed the options. Never mind that he'd made his decision days ago, this letter reflected the thoughts of the council.

"Daniel?" His half-sister's voice broke through his foggy mind.

"I'm just..." He slid one of his fingers under the lip and tugged. The wax gave with a barely audible crack.

Everything around him was happening in slow motion.

The door opened again and Javed entered his office. Daniel noted the way Javed slid an arm around Celina and reached out his other hand, setting it on Daniel's shoulder.

"We're here to support you."

He looked into Javed's eyes and nodded. "I know." He took a deep and unsteady breath and opened the parchment. He scanned the words.

It is my decision to accept your petition for The Change. You will be required to undergo the mandatory genetic and psychological testing within the next seventy-two hours. Details of your scheduled appointment and locations are attached. Should we receive a positive test result, your House Master

will advise the details of your induction, which will be carried
out by Councilor Cressida...

He released the pent-up oxygen in his lungs. "I've been given the green light. I'm to undergo the genetic and psych tests."

He felt numb. As if nothing could touch him.

"Daniel? Are you sure you..." Celina's eye sparkled with unshed tears.

"There really isn't any other option. I'm the only human and the weakest link. I can't help if I don't—"

"That's not true. You have magic. You aren't unable to protect yourself." Celina leaned in, tugging away from Javed, and hugged him tight. "You have magic."

He waited through her hug, his gaze on the ceiling while he fought the sting in his eyes.

"It's not enough. We have to beat him. This is the only way."

"If you are sure?" Javed spoke, breaking the emotion-laden moment. "I'll take care of things here."

"Thanks."

Celina and Javed drew away, and Daniel felt the loss of their physical support.

"If you need anything, anything at all, you let us know." His sister turned, and, with her partner, left him.

As the door closed, the loneliness settled around him like a cloud. Cold invaded his bones so quickly that it left him gasping.

He couldn't share any of his emotional turmoil with his father. He wouldn't understand and, even more, had no interest in finding out why Daniel would make such a sacrifice. He still wrestled with his anger at Celina and Daniel's long-dead mother.

Besides which, since meeting Celina and hearing the truth of their shared parentage, the relationship with his father had become strained. Daniel had been unable to conceal his anger at his father's careless and hurtful reaction to Celina.

She was the one who was innocent of any wrongdoing in the

whole mess. His father still treated her as someone he didn't wish to associate with, creating a schism between himself and the master of House. Things had improved though, once his father had left the nest which, Daniel reflected, was probably the only acceptable action.

Deep in his heart he knew Celina would do anything for him, and she was grateful that he'd not just acknowledged their familial connection. She respected his decisions and flaws—unlike his father.

The bond between Celina and Daniel had deepened during his time here, and he felt sure that she'd one day trust him enough to share the full truth of her cold and friendless childhood. He'd watched the blossoming of her relationship with Javed and the three children who'd become part of her family, and that warmed him. He'd seen her wrestle with the dark demons that had plagued her since her change. He only hoped he could carry it off with the same dignity she'd exhibited.

Dropping the letter to his desk, he couldn't help but wonder what Cressida really thought of it all. "Ah well, what's done is done."

He turned away and looked out over the dark garden. There was much to do to prepare.

THIRTEEN

Daniel looked around him. His things were packed and the room felt empty and devoid, as if he no longer inhabited this place.

"I guess I'm not really. Not after tonight." The clothes he'd chosen to wear in the morning lay across the chair at the end of the bed, mocking him.

Javed had given orders that the shutters be pulled on Daniel's suite so he could rest one last time.

But rest was the last thing on his mind.

He looked to the cradle of the phone, wishing he could have spoken to his father in a calm manner, but nothing about this whole situation could be classified as easy. He'd made one last-ditch attempt to talk to the man, even going so far as to travel to his new nest, but the interview had been a disaster. His father had yelled and stomped, demanded and wheedled. At the end, when nothing went quite to his plan, he'd left Daniel in the room by himself.

A knock at the door surprised him. "Come."

The wooden panel slid open easily and Kharisma entered, bearing a tray. "Celina thought you might appreciate warm milk and something to eat." On the plate he saw several chocolate biscuits and he laughed in spite of his mood.

"Yeah, it's pretty hard to be angry when you have chocolate biscuits on offer." A ghost of a grin crossed Kharisma's face. "But that's not the only reason you're here, is it?"

She shook her head and he settled down on the bed, sure Javed's second would have some pearls of wisdom to share.

"You've lived in nests your whole life so you know a little about the way tonight and tomorrow will play out. I've come to prepare you. To give you some idea of the changes you will undergo, both physical and emotional." He arched one eyebrow and waited as the woman hurried to reassure him. "It isn't appropriate for either Javed or Celina to do so."

"All right, so what don't I know?"

"As you know, tomorrow, when you leave here for the last time, the household will form a guard of honor. It is the way of the change."

He'd seen it before, so that wasn't new.

"You will parade past them. It's grueling and emotional, Daniel. They will know that your humanity is ending. That it's only a matter of hours before your body dies. To be clear, that's exactly what happens."

He wanted to laugh off her words, but there was no mirth to call up.

"Then?"

"You will be taken to Cressida's and she will be handling the change herself."

Daniel's brow furrowed. "It's usually...?"

"Yeah, normally it would be Javed, or his female equivalent. But it's an intensely sensual act. It, uh..." She pinked a little under his scrutiny.

"You have sex afterward?" Her gaze slid past him to a point over his shoulder.

"No. But I would have. Many do. It's not a part of the ceremony, but... Many are aroused by the scents and smells. Javed and Celina couldn't. You're her brother and Javed... He couldn't change you. He promised your sister he wouldn't. It's not unusual that partnered vampires refuse to participate in changing ceremonies. I don't have the standing or the power to change you, so this had to be Cressida."

He wasn't sure he needed to hear that Cressida had likely participated in any sexual gratification with those she'd changed.

As if she read his mind, Kharisma sighed. "To this day, though, I don't believe Cressida has completed any carnal acts with her neophytes."

The lump of concrete in his belly lessened a little. She didn't take her responsibilities lightly, he knew.

"Once you arrive, you will be escorted to the room set aside for initiation. It's where all our new vampires are born."

Now his belly wobbled ever so slightly. "Will it...?" He licked his dry lips, unable to complete the question he needed the answer to. Instead, he shook his head and changed tack. "She'll be waiting for me?"

"No. A witch will be there and she'll cleanse the room. She'll prepare the circle where the act will take place." Daniel must have moved as she laid a soft hand on his shoulder. "It's necessary to help keep you passive while she begins. Unlike Celina and Hope, you will know that your life is ending at the hands of a vampire. You are choosing it, but your spirit will fight it. It's inevitable. So we keep a circle active so we can contain your spirit until such time as it returns to you."

"And it will return to me?"

Kharisma stared at him, unblinking. Clearly, not all did, if he read her reaction correctly. That scared him more than hearing the words.

He picked up the mug, looking for some way to control his reaction. Drinking deeply helped as he let his mind wander, blanking out everything Kharisma had said. He knew she was watching him, but now the decision had been made, he couldn't—he wouldn't—change his mind.

He lifted the mug to take another deep gulp and realized it was empty, so he thrust it at Kharisma. "Thank you. This will help me." He shoved the mug into her hands and she accepted the dismissal with a deep bow.

Just as she made to close the door he heard her whisper, "May God be with you."

Glancing at the clock, Daniel sighed. "Time for bed."

He dropped his clothes to the floor, aware that he would clear them away when he woke, and laid down.

He willed sleep to come.

It did by gradual degrees, and he let his mind float free.

THE ROOM WAS IN DARKNESS, BUT HE COULD STILL SEE. IT WAS odd. Cressida lay on the chaise , huddled into a ball.

"Cressida? What's wrong?" He flowed in her direction and reached out a hand.

Her stomach was rounded and he recoiled.

"The child. It is dead." Tears left a trace down her cheeks and he noted for the first time the droplets of blood that festooned her collar. "Why? Why did they do this to me?"

The wail was heart-wrenching.

"Who? Who did this to you?"

"My-my sire. He called himself Sampson. He came in here and he did this to me while his friend Estersham watched!" She howled her rage and pushed from the chair, hands balled. "He said... He told me he wanted my husband, and when I couldn't tell him where Etienne was, he bit me. He changed me."

Daniel's heart thudded in his chest. "Your husband?"

"Etienne is a Godly man. A priest! He's never done anything wrong, and now this! How can I face him and myself? My soul is damned eternally!" Her anger built and in her eyes he saw the tinge of red as the hunger rose.

The door rattled and he stepped back, seeking a dark corner of the room as a man entered. "Cressida, my love. I should never have trav-

eled to the Abbey. I came as soon as I received the missive. What's happened...?" His steps took him to the chaise where he dropped to his knees. His hands touched her belly and Daniel felt a hiss of anger and jealousy rising in his chest.

The man reared back. "Cressida?" She looked at him, and his gaze seemed to center on her teeth, which descended ferociously, and the red eyes that glowed in the dimness. He gasped. "What have they done to you? What have you become?"

Horror dripped from his lips as he spoke. His hands slid from her stomach and he scooted backward, fear a palpable emotion as the room grew close.

"I didn't do anything." Her wail shredded Daniel's insides. "Don't leave me alone. Please, Etienne!" Her words were mesmeric, but the man, this Etienne, flung his hands into his pockets as she rose and advanced on him.

Daniel's stomach turned as he watched her. She crouched over him. "I'm hungry and I need you."

Etienne raised his hand, a crucifix clutched tightly in shaking fingers. "Get away, demon! I bind you! In the name of all that is holy, I bind you and cast you out!"

She laughed, mirthless and cold, her spirit clearly shattered by the pain of the loss she now suffered.

"I'm no demon. I'm your wife."

The man standing before her shook his head and reared farther away. "You're naught but a monster now."

Her fingers caught him, clutched his body close as her fangs extended further. "God help me."

She dove in, her teeth sinking deep into his body.

Etienne fought and Daniel watched, horrified, as the man struggled, his hands fluttering. The crucifix fell to the floor, the clang loud. The sounds he made—screams and moans that died away to nothing. His movements became weaker until they finally stopped.

When she dropped him, pink tears trailed down her cheeks. In anguish, she turned toward Daniel, reaching out to him. "Now you see."

Then she collapsed.

He woke as the final fingers of daylight stretched across the sky, his heart pounding.

It was time to rise.

Cressida woke with a start and tears on her cheeks. The dream hadn't disturbed her in so long. Why now? And why had Daniel been there? It wasn't... She shied away from the knowledge that it could be the mating dreams.

She knew both Hope and Celina had experienced them with Xavier and Javed. She'd shared some highly erotic dreams with Daniel, but why this? And why now? What trick did her psyche want to play on her?

The pounding of her heart sounded loud and she needed to calm herself. Perhaps it was related to her preparation for changing Daniel?

She cast away the thought. Clearly there were too many questions and no answers in her beleaguered mind.

The thudding of her heart finally slowed to a more realistic speed and she stopped, gasping like a fish out of water.

"Oh God! Why do you do this to me?" But railing at some higher force had never before worked and she doubted it would today.

Cressida swung her legs to the side of the bed and glanced at the clock. It wasn't yet dark, so what had woken her? *It must be nerves,* she told herself. In all her years of changing humans, for some reason Daniel was different.

Because it's Daniel, her heart whispered. *Then maybe...* Her heart stuttered as she stopped the thought in its track. "No. He will be a warrior. One of Gianna's men."

Instead of stilling the nerves, the knowledge left her uneasy and bitterness welled. She'd been a good wife. Wanted the child her husband had given her.

She'd tried so hard to be perfect for Etienne. Devout and devoted. The change had shattered her illusions and beliefs.

After his death, it had taken a long time to come to terms with what she'd done.

Over the centuries that had passed, she'd learned to be a warrior, had taken up arms and made her oath of fealty to her overlord.

She'd be faithful once more.

In the last few decades her role had again changed and she'd become more than a mere soldier. Now she was a counselor. A leader. A protector.

So much had changed when Hope had been born. She'd reminded Cressida of all she'd once dreamed of. It was the saving of the innocent child that had healed sections of her soul.

Then Celina had taken her place in Cressida's affections, and things had become difficult—she'd no longer attempted to deny the wisp of humanity that remained within her. She'd fed the hunger, hoping one day, she'd find redemption.

Daniel. Now he'd been different. She'd been attracted to him from the beginning and felt so personally invested.

A knock at the door broke through her introspection. "Who is it?"

"Samra. I have your blood wine."

She should have known. Should have felt her presence, but since she'd had contact with Daniel, her wits had fled—or at least turned to mush. Her reflexes were dulled.

Cressida gripped the handle and opened the door. Samra entered, her long legs eating up the space. Her second pushed the tray forward with a somber look. "Drink. It will help."

"You were listening in?" She couldn't help the blush that stained her cheeks.

"Not listening, but your restlessness woke me. Do you wish to talk?"

As her second, Samra was so much more than the warrior at her back, she was also her closest friend.

"I don't... I haven't had this dream in such a long time, Samra. Why now? Is it an omen?"

Samra cocked her head to the side. "The one from when you turned?"

"Yes, but...Daniel was there this time."

"Ahh. That explains it. Your subconscious is doing your job for you. I'm not really surprised. After all, you want him. It's more than sex though, Cressida. Your whole attitude toward him reads as protective and caring. I can see how much it scares you."

She really didn't want to hear anything Samra had to say about Daniel. She shook her head. This was her second, she had to trust her, and Cressida knew her emotions were tangled. "So what do I do?"

"You give in, Cressida. Because if you don't something *will* happen. It always does, and you'll never forgive yourself if the outcome is compromised because of your decision."

"But he saw..."

"What? What did Daniel see? How did he react? He knows you're a vampire. He grew up with them, so he's always known what they are and what they do." Samra leaned in, belaboring the point.

For the first time, the blunt words Samra spoke made an impact and Cressida bit her lip.

"Daniel saw you as you were after the change? He too will feel this need very soon. He's not your husband, though. Your husband, he was a priest at a time when what you were violated humanity and *his* beliefs—or so was the common belief of the time. Daniel saw that Etienne tried to cast you out? Most of us have either seen or had that happen to us. Those of us who lived through those times know that survival was difficult."

"But he saw it all. He saw—"

"He saw you at your most vulnerable. Dammit, Cressida, that's not who you are now. You don't back down from anything that would scare the rest of us, so why this? The whole vacillation and weak female act you are waving around isn't like you. It's time to pull yourself together. Because I'm willing to bet he didn't run screaming for the door, did he? Don't taint him with your own problems." Samra's chest heaved and Cressida felt foolish.

"Cressida, we have enough problems right now without adding to them. Now hurry and dress, it's nearly time."

Cressida wasn't sure if Samra's plain-speaking was good or bad. Just that she spoke the truth. The truth she needed to hear. A truth she needed to act on.

"I... Samra..." She couldn't complete the thought. The words wouldn't push past the lump in her throat.

"I know. When we love, it's deep. Remember, I've been there too."

Cressida realized with a start Samra had. Until Samra's life partner had been killed. Shame filled her. "I'm sorry, Samra."

Samra turned, her eyes glittering with tears. "I know. I understand. Now it's time to prepare."

With savage moves, she stripped and dressed in the simple garb she'd chosen to wear. *Samra was right*, she thought, looking again to the clock. He'd be here soon. She'd had enough time to consider what was to come, now she had to follow through.

FOURTEEN

Daniel's muscles ached with the necessity of holding his breath. His glance took in the dark room, the flickering lights of the candles and the large glowing mark on the floor.

The witch circled, chanting in low tones. At the center was a chaise longue. The only difference from the one in his dream, the metal construction, though deep cushions lay upon it. In the half-light, the gleam of silver glinted menacingly.

His stomach clenched. *You agreed to this. Time to see it through.*

Cressida caught his glance. "You still have time to change your mind."

It was as if she read his thoughts, and he gulped. Nothing would ever be the same after this, and that knowledge settled heavily in his stomach.

Gazing deeply into her eyes was like being carried on a current of magic. "I do, but I won't."

She nodded and Daniel sucked a deep breath into his lungs, feeling them expand as Cressida reached out to him. The witch must have heard some unspoken command or finished her cleansing, as she straightened and backed away. She made a careful bow in their direction, then retreated.

He and Cressida waited as she exited the room. The bang reverberated through the dimness.

The finality made him flinch.

"Come." The words were thin and reedy, and he looked at Cressida. Her face was so pale in the darkness.

Cressida made a motion as if opening a door on the faint, blue and glowing flames of the casting circle.

He allowed Cressida to lead him to the chaise. Each step, on shaking legs, felt like walking toward his doom.

One small shred of whimsy reminded him that was exactly what he was doing.

"Be easy, Daniel." He let the words wash over him as he leaned over to the chaise. As he lay back, the material beneath his nearly bare body surrounded him like a soft cloud.

She took one hand in her grip, giving him the unspoken question he was too afraid to answer, lest he change his mind. Daniel thanked the gods he didn't shake. "I trust you, Cressida. I always have."

A glint caught his eye before she turned away to fasten his hands carefully in the silken bonds.

He instinctively flinched, then released the tension in his body, but she hissed unevenly. As she leaned over him, something wet dripped to his torso.

She was crying.

"Cressida?"

"I'd rather it never came to this." Her muffled words cleaved his heart.

"This was my choice. I wanted you to change me, not anyone else. We both know this was inevitable."

Daniel waited for her to glance at him, but she didn't. "Cressida? Talk to me." Now that his hands were bound, he couldn't reach for her. Could offer her no comfort other than his words.

A sob erupted and she shook. He tugged against the bonds, but they were too strong. "Don't. I don't regret this."

The sounds subsided and finally she sniffled. "I shouldn't have done that. I didn't mean..."

For the first time since he'd met her, she sounded uncertain and lost.

"Cressida..."

She didn't respond as expected, just turned away, her spine straightening. "We should begin."

Those words filled him with trepidation. *Nothing will ever be the same once this is complete.*

With great care, Cressida lowered herself beside him, an apology glowing in her eyes before it faded away. Now there was heat and need.

She caressed his chest and his skin turned to fire, her touch skating over the muscles. They clenched at each pass and his breathing slowed as his body warmed from the center out.

"I've wanted to touch you. After we met at the house, I had this need to know you. To be near you." She raised her gaze to him. The mesmerizing power of her stare drew something deep inside him close to the surface. "But you were human. Fragile."

The smile that blossomed on her face scorched him and arousal shimmered between them.

"No more than I wanted you." His honest answer filled the air as molten lava coursed through his veins. She leaned forward, her honeyed breath bathing him, and his eyes fluttered closed while the rapid tattoo of his heartbeat fluttered in his ears.

Cressida kissed him on the lips, the soft touch stealing a part of his being. The emotions deepened and she clutched him to her, and the discomfort of the bindings melted away.

She invaded his mouth and the taste of nectar on her tongue overwhelmed his senses.

The kiss turned fiery as hunger flared. When she pulled away, he breathed heavily, chest heaving. Once again she ran her hands over his musculature. "I want to touch you."

Carefully she nibbled her way to his throat, laving the sensitive skin while he writhed, hunger filling him. "Oh God!" The utterance tore from him. "Kiss me now."

She fastened her lips below his ear and sucked lightly. He tugged against the bindings, his body on fire.

She pulled back, her gaze mesmerizing him while his body sang with arousal. Then she struck.

An instant of pain tearing at his vein shocked him momentarily. All too soon, the lethargy trickled through his being.

The dragging pulls, the drawing of blood, continued strong and sure. The pleasure he'd heard of speared him to the core as the cold he'd been warned of crept up on him. Time slowed.

The pinprick of awareness shimmering before withdrawing.

This is it.

Any intention of fight fled in time with the slowing of his heartbeat. That too slipped from his grasp.

FIFTEEN

Cressida heard the last faltering thud.

She breathed raggedly as it faded into silence, then she moved. In an instant, Cressida had torn the vein in her wrist. A spurt of bright red welled and spilled.

She held the dribbling liquid to his slack lips. They didn't open, so with a quick and practiced move, she slid her fingers between his teeth, levering his mouth wide. "Let this work." She'd known the risks all along, had held great fears that this wouldn't succeed.

The bleeding stilled as she waited, and with a curse she tore again at her wrist, widening the gash, and the blood flowed. It covered his lips and tongue and she waited for the first draw.

Nothing.

Her curse was loud. "Come on, Daniel. Drink so that you may live." The demand, imbued with magic, echoed in the cavernous room.

She waited, head cocked as she searched for the heartbeat that should have sounded. Nothing.

A teardrop made its way down her cheek as she ripped at her

flesh again. The scarlet blood gushed and she held her arm over his slack mouth.

Just as she was sure it hadn't worked, his lips moved, seeking the sustenance she offered.

At last! She'd feared he wouldn't make the turn. The more senior the vampire, the quicker the change should occur according to Gianna. Something to do with the blood of so many having suffused their veins with their combined strength. For her, it meant that every Master and Mistress who'd ever been made coursed through her.

With a shake of her head, Cressida laid her wrist to his lips, while he sucked at the slash, feeding in a frenzy.

The feeling that wove through her like a ribbon of heat and hunger was shocking but not unwelcome. When his eyes flashed open, she couldn't help herself. She tugged her arm away and kissed him, glorying in the sensations and tastes that exploded inside her mind.

The arousal that had been flaring between them became an explosion of wanton need as the pulsing of her sex and the curling of her belly betrayed her emotions.

She pushed closer. He muttered a word. Suddenly he tore the silken bindings with a resounding rip. They wound around her, tugging her closer. Deeper into the morass of need.

As skin collided with skin, the knot of desire in her belly tightened.

"I want you. Now!" His voice was deep and dark. She tried to suck in a breath and the sound that filled the air was ragged.

He pulled at the simple gown she wore. It tore with a loud rip, laying her bare before him.

Her nipples hardened to urgent peaks of hunger and he raised a hand, cupped her breast, his thumb rubbing over the engorged nub he'd found.

Her eyes drooped heavily before closing, her arousal purely elemental now. Daniel dragged her closer and she gasped.

Dancing flames of heat licking at her skin.

"Daniel!" His name was a long, thready moan.

His mouth ranged over her, muttering inchoate words as she gave into the sensual web he spun on her senses.

He trailed his fingers down her body, gliding and exploring dips and hollows before moving farther.

"So beautiful."

Tears spilled down her cheeks as she arched, unable to form a word, let alone tell him of the sensations that exploded in her body.

He found the tuft of hair at the junction of her thighs. Combed and quested before he found her core and lightning streaked behind her closed lids.

She trembled as he slid a single finger between her folds, wiping the moisture he'd found there. "So wet. So hot. So ready for me."

Her body burst apart as the orgasm rocketed, her senses overwhelmed. Time passed slowly as she opened her eyes. His gaze was steady, yet she detected the glint of well-restrained desire.

Cressida reached out, and she noted dimly that her hand shook. The force of her emotions crashed in her mind. "Daniel, I—"

He stopped her words in the ageless way men have always done —by feasting on her kiss. Any sense of urbanity was shredded, leaving behind a man who starved.

He tugged her down to the chaise, and rolled until she found herself beneath him, the light cotton of his pants the only barrier between them, and she reached for them. Shoved the material out of the way as he hissed.

"I want you, Cressida. Now."

Once more she arched and he moved between her legs, the thick, bulbous head of his cock nudging at her abdomen. A small flex of her spine and she shifted position so it sat at the entrance to her sex.

"Let...me..." He forced out the words. She heard the strain in his voice.

Determined to have her way, she hooked her legs around his waist and flexed again.

A groan tore from her throat as the sensation of being filled overwhelmed her mind. "No more waiting."

They moved. She didn't care who started it but she urged him on, rocking against him as she welcomed the maelstrom.

He ground and bucked as she tugged him closer. He slammed into her again. "Come for me." His gravelly words abraded the last shred of sanity.

She convulsed, giving in to the pleasure of orgasm, milking and demanding his all.

Suspended.

Breathless.

In the distance she felt him moving harder and faster, as Daniel grunted and held himself still, deeply embedded in her.

Her body relaxed as he finally emptied himself, every spurt sensitizing her further.

Daniel groaned and collapsed on top of her.

Running her hands up and down his back, she registered the warmth of his body, the growing heat, and reality raised its ugly head. "Oh dear God! What have I done?"

It was too late. Nothing that had been done that day could be changed.

Daniel woke to noise that battered at his brain. "Argh!" That sound reverberated through the room.

"Stop..." His entreaty was so loud, but it couldn't possibly be him, could it? The voice didn't sound like him. It was gruff. Deeper than he usually spoke. A little lispy even. No, it couldn't be him. So who was it?

He slowly opened his eyes, expecting to see someone standing over him. There was no one there, but everything was so *clear*. So crisp. He moved his head, expecting pain from the lacerations on his neck. The ones he knew Cressida had inflicted.

The tension seeped away as he felt whole. Good, even. Better than ever before.

"Daniel?" The hesitant voice was Cressida's.

"Yeah. How are you?" He drew a deep breath. She moved into his view.

"It should be me asking that question."

She sat beside him, the cushions of the chaise dipping to cradle her body. Cressida raised her hand, cupping his cheek and turning it slightly. "You've healed completely."

For the first time, her gaze dropped to his chest. His *bare* chest. Now the memories of what they'd done in this room, on this couch, invaded his mind. *We had sex.*

He wanted to wince at the harsh thought. It had been more than that. He was sure of it.

Was it?

For a moment he was startled. He could have sworn he'd heard Cressida in his mind.

I am.

"What?"

She jerked away from him, her vision clouded. "They...they didn't disclose the ability to mind-talk to you?" She worried her lip with her perfect teeth. Her agitation and concern washed over him in greasy waves.

There was that voice again. "Uh, no. No one said anything about that." He frowned.

Ah, you have so much to learn and so little time. She sighed. *As your sire, I am able to converse with you like this. I can converse with all I have changed or who owe fealty to me, and as the Head of the Council, I can also talk to all those from within the nests who owe me fealty.*

In ages past, it was how we taught our newly turned while they hunted for the first time. It was how we ensured the safety of our population. Cressida blinked as she imparted the wisdom of her many years.

Jealousy flowed through him.

She'd changed others. Enjoyed the same level of intimacy. She could talk to many.

A snarl erupted and he tried to stand. She pushed back, holding him against the seat. *Wait, Daniel. It isn't like that. I have changed many over the years, but never have I enjoyed what I found with you. I don't...* Cressida scrambled, and he had the feeling she hunted for the words that would allay his fears. He felt the confusion and anger that stabbed her deeply. *I mean, I've never done this with my changelings.* The agitation in her voice stilled his movements. *With those that came before, I felt no such hunger to investigate the more physical side of the change. I don't do that.*

Her thoughts confused him.

But with you it's different, isn't it? What makes you different?

She turned away, made to stand, but he grabbed her hand and held her still.

"Cressida?"

I don't know...

But she did. He could see it in the careful way she hid her face.

There was a seed of something hidden from him. Instinctively, Daniel sought it. Something lay beyond his grasp, but in her mind there was a veil obscuring his ability to understand her thoughts. He caught a wisp of fear and another of self-hatred—

"Don't seek knowledge you are not ready for." Her voice was rusty and this time she tugged away. "Rise and dress. I shall arrange sustenance for you." She didn't look at him, though, and her avoidance annoyed him.

"Cressida..."

"Come, Daniel. Others await your resurrection."

"Like this? Naked?" He heard the petulant tone and wanted to scream. He was an adult, so why was he acting this way? He'd not spoken to others like this since adolescence.

Everyone reacts in his or her own way to the change. Now, there is a set of clothing for you behind the screen. I will wait outside.

The petulance melted away, replaced by a warmer, more balanced emotion. "Cressida? Thank you."

This time she did turn back, her face a picture of surprise. "What? Why thank me? I'm the object of your doom."

He smiled. "Or the object of my salvation."

She shook her head and retreated from the room. The blanket that covered him fell away as he stood. He was woozy. *Hungry.*

The sides of his mouth ached. Each of these things he accepted as part of his new life—the things Kharisma had warned him of.

With a shrug, Daniel made his way to the dressing screen. It was so feminine, and for a moment he wondered if it was Cressida's own.

On a hanger he saw one of his black tailored suits and a snowy white shirt. Below sat his favorite wing-tipped shoes of black leather, and on a small stand he spied underwear. He tugged on the pants and shirt, ignoring the suit jacket. The slide of the material over his body made him moan as unfamiliar sensations crowded his mind.

That too, in time, will pass. Now, come to me.

Without conscious thought, he followed her demand.

Her body tingled in a most unfamiliar way and muscles long unused ached as she made her way slowly to her office. *Better to keep this official,* she advised herself.

It was difficult to maintain that icy barrier when memories of what they'd done kept rising to the surface. He'd been an accomplished if somewhat voracious lover, something she'd never before experienced.

It was a revelation.

Etienne had been kind and considerate, but he'd never made her burn. Not like Daniel. She wanted to shy away from the comparison, but it hovered there in the forefront of her mind.

Cressida ran a shaking hand through her blonde hair where it lay like a cloud against her skin. She needed to rein in her emotions, to react as she always had.

She lowered herself to her desk and the urge to cry rose. "You can't be like this, Cressida. Get control of yourself, otherwise we're all doomed." The weakness that seemed to have assailed her lately angered and infuriated her, yet she struggled to keep her thoughts and libido in check.

The photo of Gianna on the opposite wall made her straighten. It was as if she'd been slapped in the face with the memory of the vampire she owed fealty to. The woman who personified beauty and grace along with power. She could have any man—vampire or human. Was that the root cause of how she felt? Was it inadequacy that gnawed at her? Cressida grunted and put aside the thoughts.

Her mind instead sought Daniel and she smiled. He was dressing. She had a minute or two to find her inner balance. Seek it she did, breathing deeply and reminding herself of those she was to protect. It was enough to allow Cressida to reinforce her defenses.

The computer buzzed and she checked her emails, grimacing at the number that downloaded containing the subject header *Attack by Attar*. It had been at least a week since his last attack. She'd known this brittle peace couldn't last long, as she tapped her long fingernail on the desk. Cressida settled back in her chair, needing to focus on the problems that had surfaced.

A knock on the door echoed and she gave the command to enter. She watched as Daniel stepped into the room. There was a new grace in the way he moved—*flowed*, her mind corrected. It was as if he'd been born for this moment, and she swallowed.

His face, finely chiseled before now, seemed stronger and more angular, and his eyes glowed with a health and vitality.

"Cressida?"

She indicated with a languid hand that he should take a seat opposite her.

"I will do the formalities first, then we can get down to business."

A half smile emerged. "I thought we'd done that already."

Oh God, help me! That smile and the smoky way he spoke... She had to grip her desk, her fingers finding purchase as they gouged the grain, otherwise she'd have leaped the table and set upon him. She'd allowed herself *once!* And now she'd tasted heaven, she feared it would never be enough.

"I... Yes, well." She cleared her throat and a rumble grew in his chest. "I know Celina and Javed have spoken to you, however, I need your oath before we go any further."

He stopped, his gaze watchful. "And if I don't?"

"If you don't I cannot..." She stumbled, as if the words she had to say struck at her. Pain filled her features, more telling than any other action. "I cannot allow you to...to continue."

"This hurts you." His soft words were no balm. They clawed deeper, beneath the surface pain to where she tried to hide the truth.

She had to be honest. Brutally so. It was their way. And hers. "It does. Any who cannot make their oath..." She stopped because the words she was about to say tortured her. "It hurts me to say these words to you. Please, Daniel."

"Cressida, I would never hurt you. Surely you know this now?" He strode around the desk, the wooden structure that she'd used as a shield forgotten as he squatted. He raised his arm, then rested the palm of his hand against her cheek. "I would do anything for you. All you have to do is ask."

"I formally ask you to declare your oaths to Javed as your Master, to me as your council member and to Gianna as Overlord." The magic swirled through the air, capturing them both in its grip. His face glowed, and she knew he too felt it.

He gave a small nod, as if he'd come to some conclusion. "I will pledge myself to my house and my Master, to you as council member and to Gianna as our Overlord."

In his eyes, she caught a flash of deep emotion. He opened his mouth to speak again and she couldn't have stopped her action. She laid a finger against his lips, and for a second gloried in the feel of him against that small bit of flesh.

"Can you and will you uphold our hierarchy, our way of life and our commitment to the common goal of a peaceful existence? Will you give your future service to those who would guide and protect you? Will you give your life for your brother and sister vampires, and for the protection of the nest you are assigned to?"

He watched her as he spoke. "I will and I do."

A frisson of electricity sparked around them. Magic had been imbued in every word and every undertaking given. The bands that had tightened around her chest loosened their grip. "I welcome you to our world, Daniel."

He leaned in. She didn't know how he moved, but he did, the whisper of his breath brushing over her face. "Thank you." He kissed her.

This kiss was butterfly soft, a touch that melted her. He wound his arms around her waist and she let him draw her closer. *This is all I've ever wanted, Cressida. You.*

His thoughts drugged her, filling her senses in a way words never could. The vortex of emotions crashed over her as she twined her fingers in his hair.

How can you want me? I'm a monster!

The cry came from her soul, and she tugged away. "I never wanted you to see…"

"Ah, Cressida!" He pulled her close again. "I know. I understood that once I saw the dream. I could tell what you thought and felt. But it doesn't change anything for me."

The door crashed open, then a gasp, feminine and rather pleased, shattered the tableau. "Well, this is awkward. Just…just let me know when you're done."

Cressida laughed at Samra's dry words. It was a quaver of noise that erupted from her lips and chest, making her double over even as the door slid closed with a snick.

"Well, it was pretty funny." She raised her head as the paroxysm ended and she saw the smile on Daniel's face.

"Now, I think it's time we got a few things straight. I want you.

I've always wanted you and I know you want me. So don't push me away, Cressida." The intention in his words laid to waste any last illusions she had that he was unaware of her hunger.

The tension was back and she gazed at his face. On impulse, she reached out and grabbed his hand. "I don't want you to go anywhere. Stay here. In this nest."

"That's good, because I wasn't planning on leaving." His face relaxed and she suddenly realized he'd been worried she would send him away.

It was sobering.

She could hurt him so easily, if what she was reading was correct. "Don't ever let go," she whispered. Now he dipped his face again for a last quick, soul-searing kiss.

SIXTEEN

She dropped the receiver into the cradle. "Dammit, how could he strike again? How could we not know?" Her head ached and she rested it against the wall for a moment.

"Where?" Samra stalked closer. Cressida had been making plans with the woman when the call had come through and was thankful for the soothing touches of her second in her mind.

"New Orleans. One of the oldest American houses. They had four hundred and eighty-two nestlings. They killed all the warriors." She stared blindly at the wainscoting.

The sound of feet slapping on tiles made her turn and there was Daniel, in the doorway. "What? What's happened?"

"There's been another attack," Samra answered, and Cressida turned blindly, needing his support.

"He killed all the nestlings over thirty and any under fifteen. They said the carnage was unbelievable. The rest are gone. No one can understand where they could be." Cressida had to bite her lip as a spasm of pain flashed through her. Her connection to the senior councilors from other regions fed back into her mind.

Immanissimum ac foedissimum monstrum.

Cressida laughed. The pungent phrase denoting Attar as a gross and putrid monster seemed appropriate.

"Oh, Samra, where would I be without you?" The laughter died as she looked over to Daniel. "He staked the master outside, where the sun would find him. He was found at dawn, screaming and burning alive..."

No one asked if he'd survived. They all knew that he couldn't have. Once the ultraviolet rays of the sun had touched him he'd have suffered a reaction to the toxicity that built up quickly in their cells. Death took mere minutes to come, but it would have been excruciating.

"Where is Gianna?"

Daniel's words left her flinching. He touched her shoulder and she reached up, holding him close. "She's on her way. She said she'd found something that might help. The witches are coming too."

"I will summon Celina, Hope, Javed and Xavier, then." Samra left the room, though it was clear she understood how much Cressida ached at the knowledge that Daniel had asked after Gianna first.

"You should sit, Cressida." He tried to push her back to the seat, but the build-up of pressure seemed like too much. She tugged away from him, batting at him.

"Don't handle me, Daniel. You forget, you are a neophyte only." Her cold words shocked him as much as her. She could see it in the way the color bled away, leaving him pale, his skin close to translucent in the feeble and false light.

Without a word, Daniel blinked. He stepped back. His deep bow reeked of hurt.

The air was ripe with anger and frustration. Most of it on her side, she sourly concluded.

"Forgive me, Councilor. I thought I was also your lover." He kept his voice neutral, but she could see the flare of his nostrils.

"Dammit, why can't I...?" Flinging her hands in the air didn't help but for a moment she was at a loss to know how to continue.

Every conversation with him went awry, it seemed. She growled low in her throat.

"I will leave you to your plans." He started backing away and with quick steps she caught his hands.

"No. Stop."

He did, but there was a tension in his shoulders—the way he held himself so still twisted the cord of frustration that lodged itself in her chest. Cressida wanted to scream.

"I need your help. I...I need you." Her words erupted in a tight snarl.

"Of course, I am at your service." The old-fashioned phrase left her scowling with confusion. The anger loosened a little, or at least enough so she could breathe.

"We need to arrange for a clean-up crew to head to New Orleans. There were some nestlings that weren't home. There were a few children, including the *Yeux Secondes'* youngest daughter, who was attending some kind of overnight gathering. Some older members were attending a play and those who worked nights outside the actual house. They were spared, but their needs now will be urgent." It was difficult to think straight when she had to deal with her own jumbled emotions, but she managed.

"How many?" His gaze bored into her.

"Survivors, you mean? Twelve, maybe fourteen." She grabbed a pad from her desk and thrust it into his hands. "These are the details that we have so far. The number at the bottom of the page is the direct line to the most senior vampire relations officer in New Orleans. Get on the phone and see how we can help. Not only our nest, but—"

Daniel dropped the pad to the desk and tugged her close. "Do you realize what you just said?"

Cressida heard his sharp inhalation and wondered what she'd done now. It bewildered her, and she tasted his emotions. The anger had dissipated, leaving another, more unfamiliar emotion behind. "*What?* What did I say?"

"Our nest. Yours and mine." He kissed her gently, a soothing balm to her aching soul.

"Daniel, I can't..."

"I know. Someday soon, when things are settled, we'll work out what is between us. Until then, my promise to you is that I will be by your side. Whenever you need me, I'll be there, and I'll never turn you away."

He rested his forehead against hers, and the intimate gesture left her without the words to express herself adequately.

"Now you do your job and I'll see to this." He slid away from her. She mourned the loss of his physical support and dropped into the chair. "I'll get on this and see what I can organize between our nests."

"Fine. I'll also send for blood wine. I daresay we're going to need it before the night is through."

One week later.

CRESSIDA SLUMPED BACKWARD, HER EYES CLOSED AS SHE considered the Daniel situation. She needed something, some kind of closure, then maybe she could turn her mind to Attar. The thing that rode her, though, was that this was never the way she'd worked before. She'd always been focused. For the first time she wondered if there wasn't more to the situation than she could see or understand. "In such a short time he's become important to me."

She'd fought against it, and heavens knew she'd tried to avoid this kind of entanglement with anyone. *So why didn't it work?*

Because he's committed to you and you need him. He completes you, I think.

Samra's thoughts floated into her mind.

Now, trying to see it objectively, she had to agree, but for all she considered, there didn't seem to be an answer. Not yet.

"I need to work." Her muttered words filled the air, but nothing stopped the whirling of her brain.

For an instant she inhaled, hoping a cleansing breath would calm her rapid pulse, and with a tremendous effort she realigned her thinking and looked at the computer screen.

The blinking window told her there was a video waiting, the timestamp informing her it had been sent while they'd slept. While she'd been wrapped in Daniel's arms.

She opened the message and the video started automatically.

The room was dark, but she could make out doors, and people standing against the metal walls. "Councilor? If you get this, you have to see. You need to know. Someone from within must be sharing information, because otherwise they wouldn't know about our reinforced safe rooms!" The man, *Yeux Secondes* of the New Orleans nest that had been attacked, was clearly afraid. "No one here knew, except my family, and of course the Master and his Second." The terrified man glanced over his shoulder to where several huddled against the wall, the whites of their eyes glinting in the darkness.

"This room was built to hide slaves and over the years, generations of my family have reinforced the rooms. But *we* never told anyone about the hidey holes."

The man's movements were jerky as he rubbed at his eyes, horror making them wide and wild.

Cressida punched the button on her phone, her eyes never leaving the screen. "Samra, come to my office, now."

"We're under attack." The white-faced man panted as thuds and screams rose in the background. The video was grainy, but it was clear he despaired. "My daughter is at camp. I sent her, knowing that the situation was precarious. One of our seers warned me... If I don't get out of here, please attend to her safety, Cressida, I beseech you."

A tremendous bang sounded and Attar's vampires pounced. "Save her!" The screen went black as vicious creatures lunged.

Cressida's heart raced like a freight train. Samra arrived at her doorway. "What?"

"We've been sent a video."

The sound of it left her nauseated. The terror refreshed memories she'd hoped were forever behind her. Recollections of massacres she'd come upon rose. The scent they always left behind had affected her badly. It wasn't a relief, though, to be spared it this time. The stench of spilled blood wasn't something that could be overcome in a mere millennium.

Maybe it was because of her unwilling change... For an instant her hand rose to her flat belly before she acknowledged her actions. Her hand dropped away as she noted Samra's shocked glance in her direction.

Without a word, Samra strode over and took up position behind Cressida's seat. "Show me."

Cressida ran the video again. This time she could be more detached about it. She sought to pick out particular people and actions. But none of this made sense.

Filius canis. Samra's oath almost tugged a smile from Cressida.

"My thoughts entirely." Cressida raised her hand and wiped it over her brow. "We need to get this to Gianna quickly." It was the sudden intake of breath that had her turning in her seat. "Well then... that's... It's a good thing she'll be here later tonight."

Cressida felt as if she'd been turned to stone. "Why?"

"Her second told me it was so she could check on the preparations we'd been making, and she wanted to see Daniel, Hope and Celina."

Gianna wants to see Daniel.

Clearly her thoughts broadcast, because Samra's lips firmed. "All three of them, Cressida."

It took a minute for her to process Samra's words, then she shrugged. She'd wasted so much time, and if Gianna wanted him, she'd take Daniel. There wasn't much she could do. Realistically, there also wasn't time for her to descend into another fit of doldrums. She had irrefutable evidence that needed to be acted on. "Fine. You'd better warn him and arrange for the weres to be here as well." She spoke through stiff lips and felt Samra's frustration.

"He's not interested..."

"Just... Not now, Samra. I need to concentrate on this."

Samra left her office and Cressida busied herself, contacting the Masters and explaining what she needed and collecting updates. However, she avoided details of the video. That would need to be dealt with later once they knew exactly who was giving away information. That would be their death knell. Nothing else could be acceptable to all of them.

By the time Gianna arrived, Cressida had harnessed her wayward emotions and could look dispassionately at the situation.

"So, Cressida, you've already been in contact with the others? They will be here soon?"

"Yes, in fact, they should be here already. But before we get to that, there is a further complication. Could you... Would you spare me a minute?"

Gianna raised one well-shaped eyebrow and Cressida had the impression she was trying to work out what Cressida's problem was. Now that she had her fears and frustrations under control, she intended to lock them away.

With a tiny shrug, Gianna dismissed her entourage and took a seat opposite Cressida.

She turned the monitor around and played the scenes. Gianna's expression didn't change. *Not once.* However, Cressida had the impression that this haunting footage had angered her. Particularly if the icy tendrils of power were indicative of Gianna's emotions.

"Within the council or councils we have one aligned with Attar. We must weed them out. How do you plan to attend to that?"

Cressida gaped at Gianna's question. Gianna wanted her opinion? When it came to battle, Gianna was a fearless but determined leader. Her forceful nature had never allowed any other to extend their ideas and plans. Something had clearly changed.

"Well?" The tapping of fingers on the tabletop reminded Cressida that Gianna was waiting. "I... Uh, breadcrumbs."

"Breadcrumbs?"

"Yes, like in the story..." Gianna's blank look reminded her that she hadn't been in the company of children in a very long time.

"In the story *Hansel and Gretel*, the children find their way home using breadcrumbs after they are abandoned to the witch. It makes sense that we lay down a trail of 'breadcrumbs,' or false information in our case, so Attar and his minions come to us."

"It certainly has merit. But tell me, what happens to Hansel and Gretel? Do they take lovers?" Gianna's eyes lit with interest.

"No. It's a children's story."

Gianna's eyes widened. "Oh! And you know this why?"

"My nests have traditionally harbored children. I spend time with them."

"Hmm." Clearly Gianna questioned her sanity, but she shrugged. "Fine. Show me to the room where I can find the neophytes."

Cressida rose and led the way to the small meeting room where Hope, Celina and Daniel waited.

The sounds of chatter from within died away as they opened the door. The three stood, clearly worried and unsure about why they were there. The tension in the room left her as confused as them. As she made to step away, leaving them to Gianna's less than tender mercies, Gianna stayed her with a sharp movement of her hand.

"Cressida, you will stay too."

Gianna indicated they should all sit and, as one, they lowered themselves into the seats. "So, things are escalating, but until now I wasn't sure we had any advantage. However, today one of my contacts handed me something I believe will give us the upper hand."

The three sat forward, their eyes alight with interest. Cressida too was intrigued.

The warrior overlord reached into her pocket and withdrew a

large velvet pouch. "I'd heard of similar things, but never seen them. Not until today." The strings were frayed and the velvet well worn, but inside the bag something disk-like pushed against the material.

"Liege, what have you got there?" Celina pushed forward now and a ripple of power undulated through the air.

"Well, interestingly, it seems to be reacting to you. I wonder?" Gianna pushed her hand into the bag and drew back a set of necklaces of black and silver metals. She dropped them onto the tabletop as Cressida breathed deeply.

SEVENTEEN

The instant the disks fell to the table, Daniel felt the buzz of power. It drew him closer, as if his whole psyche needed contact with it. Without thinking, Daniel reached for one of the silver charms and it warmed gently in his hands.

Celina grabbed a black one before dropping it with a cry. "*Oh my gosh*! It's so cold!"

Gianna laughed, the sound tinkling in the air, and Daniel smiled, unable to ignore the feelings she evoked. A cold shaft sliced at him and he glanced to Cressida. Her face was set in stern, forbidding lines as she watched from the end of the table.

He ached for her.

Having been part of the dream the night before his change, he now understood. She felt too much and had locked parts of herself away, hoping to protect her heart and soul. There was a deep empathy, but it made her vulnerable, and she would never allow that. Many would think her remote and unapproachable, but he knew better.

"Cressida, I think you should hold one, so we can gauge if they only respond to these three."

She jerked and her gaze locked with his.

Go on. Pick one up.

She extended her hand and he felt a momentary compulsion to grab it and tell her what was in his heart. But he didn't. Not even with his mind. He instead imagined a wall, with his feelings hidden behind it. He'd tell her in his own time and in his own way, without a damn audience.

Instead, he watched as she traced her fingers over the scrolls and the tiny gems in the center.

"Warm." Her voice was soft and surprised.

"No. It's cold."

"Celina, I think I know the difference between warm and cold. This is warm and that warmth—" He furrowed his brow.

Celina whispered, "It's like it's climbing up your arm?"

Cressida nodded.

"Now that is interesting, because I only had the impression of cold. Cressida, call your second."

"Of course, Gianna." Her forehead crinkled and he noted the way her gaze almost turned inward before the door behind her opened and Samra entered.

"Ah yes. Samra, could you pick up one of the white ones?" Gianna gave her sharp demand and Samra reached out, plucking the amulet from his hands.

"It's cold!" She thrust it back at him and he smiled.

"Now one of the black ones."

Samra followed Gianna's command. The instant her hand touched the round metallic disk she pulled back. "Cold again. Am I supposed to—"

"Thank you, Samra. If you could wait outside." Cressida dismissed her with a smile and Samra left after shooting a searching look at Cressida's face.

He sighed inwardly. At every turn, the game changed. Whatever these artifacts that Gianna had presented were, she clearly thought they were important, so he'd go along with her. For now.

"So they only react to certain people. I find that intriguing, don't you?"

He glanced to Gianna, who tapped her long finger against ruby lips.

"Then who are the others intended for?" Cressida rose, her every motion carefully controlled.

"For the neophytes and their partners, I would think."

Cressida stilled, body stiff and radiating her shock. "What?" She turned and her hair tumbled loose from the confines of her bun. It lay around her shoulders like a cloud of golden silk.

"Yes, Cressida. I think they—the amulets—choose the people who command them. Go on. Pick it up."

Cressida's gaze was steady, but he detected something in their depths of her eyes. "But..."

"Do. It." The words were a command and the air rippled once more.

Cressida slowly walked to the table and lifted the amulet. Peace flowed through him at her sigh. She clutched the amulet, then looked to Gianna.

Hope and Celina rose. "We're going to contact Xavier and Javed," Hope informed him and left the room.

"Take a break. The others will be here shortly."

Daniel imagined a vision of them leaving the room, a large wall separating them from Gianna. In his mind, he rose, gave a short nod to Gianna, who took Cressida by the hand.

"Come."

She did. Without a murmur, she followed him to the office. The soft whiteness that edged her thoughts reminded her this was taking place in her mind, yet she was sure and could sense everything said and done as if it really was what she was doing.

"Cressida, I understand your uncertainty before. Now, here, before the others join us, I need to tell you. I am yours and you are mine. Never question that." His lips covered hers and the emotion was so deep that he felt every atom of his body participate. He tasted and sipped at her, then allowed his mouth to follow her jawline, the long arch of her neck and down to the fine collarbone, hidden beneath her black jacket.

He took his time. Finding the button, he pulled the material firm while she moaned. It gave with a jerk and sag, before he slipped the heavy wool item from her shoulders.

He set his lips to hers, as her body quaked and he whispered, "This seals it. We belong together forever."

By the time he'd kissed her lips again, his body raged with a fever, hot with wanting and heavy with desire.

He drew back. The glint of her heavy-lidded and smoky eyes was the knowledge that she too yearned for him. In her gaze he read the promise of passion, but also her fear.

With great care, Daniel pushed aside her golden tresses. "Don't fear what we have, Cressida. Forever is nothing to be afraid of when you aren't alone. I will be here, by your side. Evermore, my love. Evermore."

Her hands slid around his waist. "Then don't let go." She sobbed and the control, iron hard, shattered and she shuddered in his embrace.

Under the onslaught of their shared passion, his mind fractured and the wall surrounding their thoughts dropped, leaving them open to those around them. A firm *ahem* sounded. Gianna.

If you are finished, perhaps you can concentrate on matters at hand?

Daniel cursed as Gianna spoke in his mind.

"God damn... Does she do that to you too?"

Cressida flinched at his mutter and struggled to regain her composure.

He glanced in Gianna's direction and couldn't help but notice the way she looked at them both, her grin knowing. Embarrassment flooded him for an instant, then melted away. "I really don't care who knows of my feelings."

Cressida blushed deeply as Gianna's laughter tinkled through the air. Not unkindly, he thought with amusement. It was more a sound of acceptance and that settled their future in his mind.

I do hope you've sorted things out.

His grin died away. *The witches are here, as are Xavier and Javed.*

THIS TIME CRESSIDA WATCHED HOPE AND CELINA ENTER THE room with their mates, extended her senses and *tasted* their reactions. It surprised her that there was desire and happiness exuding from them. They were exactly the same emotions she felt whenever Daniel was near.

It was an uncomfortable situation, sitting there with Daniel beside her. His eyes met hers, and she could sense the dare.

Will you acknowledge me and what is between us?

His thoughts battered her. She wanted to, but fear held her in its grip. She wanted what she *thought* he offered. But was it really that? Could the passion that seethed be more than just sex?

After centuries of loneliness—and she allowed herself to acknowledge that was what her dominant emotion for so long had been—that fear of intimacy had driven her to deny herself any possibility of a relationship in such a cowardly fashion. She continued to bury herself beneath layers of responsibility.

For a minute she critically examined these men who'd taken on the responsibility of nests and partners. They were clever, resourceful and happy, that much was clear. But they were also strong and wiry of body, with charismatic presence.

She understood why the women were attracted, yet they were missing the something that made Daniel who he was. His earnestness and his attention to detail had been early indicators for her. His commitment to their cause and the sexuality he exuded whenever she was near had sealed their fate.

"Javed and Xavier, we need your help. We've accessed some amulets that we believe will help us in the battle against Attar." All eyes settled on Gianna now, including Cressida's.

Xavier reached out, his hand hovering above the two amulets left on the table before he grabbed for one. "It feels warm."

"Javed? What's your reaction?"

The dusky-skinned man scooped up the other and his eyes closed.

"Power. Warmth." His muttered words broke off as he opened his eyes, pinning Gianna with his searching gaze. "These are meant for us?"

"I believe so." Gianna rose. "In fact, the witches will be able to explain better. I've asked them to await us down in the dungeon."

"So we should...?" Hope stood, the leather of her pants creaking slightly.

"Yes, we should wear them." Cressida spoke quietly as she lifted the metal chain over her head. Against the white of her blouse the black and diamond amulet seemed to shine, and she noted the six tiny diamond points at the outside and the single point in the center. *I wonder what they mean?* She shook her head. *I'll no doubt find out more later.*

EIGHTEEN

As he slipped out the door, Daniel reached for Cressida's hand and stopped her at the old stone steps hidden behind a metal grate. "Wait. Cressida."

She turned her gaze on him and in her eyes he saw a little fear but mostly a burning excitement. "We're meant to be, aren't we? That's why there's six amulets. Six points. Six of us."

"Meant?" A thrill punched through him. Her words contained the breathless quality of someone laboring hard.

"You believe me only after someone hands you an amulet?" He couldn't help himself, the tone of his words teasing as he leaned over and watched her eyes dilate. "I'd been hoping you'd work it out. Without any outside intervention."

His gaze narrowed on her lush pink lips. He wanted to kiss her. His body urged him to, but he held back, knowing they'd be missed.

"Dan-iel?" That tiny break as she spoke his name propelled him.

She tasted sweet, and a moan broke the air. His body ached with instant need. He curved his hand around her buttock and pulled her close as his will melted away.

"Daniel? Cressida? Stop that, and get down here!" Celina called them, smashing the blissful cloud that surrounded them. He pulled away and she blushed, a red crest rising over her perfectly pale cheeks. Her eyes sparkled and her lips, now lush and slightly swollen, parted enough to entice him.

It was a struggle to settle himself.

"We should..." He panted, chest heaved from the quick lightning flash of passion, then he tugged her after him, down the stairs, their steps echoing in the darkness.

The low light that would have bothered him before his change was now akin to a high-wattage globe and he smiled, realizing that he could move swiftly in such situations. It was a reminder that he was now a predator, and that fact no longer carried any cause for qualms.

Sleepless nights are a thing of the past. Or days...

A smothered laugh caught him unawares. "That's why I lo..." She cleared her throat and the tension inside him returned.

"We'll have to finish this discussion later."

He sensed rather than saw her nod as they entered the large dungeon room.

The three women, the three witches stood waiting for them while Hope, Celina, Javed, Xavier and Gianna looked at them expectantly.

"So you have the amulets. We'd heard of them but have recently come across a tale foretelling that they will herald the beginning of the end."

"They are ancient artifacts from somewhere else." Selena waved her hands in the air and it made Daniel want to growl at the careless way she clearly shared only a section of what she knew. The way she avoided looking at those gathered reinforced his deduction.

They could be from outer space for all he cared.

"From the stories we'd heard, they were hidden away from sight until such time as they were needed." Selena scanned their faces, her posture straight, and he was reminded of an old-fashioned schoolteacher. He wondered for an instant if that was one of the many incarnations she'd assumed over the centuries. She glanced in his direction and smiled. The action didn't ease his nerves and he shuffled on the spot.

The one he knew as Jemima stepped toward them. "Each of you was chosen by an amulet. They called to you, didn't they? You felt the singing of them in your blood and your heart." Her soft words and gentle smile eased the tension the others exhibited and she stepped around the gathering, rubbing a soft hand down their arms. "Yes, they are magical things, gifts from other beings. Ones you don't yet know."

"Well, that's great, but what do they do?" Celina demanded.

"Do? Yes, they do many things." Jemima's eyes took on an unfocused quality. "Communicate. You will be able to communicate with the others through them. I believe…"

Cressida flinched, the intimacy of her ability to communicate with others having been an issue with Daniel. The others who'd gathered tensed in reaction to her palpable concern.

"What she can't tell you is that we believe they will help you bond your skills, share them. Enhance them."

Daniel frowned. "Why?"

"Why can't she tell you? Because she doesn't know." Danicka inclined her head slightly to the side.

"So why did she react like that?" Cressida's eyes narrowed and Danicka smiled.

"That's simple. Each of you"—she pointed at Hope, Celina, and Daniel—"has a skill. Those skills are mirrored in ours." Her enigmatic smile left Daniel's mind whirling. "Ours are a pale imitation where yours have been developed by harnessing and finessing them. Only you can achieve a true mastery. Jemima's true skill is foretelling, but she can heal things in the blood. She can't read their use because while she can foretell, she, as with all of us, is connected to you at a certain point in this journey. Her time has been and gone. My ability to control objects is strong, but with finite limits. I can boost others' use of magic. My connection is the last and only assistance we can offer you. Our sister's…" She grinned at Daniel. "Hers is a reflection of yours. Her magic had to be encouraged to develop, yet once it did…

Again, it's with limits. But planning, well, she's very good at that." She shrugged.

"So, what can we do with these?" The demand escaped.

"Well, that's up to you and what you learn to share."

Frustration welled, but he tamped it down. "So how do we...?"

"We don't know." Jemima shrugged.

"Wait, Daniel." Celina extended her hand, ceasing their questions. "I think I understand. The skills of communication would be the easiest, because it's something we already do, I mean, amongst ourselves and our partners. Would that be correct?"

Jemima inclined her head.

"I believe so. However, the only way to *know* is to try."

Cressida sighed and she stepped in front of the diminutive woman before him. "I think I can work this out. But for it to be effective..." The innuendo, that it was their intense sexual connections that empowered them surprised him.

Cressida whirled and grinned at the other couples. "Go home and we'll be in touch."

The rest of the group caught on and the men grinned at their women. "Fine. It's drawing close to dawn, so we should be away."

Cressida held up a hand. "Before you leave, there is one other thing. Something I haven't yet shared. Tonight I received communication from the nest in New Orleans. The one that was attacked. It's..." She sucked in an unsteady breath and Daniel moved closer, winding his arm around her waist in support. "It's not something I can share widely. I'm concerned someone in a position of knowledge is feeding information to Attar."

"You've intimated that before, Cressida." Xavier frowned deeply.

"I have. But this... He knew of the panic room in the nest. It's one of the oldest nests in America, and most of the Masters and Seconds would be aware of it. All the oldest nests do. It's a matter of knowing where they would be."

"That means... Cressida, the councilors and other nests can't be trusted. Not until we can be sure."

Her jaw firmed. "That's exactly my point. I need you to delve into their backgrounds, Javed. No one would question that, as your nest is still in its infancy. You are still taking on nestlings and can ask such questions. Find them for me. Bring them to justice."

He bowed without a word, accepting Cressida's decree.

Gianna stood silent during the whole discussion. "Excellent. I can see you will deal with this, Cressida, and I am no longer required. I have other councils I must consult with."

Cressida opened her mouth and closed it just as quickly. "Yes, Gianna."

"Good. If I hear anything, I will inform you." Gianna spun on her stiletto and left them there in the cool dungeon.

"We will bid you *adieu*, as well. We have things to prepare. The time is growing near and we must all be readied for the battle." Danicka slid a gentle hand over Daniel's cheek. "*All will be well between you now. Just don't let her backslide.*" With that, they too melted away.

THE OTHERS HAD LEFT AND CRESSIDA BREATHED DEEPLY, taking a moment to settle herself. The scents of summer were gone, replaced now by the wintery chill in the air and the woodsy smell invading her senses.

Since Gianna had left she'd locked herself in her office, asking Samra to keep everyone away.

"Come to bed, Cressida." Daniel settled his hands on her shoulder, turning her gently in his direction.

"I'm wondering how we can beat him. He's out there, somewhere in the darkness."

His lips were warm against her ear, his breath playing over the sensitive skin. "I know. But right now, there isn't much we can do and you need rest."

Each pass of his hand started tiny sparks of electricity coursing through her system.

A deep sigh escaped and she shuddered as it ended. "I know. I feel like my future—our future—is in abeyance until this is done. It's wrong, but..." Lost for words, she scanned his face and his embrace loosened. She turned, seeking the comfort she could only find in his arms.

"God knows I've fought against this, Daniel. I didn't want it. I thought..." She shook her head, clearing away the cloud of doubt. "I thought my role was that of a protector, and that my chance of love was gone. Murdered by my own hand. I've weighed and questioned this whole thing in my mind over the last few months. Ever since we met." She searched his face and he smiled slightly. Just a tiny movement at the corner of his mouth.

"I know. But, Cressida?"

This time she shushed him with a soft finger that played over his lips, caressing them with light strokes. "I need you to understand why. I want you, Daniel. But I had to understand how this happened. How I came to be here, now."

She'd needed to understand before she could commit to Daniel, and it had been a journey of discovery. It had been Hope, the young child who'd opened the chink in her icy wall, who'd brought her peace. The ability to love and heal was a magic that altered her very existence. The need to connect herself to one person had been buried deeply, and it had taken a child to unlock the truth. Until she'd experienced love from someone innocent, she'd been unable to embrace that emotion and give it. Without Hope, she knew, there would have been no chance of experiencing what she did with Daniel. That *true* bonding of souls could never have occurred.

"Hope gave me the chance to love again. I didn't understand why I felt this connection to her, but now I believe it's because the magic knew and understood that the imbalance had to be corrected. And I wasn't ready for that. She needed to grow, and so did I." She laughed harshly.

"You're a strong woman, Cressida, but you can't stand alone forever. No one can."

"I know. On one level that scares me too. To love deeply means to surrender myself again. I loved Etienne."

He clasped her now, sliding his arms around her waist.

"But it was a flawed love. One where I wanted to be what I thought he wanted and needed. It was shallow and selfish. This isn't. This is more. And it's a leap of faith. One I believe I'm finally ready for."

The smile on his face was breathtaking. "So...?"

"I want you as my life partner, Daniel. I want to share everything. Your joys and your sorrows. They will be mine as much as mine will be yours."

"About bloody time." Daniel shuddered and she laughed, letting go of her fears. "So, now I think it's also a good time to tell you I love you *and* lust over you too, Cressida."

Her mirth leached away, replaced with a deeper and more compelling emotion. Desire welled and her body warmed in response.

The sound of the shutters falling heralded dawn, but she knew he paid little attention to the break of day as he kissed her.

Come to bed with me and love me.

Daniel moved swiftly, lifting her into his arms, and she laughed. "Put me down!"

Why? We'll get there faster this way.

At the top of the steps he pushed the door to her suite wide and carried her in, slamming it shut with a swift kick, then he strode in the direction of her chamber.

She slid her way down his body, clothes catching between them, but she felt his heat, the need that they shared. He was so hard against her softness, the difference seducing her as surely as any words.

Already burning for his touch, she raised shaking fingers, looking for the buttons and zips that kept everything in place. He caught her hands, stilling her.

"Tonight, let me."

His eyes were heavy-lidded and she could feel the power that whispered between the two of them. His movements were slow, and the eroticism drugged her mind.

His every move was unhurried, as if he'd studied her needs and was primarily directed to fulfill them.

"You're such a beautiful woman, Cressida. Every inch of your skin is soft and silken. I want to wrap myself up in you." The hoarse words left her shaking.

He placed tiny kisses against her throat as he pushed the blouse from her shoulders. He found and worshiped the sensitive skin at her collarbone, giving the tiniest of flicks with his tongue while she shivered.

"So. Beautiful."

She clutched his shoulders, needing the support only he could give her. "Dan-iel..." The cry was soft, torn from her throat as the pressure of her arousal grew. Her sex melted while he ravaged her senses.

Her blouse slid to the floor, forgotten, and he smoothed his fingers over her skin, following the band of her bra. "You really don't need one." His finger skimmed below the lacy cup and she hissed.

"I..."

"Let go, my love, and feel." He kissed the hollow beneath her ear, a sensitive spot that left nerves jumping.

I... Oh, do that again.

Anything my lady desires. And he touched her again, the glance of his lips over her flesh drugging her senses.

His kisses were magic, tracing back across her jaw before he settled his mouth on hers.

The pop of her bra strap impinged and her breasts, the size of ripe grapefruit, swung free.

"Oooh..."

"Every inch of you is perfect. Made for my touch."

Touch he did, sliding his hands down her lean sides to bury them in the waistband of her long pants and push them away.

"Your..." Her breath caught as the whisper of air caressed her bare skin. *I want you naked too.*

His chest rumbled against her as he laughed, a deeply erotic sound. "As you wish."

He tugged away, and she wanted to complain, but the planes of his face, tight with emotions, stopped the words before she could speak.

Daniel's glance caught hers while he tore at his clothing. Buttons popping to the ground as he pulled the shirt from his body. Even in her state of arousal, she could appreciate the hasty striptease.

Soon he was naked in front of her, his cock erect and ready.

The corresponding part of her body was molten fire and her nipples stood proud, ready for him.

Eager for his touch.

They came together, hard to soft, skin to skin. A moan rose in the air as they kissed deeply. He caressed every inch of her, hard and knowing touches soothing the ferocity of his grip on her flesh.

Finally, he lifted her and carried her to the bed, but she pushed against him with her hand.

"No. I had things made ready." He quirked his eyebrow and she giggled. "Romance hasn't died because we're vampires, you know."

He gave a choked cry that she was sure was a laugh.

"In front of the fireplace."

A deep pile of blankets had been laid in readiness, and on the low table stood two goblets of blood wine. He smiled.

"Indeed. We can't let such a scene go to waste."

She gulped as he settled her on the soft pallet before lowering himself. "There is another nectar I plan to sip tonight."

Her mouth dried as he kissed between her breasts. His hands covering them as if they were the most precious things in the world. Then that thought splintered as he kissed his way down the center of her body. He rested at her navel, dipping his tongue into the depression while her thighs quivered in time with the hot pulses of her sex.

"Daniel? Please." She arched, not sure what she wanted. When his hot breath whispered against her labia, she shuddered. He touched her so agonizingly slow she was sure the earth stopped spinning. He opened her and finally kissed her tiny bud.

Sensations rippled through her, ones she'd never known before, and Cressida cried out.

Let it go. Feel the pleasure I want to give you.

Her thoughts splintered while her body convulsed, lost in her orgasm.

More!

His demand rang through her mind as he ruthlessly started arousing her again. She gripped his shoulders as she rode the wave of desire. With his teeth, he nipped at her sensitized flesh, enough to make her gasp and writhe, and she scraped her fingernails over his biceps.

He hissed, stilling for a moment before gazing into her eyes. "I want all of you. In every way."

He crawled up her body and when he kissed her, she tasted the muskiness of herself on his lips.

"More!"

His demand spurred her on. Mindless now, she writhed against him.

Cressida's teeth descended and she couldn't contain herself, manipulating her body into position before sinking them deep into his shoulder.

His essence, so male and full-bodied, spun in her brain, and she dimly noted he'd reciprocated, the slight sting leaching away as pleasure, deep and heady, bloomed again.

Still drinking deeply, he positioned himself between her legs. He thrust hard within her, and Cressida's body stretched to admit his cock.

Together they moved, undulating wildly while they drank deeply of each other. When the precipice loomed she welcomed it, her body little more than a tight coil of need. Every inch straining for the release she'd experienced before.

The orgasm came. Crashing down on her.

One body.

One mind.

Bathed in pleasure.

The milking of her orgasm and the jetting of his release overwhelmed her, then even that tiny thread of consciousness fled.

NINETEEN

His body ached. All over.

The early evening had been filled with training in swordplay, honing the skills he'd been steadily improving. From there he'd taken a pummeling on the wrestling mat, and he felt the location of every grip and throw right down to his bones.

Now he stood in the dungeon. Celina closed the circle, its shining light bright to his enhanced sight.

She's come a long way.

He grinned at Cressida's thoughts. In the past few days, he could have sworn she'd mellowed. The frequent touches, and even the soft look in her eyes, betrayed the fact that she was already more relaxed, which filled him with a sense of accomplishment. Yet even with her edges dulled by love, she remained the ultimate commander, firm in her demands that he train and practice. She expected no less from the others.

"So what do you think we do now?" Hope screwed up her nose, clearly unsure, as they all were, with how to proceed.

"Maybe if we begin with communicating... I know I can mind-talk to Daniel, Javed and Xavier. So perhaps, Hope, you could begin with contacting Celina?"

They all watched as Hope gripped the round amulet in her hands, her eyes closed, showing the intensity of her efforts. Celina grinned, and it became a loud guffaw.

"You want to buy what?"

Hope blushed deeply. "Well..."

Xavier whispered into her ear, and Cressida released a snicker—no doubt in amusement, and it warmed him..

Hope squeaked with embarrassment. "I can't tell them that!"

Cressida cleared her throat, realizing that this wasn't helping them to achieve their goal. "Okay, so I'm guessing that worked. I'm going to propose that the three women form a group and the three men another. We need to see if we can merge enough of our consciousness's to communicate with more than one other person at a time."

They moved into groups, one at each side of the room, and the other two women looked at Cressida, gripping their amulets. "Hope, you've managed to talk to Celina so you go first."

She nodded with a jerk and concentrated. *"All right, nod if you can hear me."*

Cressida nodded and Celina gave a toss of her head.

Celina, can you hear me?

Yes, I can, and Hope too. But I'm also—

Celina? What's wrong?

I'm—I'm feeling this pressure. It's just at the back of my mind... It's... Ahhh!

Celina pulled out of Cressida's mind, and the impression of a rubber band breaking flicked through Cressida's brain.

Celina lifted a shaking hand while her face took on the shade of winter snow. "Sorry about that."

Cressida wanted to say it was nothing, but even as she opened her mouth, Celina's eyes rolled backward.

Before the two women could reach for her, Javed was there,

sliding his arm around his mate, physically supporting her as she slumped to the ground.

"What went wrong?"

"I don't know. Hope was able to open the communication links, but when Celina went to do so, it just...it went wrong."

Daniel laid his hand on Cressida's shoulder and she covered it. Fear settled itself like fat dollops in her stomach, and the queasy sensation that came with it wasn't welcome.

Celina moaned and Javed exhaled heavily. "I'm taking her home. I suggest we finish up for the night."

They all nodded silently, understanding that nothing more could be achieved tonight.

"Javed? Let me know how she is later."

"I will." With that, he lifted his mate into his arms and headed up the steps. The four of them watched him leave.

"I wish I understood what happened. How we could avoid it." Cressida worried her lip, feeling the pinprick of her feeding teeth breaking the surface.

Daniel drew a deep breath and his body stilled.

"Well, we should go too." Hope smiled, then Xavier took her hand and they too left.

"What's wrong, Daniel?"

"It's not what's wrong, it's how you taste. The scent of you catches me unawares. Like..." He dipped his head in her direction. "Right." Closer he loomed, his eyes brilliant orbs in the low light. "Now..."

The kiss was soft and he gloried in their connection. When he finally pulled away, she was breathless. "Well. That was quite a way to end the day."

DANIEL MIGHT THINK HER SCENT SURROUNDED HIM, BUT IN HIS mind, he read how his stole along in her brain, enticing her all over again.

She slid her hand along his shoulders. "I can leave Samra to attend to preparing the nest for the day, but I think you need a shower, as do I. Let's retire."

His gaze searched her face and he noted with joy the glint of interest that lit her from within.

"Well, I'd hate to ruin your plans."

She grabbed his hands, towing him up the stairs. *Samra? Can you take care of the house for tonight?* Her thoughts echoed in his mind.

An echo of a laugh chimed in behind it. *Sure, and as I can guess what you plan, I think I'll make myself useful in another part of the house!*

Cressida snorted and he grinned, hearing her vow, *I'll talk with her about that comment. Tomorrow.*

Consciousness rose slowly. The warmth in his bones left him tingling as he rolled. A body lay beside him and an instant of disorientation flooded him. Where...? Awareness came and he smiled. *Cressida.*

He ran a hand over her curves, enjoying for a moment the pleasure of simply touching her silken skin before she woke.

"Oh... That's nice." She moved languidly until she'd turned over to face him.

"Good morning, my love." He caressed her cheek and she nuzzled against his touch.

"This is the nicest way I can think to wake." She grinned, and he loved the brightness in her gaze. "Sadly though, we don't have time to lay here."

He laughed. "I don't only want you for the sex, you know?"

She snorted inelegantly, something she would never have done months or even weeks before, he was sure.

"Though as an added benefit—" Cressida tossed the pillow at him before he could dodge, as the phone rang.

"Ah well, I said, we couldn't just lie here." She reached for the phone and he enjoyed the sight as the sheet fell away from her, exposing her breasts. Her plum-colored nipples puckered and for a moment he was tempted to bend over and suck. His waking erection was urgent and he knew it wouldn't take much to entice her to dally a little longer.

"What?" Her words stilled his movements and his gaze flicked to her horrified face. "When did you realize?"

She reached up, fingers threading through her long blonde hair. "We'll be there as soon as we can." She slammed down the receiver and turned in his direction. "The girls are missing. They were outside and Celina sent one of the nestlings to round them up. They can't find any sign of them."

His heart thudded. Marian, Rachel and Lucy were Celina's foster daughters, found during the Slaughterhouse Rout. She'd be devastated if anything happened to them.

"We better get moving."

They rose and hurried to their shared dressing room. It was huge, with tall mirrors, seating and floor-to-ceiling doors. Behind the doors hid hangers, drawers and shelving stuffed with clothes sorted by summer, winter and temperate piles.

Cressida was controlled even in the way she stored her clothes, he'd already learned. This time that attention to detail was more than welcome.

He tugged at the leather pants Cressida had told him were best for combat and pulled on a white T-shirt, realizing that if it came to a fight, his ability to move might save his life. The belt he fastened at his waist carried the ornately engraved silver dirk Cressida had presented him with after his change. He grasped the hilt for a second, testing the grip, then he dropped to the plush seat.

As he pulled on his boots Cressida hurried around the corner. For a moment he was unable to talk, sure he would swallow his tongue. Even in the face of a catastrophe she still had the ability to leave him speechless.

Her formfitting leather suit molded to every inch of her body, the ruby red of it the perfect foil for her carefully braided blonde tresses.

"Come on, Daniel, we need to hurry." Like that, he snapped out of the trance.

He followed her down the stairs to where Samra and several other warriors waited.

"Cressida? The cars are ready and I've already sent a contingent ahead."

A tall, pale-skinned woman kept pace with them as they raced down to the steps to the heavy black cars. They started and moved down the long drive with barely a sound, just the tiniest sensation of movement. It was the first time since his change he'd left the estate, and he considered it certainly wasn't the way he'd hoped this would have taken place.

Worry gnawed at his gut, bitter and acidic. "There's no more news?" His hands curled into fists as he thought about the three young girls who were nominally his nieces. They'd taken an oath to protect the innocent, and these girls numbered at the top of his personal list.

"Nothing. But what's odd, is that there is no sign of..." Samra stopped and straightened, as if what she was about to say was more than just unpalatable. "His usual modus operandi is to kill everyone in the nest. It doesn't fit his style. To only take the girls...?"

Cressida shook her head, her eyes stormy with concern and her body stiff. "No. That worries me more than anything else."

The rest of the journey took place in silence, each of them lost in their own thoughts.

TWENTY

The cars swept up the drive and Cressida leaned forward, silently urging the vehicles to hurry a bit more.

That the girls being human was only one part of the fear that rode her mercilessly. It wasn't that they'd survived the Slaughterhouse Rout, fought to stay together—something she appreciated more than she'd revealed to anyone—or even that at the end of the day, they were children. No, it was that in her very private mind; they reminded her of the child she'd longed for all those years ago. The child she'd lost.

The pain in her heart never left, though it had dulled. She would use the tendrils of grief instead and focus on using her enhanced senses to seek them out. She'd look for the trail every human left behind.

Like the breadcrumbs in the story she'd spoken about to Gianna.

At the estate, Cressida snapped open the door and was out as the car came to a halt. At the top of the stairs stood Celina and Javed. Their faces were drawn with fear. "Thank you for coming." Celina reached out a hand and Cressida grasped it.

"You don't need to thank us. Just tell me where, when, and we'll go hunting."

"They were in the rose garden, reading. Karen went out to call them in for their meal when... She came back in and said they weren't there."

"Where have you looked?" Daniel inserted himself between the two women and hugged Celina.

"The grounds. I have warriors walking the perimeter and even the witches are busy with spells. We've also reinforced the wards."

Cressida nodded. "Fine. Daniel? We'll start at the rose garden. Celina, Javed? Have you called for Hope? She may have seen—"

"We contacted her first. She had a flash of faces followed by darkness. I think she's trying to shield us from the worst." Celina's face paled further and a single tear dripped down her cheek.

"And you have no trackers here at your nest currently?" She had to ask, unease settling in the pit of her stomach.

"No. We sent them to New Orleans. We never expected..." Javed's broken tone died away. "Dammit, Cressida, we would never have placed the children in jeopardy."

With a steady hand she reached out, gripped his fingers then Celina's. "I know. We did the same, hoping to track Attar and his warriors. Had you told anyone what you'd done?" They stared at her, questions in their gazes.

"Never mind. We'll find them." With that she spun and headed for the garden, knowing that Samra, Daniel and the rest of her contingent would follow. Once there she breathed in and out. Seeking calm. With difficulty she focused on centering herself, opened her senses.

Filaments of power extended, touching everything in their path as she concentrated. A lick here and a flicker there.

Opening her senses like this required every ounce of magical ability that she had, but she used it, ruthlessly pushing forward.

A hint, the tiniest trail captured her attention and she focused on it. *Fear.* It was fresh, maybe half-an-hour to an hour old, yet it was already decaying and carried an overlay of anger. Vampiric anger stank of bitterness and other dark emotions. There could have been more than a touch of excitement too, which had her swallowing heavily as bile rose in her throat.

"I've…" She panted, bent double as trickles of sweat dripped under the top of her suit. She needed to find her balance.

Inhale.

Exhale.

She straightened and pointed to the rear of the house. "That way." She took an extra second, hands firmly pushed against her side, washing off the miasma, then she strode off, needing to find the girls quickly.

It hadn't just been one attacker, but a group, each carrying their own individual scent. The trail was growing cold, but enough remained for them to follow.

The terrain was flat, with some bushes here and there, but she cursed the designer of the landscaped gardens, the nooks and hide-aways they'd used to fashion the area.

We'll find them.

Daniel no doubt thought to reassure her. She'd kept a tight rein on her emotions after her brief search.

Cressida stopped and around her the others did too, looking at her, questions in their gazes. "I read at least nine vampires. Searching for the girls. If they find them…"

"We'll find them first. Come on." She could always count on Samra to buoy her, and a touch from Daniel lifted her spirits.

"Fine, let's go."

They ate up the ground, long strides carrying them beyond the carefully laid out gardens and into a rougher area, where rocks rested against large trees.

They slowed, picking their way along the uneven ground until they spied a small clearing. At the far end was a cave, overhung by tree branches. The mouth was maybe two meters wide, and there she spied the children. The girls had grabbed sticks, dragging them across, using them as spears and creating a rudimentary barrier, no doubt to keep the hungry predators at bay.

Quivers of fear lashed at her, but she pushed that knowledge away, instead focusing on what the girls had done to protect themselves. To hide from the vampires and to fortify their tenuous position.

Raising a hand, she halted. The vampires hadn't yet realized Cressida and her party were there and she smiled, the sides of her mouth widening as her teeth descended.

She flung her arms wide and indicated to surround the growling creatures ahead of her. The warriors nodded.

She gave a cry of battle, cold and loud, which stopped the rogue vampires in their tracks. Their eyes flashed with hatred and power filled her. Blood pumped through her veins as she stalked toward them.

"Prepare to submit!"

Daniel watched as Cressida moved. It was graceful. Balletic almost. Step then still. He stared, lost in the dangerous symphony as her nostrils flared and she weighed the mettle of her foe. Her gaze narrowed and her teeth extended fully, far longer than he'd ever seen.

This was the predator he'd sensed in her from the start.

The others engaged as he moved his way in front of the cave. He'd protect the girls and knew that Cressida had already divined that.

The sounds and smells crashed over him, and the thrumming of primal senses urged him to participate. His muscles tensed and teeth lengthened, tearing through apertures that had opened on his change. The urge to crush those who'd threatened the children rode him hard. Instead, he squared his shoulders and prepared to defend. One of the creatures, haggard and dirty, advanced in his direction.

Its eyes flicked to the children behind him, tongue licking out as if tasting the air and the essence of innocence. "Blood."

The word was slurred and his mind made the connection. It was hunger, savage and wild, that drove them.

"Cressida, hunger. They're starved. That's the key to defeating them." He pushed the thought in her direction, hopeful it would give her the advantage in beating the opposition.

She glanced in his direction, distracted for an instant. A creature stalked behind her, sensing her lack of concentration, and jumped, striking her hard from behind. It sank claws and teeth into her flesh, and Daniel tensed while fear and anger rose.

My mate unprotected.

A growl rose, splitting the air.

Cressida whirled, knocking the creature back before attacking. He stared as she tore at the creature with her hands and teeth. When the brief skirmish was complete, the carcass at her feet barely resembled a body, as strips of flesh littered the ground and blood seeped into the earth.

Around them the snapping and snarling had started to die down, leaving in its wake an eerie silence.

Once more Daniel focused his attention on the vampire before him, as it too had been lost in the wild melee before it. Its eyes flicked from side to side, watching the destruction of his cohorts. The scent of fear rose, but so too did the cry of hunger. Even as Daniel watched it warred with itself, the fight-or-flight question uppermost in its mind.

"Blood."

When the creature spoke, Daniel gave it his whole attention and moved. A step to the side, only enough to keep the children protected.

It shuffled toward the children, attempting to sidestep the physical barrier he presented. Daniel prepared himself mentally for what he was about to do

With a lightning-quick movement, Daniel shot his hand out, long nails digging into flesh as he gripped it by the wild neophyte by the neck and shook.

"Blood!" The piteous cry filled the night and he sighed, hand settling on the long dagger attached to his belt. Hunger rose, like a red wave. Long seconds where he warred with his nature passed.

"Daniel. You must destroy it."

His gaze collided with Cressida's.

"Why?"

"Because it's little more than an animal. It will only seek blood. It will kill everything in its path. Men, women and children. All it has left is primal instincts."

With a deep breath, he considered her words. He needed to know for sure, though. He used his mind, stabbing into the thoughts of the creature in his grasp.

Cressida was right. All he found was bloodlust. Nothing remained of the human it had once been.

With that knowledge came the decision.

Daniel curled his fingers around the long dagger and drew it from the scabbard with a hiss. One quick slice and in his hand he gripped the head, while the body fell away to the ground with a thud.

Silence had descended and all eyes were on him. Daniel's and Cressida's gazes met, hot and searching.

"An interesting way for a vampire to defeat its opponent." Cressida flowed toward him, a tiny smile on her face.

He shrugged. "It made sense."

Cressida grinned. "Well, that's a good thing, because now we have to collect the remains in the shade and leave them out for the sun to do its job."

Just like that, the battle was done.

A cry sounded behind him and he whirled, unsure what he expected, but the children emerged from the cave. "Y-you killed them." They weren't shocked, he realized.

"Yes. We promised nothing would ever harm you." Daniel shrugged, unsure of how the girls would react.

Rachel cocked her head, while Lucy and Marian smiled. "Yes you did, Uncle Daniel. But you see, we can protect ourselves."

He narrowed his gaze. "What exactly do you mean by that?"

"We remember." Earnestness shone in her eyes and soft smile as she touched his hand.

Confusion filled him at her words. "What do you mean?"

"Who we are, where we come from, and our parents. You see..."

The vampires crowded in and the children stood straighter, facing them. Their smiles broadened further, becoming full-blown grins. "Our parents were special. Every set of them. Ours mothers and our fathers. That makes us special. We have powers too, not the kind you might be used to." Daniel goggled at her words. "We aren't human, but we really aren't *witches* either. We can do things, *be* things."

Daniel felt the shock ripple through his mind. *Not human?* It was too much to understand that these children were more than what they'd all thought. For a moment he questioned his sanity and that of the children. It made no sense that they'd make it up. Accepting their words at face value explained far more.

"But you were born here, on Earth?"

"Well, we aren't aliens, if that's what you're asking." Lucy rolled her eyes and they all nodded smugly.

There didn't seem much else he could do right now. There might be questions and he needed to know how they came to these memories, but the main consideration was to get the children away from here.

Cressida was clearly intuiting his thoughts as she slipped her hand into his. "We need to get them back to the house, back to Celina, and call everyone in." Cressida spoke with control, as if she too was shell-shocked, but she'd obviously recovered far more quickly than he.

"Yes, you're right. The longer we stay, the greater the risk of more rogues." He grasped the lifeline she'd granted him.

The children stepped into the middle of the vampires and they marched their way back to the house.

The large, square white building came into view, two forms

sprinting toward them.

Celina and Javed. As they reached the children, they wound their arms around them. "Oh my God! I was so worried!"

Javed didn't speak, but he was just as affected as Celina. The three girls reciprocated the embrace while the adult vampires watched in silence.

"Celina? Javed? We need to talk." Their heads jerked in Cressida's direction.

"Yeah. Later, okay?" Javed faced them, his face grim. "They're home, safe and sound."

"My friends, there is so much more to this situation." She indicated the children.

Celina blinked rapidly, and he caught the shimmer of a tear on her lashes.

"What do you mean by that?" Javed's tone was adversarial and Daniel felt sympathy for the vampire. He'd be shocked to learn the truth, but right now he shrugged as Javed turned from one to another of their band. "Fine, inside then." He spun, taking Celina's arm, and the children skipped unconcernedly behind them.

ATTAR STRETCHED, ONE OF HIS FEMALE VAMPIRES HUDDLED ON the ground beside the bed he'd made. He'd fed deeply and sated his body again. Weariness assailed him, but so did great pleasure. Knowing his plans to dominate the vampire clans was moving forward at a speed that was energizing.

He eyed the ceiling, festooned with dancing humans, extended olive branches and semi-naked women. Their bodies were softly rounded and he grunted, considering the form on the floor.

"I want a woman. Another one like that."

The guard at his door stared in horror and fear. "L-like that?" The human gulped loudly and Attar's ire grew.

"That's what I said! Get me one like that or you..." He leered at the male guard, who paled.

Puny human.

If it weren't for the need to be guarded throughout the day, he'd have dealt with the fool far more harshly. As it was, the sound of the blood pumping in his veins almost enticed him to feed and take pleasure from the male. *I haven't had a male in such a long time...*

"One like that?" The strained words broke through his thoughts.

"Exactly. Find me women like that. Several." With that, he dismissed the man. He wanted blonde women, lithe and succulent. Women who reminded him of Cressida.

He'd not long been in this city, realizing that to stay in the same place would increase the chances of his enemies finding him, yet he was weary of moving and hiding. He wasn't prey. No, he was the ultimate predator, so this behavior felt intensely alien to him.

A beep echoed and he jerked, angered at the sound. He grew tired of the incessant chimes and pings that seemed to accompany technology. "Someone answer that." His roar was met by the rush of minions hurrying to do his bidding.

The woman on the floor didn't move. He slid off the bed and strode in her direction. His foot caught her under the stomach and with a swift move he rolled her over.

Dispassionately, he eyed the pool of blood congealing under her form. There was no sound of it pumping through her veins, and he frowned.

Pity. She'd been interesting, with the struggles she put up initially. I could have spent much more time searching her interesting mind and acquiring details of current human politics. With a flick of his hand, he dismissed her from his thoughts.

"Sire, your friend wishes to consult with you. Says he has information that you would wish to hear." The guard gulped again, his eyes settling on the dead flesh at Attar's feet. "Is she...?"

"Remove the carcass and let me talk to my informant" Grabbing the phone from the human's hand, he stretched, working the kinks out of his body. "Your report?"

"Attar? They've been meeting with the witches and have been given some kind of tokens."

He stilled. *Tokens?* His mind whirred to life, searching memories for what the witches may have claimed.

Long moments passed before he remembered the amulets that should have been his. The ones his mother had hidden from him. *Were there five or six? Six was a magical number he remembered, and if that was so...*

"Tell me more." He didn't attempt to hide the harshness of his demand.

"They aren't saying a lot, but I know they have been working with them. These tokens, from what I understand, will likely enhance the powers they have."

Now Attar reeled as he contemplated what might happen next. They *had* found the amulets. For a moment a shaft of fear pierced him and he had to sit down, breathe deeply and find his equilibrium.

"It matters not. They are but a motley band and I will defeat them. Go find out more, though, about these amulets. Who found them and handed them over?"

"They are important, sire? Are they dangerous?" The vampire's voice wavered, and a boiling anger welled in Attar's chest.

He growled deep in his throat.

"Anything that those witches may grant my enemies is dangerous! Go find out more. Everything!"

He threw the phone against the wall. It clattered to the ground, smashing into bits on the linoleum.

He grunted in anger.

How to defeat them? Now that was the question he needed to answer. His army was not yet of sufficient size or capability to overthrow them, and he roared with displeasure.

"Bring me food!"

The guard moved quickly at his bellow, but Attar paid him no mind, too deeply lost in his thoughts and plans. Yes, they would pay. And soon...

TWENTY-ONE

 Daniel took in the scene. It reminded him of his childhood, with the adults gathered around the children, who were eager to share the knowledge they'd gleaned from the day. Except this time, it wasn't after school; he wasn't one of the children and the information the girls were imparting was of great importance.

"So how did you work out you weren't human?" Cressida spoke gently, and Daniel glanced to Celina, who sat quiet and composed, though her face was paler than he'd ever seen it.

Rachel shrugged, bit her lip and looked down at the carpet before glancing up. She gazed at her sisters before sighing heavily. "We were out in the garden when dusk started to roll in. We love that time of day. Anyway, we were talking about our lessons when Lucy said something about missing home."

Celina gasped and Javed slung his arm around her shoulders.

"But it's okay, because we talked about it, and all of us agreed that Celina and Javed love us. But when Lucy spoke, it made me think of my mother and my head started to ache." Rachel spoke carefully, raising her hand to her forehead, and Marian nodded.

"Rachel kind of reacted badly, saying it was probably a dream but it—I don't know—it made me remember. I could see this big group of people and large animals. There were other children like us. With skills and abilities. I remember my mother. A lot of them spoke to her as if she were a leader, and some called her empress. She has this long black hair and—"

"You can tell us about your mother later, child. But right now we need to work out what you know. How you remembered..." Cressida's voice soothed the fractious children, who wanted to complete the story in their own way.

"Okay. But only if I get to tell you about her later?"

Cressida nodded at Rachel and the child beamed at her.

"I don't remember how we came to be alone. There're flashes of screaming and blood, but that's all." Marian shrugged deeply.

A spurt of surprise filled Daniel as he watched them speaking. For the first time, they seemed much older than their years. He leaned in. "But you're just kids."

Marian reached out, grasping his hands. "We are in human form, but we've lived a long time. I remember now, reading a newspaper the day I first found the others. It was over ten years ago, Uncle Daniel. For some reason though, when we were in the slaughter-house, our memories kind of faded away."

Daniel stood, needing some kind of movement to let him work off the pressure that filled his skull. Too much information, too many factors to absorb.

Be calm, Daniel. The witches will scan the children to check the facts as they have recounted them.

The door swung wide and the three witches entered, their presence a powerful force that followed in their wake.

"Where are the children?" a booming voice demanded, and Daniel turned in time to see Selena, her eyes flashing.

Celina gasped and jerked forward, no doubt to shield the children, but Lucy laid a hand on her wrist. "It's fine, Celina."

Rachel cleared her throat. "We're here, Graces." The children rose and curtseyed deeply before the older women.

"Graces?" Celina frowned.

"It's what they are called in our species. We're taught of them, but they are more myths... Or that's what we'd been told." Lucy spoke slowly, as if schooling a child.

Jemima laid her hands on one child, then the other, her slow movements careful. She nodded to Selena, who followed her actions. As did Danicka.

Once all three witches had scanned the children they sat down and sighed. "So, what we have here is...not *were*. Not human, but something different. Some would call them *changers,* but not us. They're closely aligned to the fae, if you will, though a hybrid of more than one type, nonetheless. We'd almost forgotten their existence," the witch muttered.

Danicka extended her hand. "They can change shape, wield magic and age slowly. But I don't remember an assemblage disappearing for a long time."

Selena shook her head. "Well that makes sense. With were's they are born in a single shape and that's the only one they can assume after puberty, which these three clearly haven't. But you can feel the power washing off them, which meant I knew they had more. But Fae? Hmm... Until they display their abilities, most people will think them regular children..."

"Unless something traumatic happens to push their skills into action." Jemima nodded sagely.

"What the children say is right?" Javed grunted before gripping Celina's shoulder.

"Oh yes. Assemblages of magic wielders such as these children were common before, though not for many many centuries. But it was all a long time ago, and I'd forgotten that dream." Jemima touched a hand to her brow.

"Well then, now that's settled, we should sit down and talk."

Hope spoke quietly, but it was enough to bring the various parties to an amicable agreement.

Cressida sat on the bed, waiting for Daniel to complete his ablutions. In her head, she sifted through the emotions that had stormed throughout the night just past. She'd felt pain, anguish, hate and, for a short while, even grief.

The grief was something she'd tried to contain for so long, and she'd almost given in to the crushing emotion.

Celina and Javed cared for the three girls as if they were their own flesh and blood, and that made the children even more important, because she'd been around them, knew them and understood their connection to their adoptive parents. That made them her family, too.

No matter that she'd had a nest, she'd never allowed herself to see the nestlings as her family... Until Daniel, Javed, Celina, Xavier and Hope, not to mention the children, who had become exactly that.

She'd once a family—flawed though it had been. Through no fault of her own, she'd lost it. She'd never conceived that she might have a second chance.

Daniel entered the room while she was lost in her thoughts.

"Cressida?" His voice was soft and understanding, tugging at her mind.

"What? Oh, I apologize." She was flustered. She raised her hands, smoothing the blonde hair that she'd tied back in a severe braid.

Daniel stalked to the bed, a frown on his face. She scanned the perfect symmetry of his features, no longer obscured by the wire-rimmed glasses he'd worn before the change. Wondered at the fact that he no longer needed them, pleased that the gleam of his eyes was now unobscured.

Cressida? Why are you so upset? It's clear something is bothering you. Tell me. Let me help you.

She bit her lip. *How?*

When he pulled back, she gave a deep sigh. It wasn't easy to explain, but for him, she would.

"It's the children, isn't it?"

His words startled her. It was that, partly. But there was so much more to her feelings than longing and wistfulness.

"I... Yes and no."

He barked a laugh. "Cressida, you're such a terrible liar."

She whirled around to face him, ready to denounce his words, but she couldn't discern any anger. All she could see was the softness that he only shared with the children, Celina and Hope...*and herself.*

"You know how I was turned?" She spoke slowly, the anguish welling up, as it always did when her thoughts turned to that time. She wanted to stop, to put some distance between them so she wouldn't remember. "You saw parts of it. It's all tied up in that. History. Ancient history, really."

"No, it isn't. You wear those memories around your neck like a millstone. You need to talk about them. It's hurting you deeply, like a festering poison. It's time to let it all go."

The glance she gave him must have spoken a million words, because he shook his head. "You can't fix what's already been. You have to make the best of it. Learn to live with the reality in which you find yourself."

She breathed deeply, while a million butterflies took wing in her stomach. "I wish it were that simple, but I've lived with these for a long time. During my many years, I've never found a way, or something, to ease the pain. At least, until now."

"All the more reason." He raised a hand to cup her cheek, thumb tracing the soft skin, and she nuzzled it.

"Tell me, Cressida. Allow yourself to grieve."

It was the tenderness in his voice that captured her, shook the pain free from the depths where she'd hidden it long ago. Where it had sunk root. "It was a long time ago, Daniel. Hundreds of years. I'd not been married very long. Etienne was a good husband." She shuddered as the memories battled through the chink she'd opened in her psyche.

Daniel encouraged her to lie back and she did, the scent of him on the pillow soothing her ragged emotions, as if he were wrapping her in his arms.

"How did you meet?"

She laughed softly. "His father was a farmer, but Etienne, he never wanted a life of labor. He was a lay priest and had come to our village to serve, and of course he was good-looking..." She smiled, remembering the way the girls of the village had gathered to whisper about the newest addition.

"We met one day as I was fetching water from the well. Mama wanted to scrub the floors, as she was a midwife, and forward thinking."

"Really? Were things so different then?"

Cressida rolled to her side to look into his eyes. "Oh yes. Most of the houses were still strewn with straw, and lice were an everyday occurrence. Babies died, as did their mothers, from botched deliveries. Legends held more sway, so mothers would pack themselves after birth with pig fat, or would refuse help because the pain of labor was considered God's retribution for Eve and the apple. So many things have changed." Her voice died away as she considered what had taken place. "Of course almost everyone lived in hovels, with holes in roofs where the thatch had failed and no glass for windows. That was for the wealthy. If you were lucky, like us, you had shutters to keep out the rain and wind. Etienne was determined and found a house on the edge of town while all the girls vied for his attention. The day I was carrying the pails, he offered his help, and on the way back home he told me of his sister and her death. She hadn't survived the childbed. It was so common in those times, but she'd only been fifteen."

"So young." Daniel frowned.

"It was the way of it. I was only fifteen when we met, but there was something about him. He was handsome…"

When Daniel grimaced she chuckled and smoothed her hand over his cheek. "Not as handsome as you though." But even with the words, his brow furrowed with disbelief.

"So how did you…?"

"Come to marry? We met many times during the summer, and by the end he asked my father's permission to court. By winter we were wed."

"But you were only fifteen?"

"Hmm. The cold wind blew the doors open to the church the day we took our vows. I remember the crash. So loud…" She dimly remembered clutching the tiny bouquet of winter greenery, the round red berries adding a dash of color, and her best gown, carefully refurbished for the day. Her hair caught up at the back, washed and brushed with care. Etienne in his best coat and breeches, with long, dark hair tied back at the nape of his neck.

The memory of the joy she'd felt standing there at the altar swept through her soul. He'd had his pick of the village maidens, yet he'd wanted to pledge himself only to her.

In her mind she replayed the scene—all that had remained was the final blessing, and she had been warm, so warm standing there beside the man she loved while the wind howled outside. They had been about to kneel when the bang had caused her to jump. An insidious finger of chill had advanced through the tiny chapel, freezing her to the marrow.

Afterward, the Matrons had denounced it as an evil omen. If only they'd known…

"The child?" Daniel's soft query pulled her back to the present.

"The next winter I was pregnant, the babe twisting and turning, and I was so happy. Etienne was proud and so was I, to know I'd brought him such joy." She stopped and shook her head. "But things started happening well before that. As the summer grew, he became distant. I can't…it was as if he knew what was coming. You see, a stranger came to town and the maidens, they relinquished their favors to him in a way none of us had ever seen before." The memory horrified her. She'd watched the repercussions each girl had faced. The floggings, those girls turned away from home and those who'd given birth out of wedlock. All of them had suffered the shunning of the townsfolk. The people hadn't known that Attar took the girls, then 'gifted' them to the ones who impregnated them. The girls had no choice, as they'd been treated like slaves. Those who'd returned pregnant...? The children who'd been born—not that many survived the pregnancy—were misshapen. The offspring taken into the wilds and left to perish. There was no room or care for those who wouldn't be able to support the village.

"The girls were changed, or at least the few who returned. They didn't seem to care after everything. More than one child was born from the loveless unions spawned in that house where evil lived. The elders whispered there was dark magic afoot. I know better now. But then, well, every aspect of the changes and the babes was unnatural." She shrugged, took a deep breath and glanced in Daniel's direction.

"It was clear the man was well born, living in the house on the hill. For all that, though, he couldn't find and retain staff. After the first couple joined the menagerie, none would serve, so he brought others in from outside the district to care for those who dwelled there. The few girls that got away, well, they were never really sane again.

"Until that winter, he never approached a married woman. One day he summoned me. He'd heard I was a competent cook and he had been preparing for a feast. He'd decided I should be the one to create it."

Now the memories were overlaid with the greasy fear she'd felt standing there before the man. "I told him I'd need to talk to my husband. I'd known Etienne would react poorly and hoped to find a way to refuse.

"It was during that interview that they came. I didn't know then, but they were vampires, and if I were a dramatic sort, I'd say evil traveled with them. Etienne forbade me to return, and I was pleased with that. He'd decreed I wasn't to go there, but he feared that more women and girls would be subverted. He decided he needed help. He traveled to the monastery to seek assistance and instructed me not to leave our home, which he'd blessed."

"Did he come to the house?" Daniel spoke quietly and she nodded.

"He did. When he crossed the threshold, I thought it was safe. I mean, we'd been told evil couldn't cross holy water, and I believed the myth. So I thought it would be fine, after all, he clearly wasn't evil, just..." For a moment, she was lost in the past. The weather had been cooling and the crops had failed. Food had been scarce and the gnaw of her belly was a palpable feeling again. "I decided to accept the work. After all, I'd be safe. I was pregnant and married. He'd never entangled someone like me."

He shook his head. "But you weren't. He wanted you, he'd seen you, and because you didn't lie down for him—"

"No. I mean, that's not quite accurate. The truth was, I was fascinated too, but not in what I'd call a normal way. In hindsight, it was seductive. I was with child though, so I ignored what my conscience told me. I told myself he wouldn't touch me, because I was a preacher's wife and pregnant. I went to the house and he..." She turned away, unable to see the loathing in his eyes.

You shouldn't turn away from me, Cressida. You took a chance because you honestly thought it was safe. We all make mistakes...

"Not ones that cost the lives of your child and your husband!" The shriek was wrenched from her soul as the anger spewed forth. "It was my fault. He bit me, drained me and changed me!"

Daniel wrapped his arms around her. "And it could have been nothing, just the imaginings of whatever age it was..."

"Hundreds of years ago. But the child died inside me. I had to birth it knowing it was dead and when I looked upon her face, it was perfect in every way." Tears burned her frigid skin as her chest heaved.

"I buried Etienne afterwards and left the area. I couldn't take the chance that anyone would know what I'd become. The child I bore in a hostelry far from my home and *it was dead*. Because of my foolishness. My pride."

She tried to tug away from him, but he hauled her back against his chest.

"You carried this pain within you for hundreds of years, used it to keep everyone at a distance. But now, Cressida, you have to face it. Accept your pain before you can heal."

Hot tears poured down her face while she lay there, the pain washing over her. Daniel held her close, let her release the anguish she'd buried for so long. When it was done, she felt spent. Her eyes stung and her chest ached.

She released the muscles that had tensed during her weeping and allowed him to rub circles on her back. A modicum of wellbeing crept through her, but she realized the truth of Daniel's words. She needed to tell him everything.

Before she could speak though, the rattle of his voice echoed in her mind and body. "What did you do...?"

"I left the child on the steps of a church with her name and the name of her parents. I went back much later, when no one would recognize me. They'd buried her in a baby's grave. Eventually I arranged for a headstone. It's still there." She knew, because she'd bought the land, ensuring it would never be developed.

"One day, when this is done, we'll visit it together and you can tell her of the life you lead. How you mourned her for centuries."

"But I can't ever have another." She breathed the most secret regret. "I mean, I had one chance and made the biggest mistake. I have to live with that knowledge forever."

"Would you?"

"Would I what?"

"Want another child. Want one with me?" His voice wavered and she felt his uncertainty. It took her a moment to consider his question, and she reached out and grasped his hand.

"I see what Celina and Javed have, with the children and it...it hurts. Here." She tugged his hand to the region of her heart.

"We could adopt, if you want. When this is over, we'll investigate it." The words enticed. They gave her hope.

But fear, particularly one held close for centuries, needed more than words. "Don't say that if you don't mean it."

For the first time she saw anger banked in his eyes. "I would never joke about that, Cressida. I'm not hurtful. I love you and all I want to do is bring you pleasure. I want to see your eyes sparkle with happiness. I've never seen you truly happy."

She swallowed the lump that had taken up position in her throat.

With a great heaving breath, she gathered her courage. "I love you." Cressida leaned in, kissing him as a tiny flicker of warmth grew in her belly.

Daniels body heated and hardened as she pressed her lips to his. *No, Cressida. Not like this.*

She pulled back and he felt dirty. He knew she was using sex to blot out the memories and promises. She needed to accept that part of her life, as much as she did his love, before they could truly enjoy the promised future. "I love you, but you can't use me to forget your pain."

Her eyes widened and for a moment he wondered if he'd pushed too hard. He'd ached for her as she spoke, marveled at the strength of the beautiful woman in his arms. The way she'd faced life, alone and with buckets of regrets, humbled him.

"I'm not..." She screwed up her face and he could feel the depth of the hurt that she hid. "I would never use you, Daniel."

He sighed, realizing that what he'd hoped to achieve had gone awry. "I don't mean—"

"You do." She slid from his grasp, making her way to the side of the bed before standing. "Please leave me."

He stared at her perfect body and face, but there was great anguish in her eyes and that firmed his conviction that he couldn't leave. Not until she knew that wasn't what he'd meant. "No."

"Leave me." She gasped.

The ripple of power stabbed at him and he collapsed backward, taking the full brunt of her anger. "No." His skin felt as if it were peeling back, and his head ached as if it were about to crack open. He ignored it, knowing that he had to stand his ground. "I told you I'd never leave you. I meant it." Breathing posed a great problem, with the magic stealing the air in his lungs, but he'd be damned if he would give in now.

"Why won't you leave me alone?" Here it came; grief crashed through her defenses as she crumpled to the ground, sobbing, and he cursed himself for the pain he was causing her.

Daniel moved quickly and dropped down beside her. "Cressida, I love you, but you have to understand, you aren't only the woman I see now. You are the sum of what you've lived through. Every experience formed the one person I want to spend eternity with."

"But I caused pain and death. How can you love such a flawed person?" It was a cry from her soul.

"The heart only sees love, and I see with my heart, dear one." He held her, while her shoulders bowed and the tears finally flowed. Before she'd been stoic but controlled, but now that stoicism was shattered into a million shards and it felt like each was driven into his own heart.

"Come to bed and let me hold you," he muttered against her hair, and she gave a tiny nod before moving in tandem with him. He led her to the bed like a child and tugged the covers over her nakedness while the streaks of her tears marred her skin.

It hurt to watch her suffering the intense pain, but he knew she needed to accept it before she could heal. Here, in their sanctuary, she could be just a woman. Here she could heal. Once outside these rooms, the warrior and general needed to take ascendency.

On the other side of the bed, he lifted the covers and slid beneath them before scooting to her side. "Just let me hold you, Cressida."

She nestled in his embrace, and he thanked every god he could think of that such a vibrant woman, even in the midst of her darkest grief, wanted him.

He lay there for a long time before sleep claimed him.

TWENTY-TWO

She woke, and awareness swept over her body. The warmth of Daniel beside her soothed the ragged edges left over from before. At the time she hadn't wanted to admit to using him as an emotional barrier, but he'd been right. The pressure that had existed in her soul was a little lighter. "It'll take time."

"Huh? Cressida?" Daniel moved, warm and solid against her skin, with an erection that jutted against her hip. Her body responded and heat pulsed through her veins.

He reached, and without thought, she moved into the embrace. When he kissed her, ripples of excitement skittered.

Good morning, beautiful.

She could so get used to this. The thought slid away as he caressed her breasts, then flicked the now hard nipples into buds of pure pleasure.

She moaned as he applied his mouth to her skin, kissing his way across her jaw, paying extra special attention to the juncture of her throat. Cressida arched when the tip of his tongue slid over the sensitive, exposed flesh and streaks of lightning flashed through her mind.

"How...?" Stringing a sensible thought together was difficult as her nerves sang their pleasure at his ministrations. "How can you," she panted, "do this to me?"

Daniel raised his head, his gaze seeing right through to the woman who hid behind the mask. "It's love."

She squeezed her burning eyes shut and when she opened them, saw stark emotion on his face.

Cressida rose to her knees, breasts jutting forward as the center of her being melted. "Let me show you my love." She extended her hand, placing her palm against his warm and hard pectoral muscle, and shoved.

Once he lay before her, she stripped the white cotton sheet from her body and surveyed the man.

Firm muscles dipped down to a trim waist and the mass of curly hair at his abdomen couldn't hide the proud thrust of his cock. Long legs, with enough muscle to entice, but not enough to be too big.

He grinned. "So, I take it you like what you see?"

One long fingertip is all it would take, she thought devilishly. With great care, she reached out and slid the nail down his length, watching as his penis jerked in reaction.

Daniel hissed and made to move. She stilled him with the palm of her hand thrust against his chest.

"No, Daniel, with us, it's all about pleasure. Pleasure and love and desire..."

Returning to the head of his erection, she stilled. Then pressed. Just a little. When she raised her hand, she glanced at his face. His eyes were glassy and unfocussed, and he breathed more heavily than before.

"Liked that, did you?"

When he slowly moved in her direction, Cressida was startled for a moment before desire reasserted itself and once more she was lost in the excitement of bedeviling him. When he touched the flesh at her core, she moaned and moved against his fingers.

"As much as you like this."

He moved his fingers so slowly she wanted to scream, but instead she bit her lip while he traced the swollen flesh.

More.

He laughed, and the rumble of his chest ricocheted through her, leaving her a quivering mass of sensation, hungry and unsatisfied.

She fastened her hand around him, the bulbous head engorged as she gave a single pump. Heard his exhalation.

Witch!

This time when she leaned forward he met her halfway, the kiss explosive and her body so alive with hunger. She moved to straighten and as her nipples brushed against his lips, he slid one finger deep within her.

She gripped his cock harder, squeezing rhythmically. Her body was a single flame, dancing as the passion rose between them.

She arched again, undulating as he tormented her, and the flames licked at her mind.

Daniel? I can't...

Let go, my love. I'll catch you.

She did, her body stilling, until she shattered in his arms, tugged away from reality as instinct took over. The primal cry she gave echoed in the room.

Blackness filled her, and when it cleared she lay against his chest. "Daniel?"

He chuckled. "Now that was extraordinary. I've never had that effect on anyone."

Her thighs quivered as he rolled her over and pushed her against the bedding. With great care, he rose and climbed between her legs.

"Let's do that again." There was devilry and desire in his tone.

His gaze captured hers as he moved down her body, until his face drew level with her core, still damp while aftershocks of pleasure rippled. She watched, unable to form a coherent thought as he applied his mouth, licking and sucking at her. All she could do was react, raising her legs, her feet resting at his shoulders.

He worked her, lapping and flicking the tight bundle of nerves while arousal spiraled once more.

"You taste so good."

She closed her eyes, but the sensations seemed stronger without the other input. He kept up the comments, telepathically.

So sweet.

The thrill rose again and she reached down. Her hands tangled in his hair as he wrought his magic and when the wave crashed again she screamed, clenching her legs against him.

Tears leaked from between her tightly closed eyes.

"I want..." She could barely breathe but determination spurred her on. "Next time, you... I want you inside me."

He rose, his face was hard and raw with desire, and she met his kiss. It tasted musky, and when he opened his mind she nearly shattered again. *This is what I see. This is what I feel.*

In her mind whirling colors spun, a multitude of red and gold hues.

He settled himself between her thighs and reached out, taking her hands in his grip before he slowly started to push his way deep within her body. "This. I want more of this."

When he was firmly seated he stilled. "I need you with me, beside me." The words stole the last vestiges of thought as love, strong and powerful, filled her.

"Forever." As if her words broke the dam he'd created, he moved, urgent thrusts that ripped free everything she had to give.

The undulations of his hips took on a wild and primal quality as he slammed home again and again while she arched, accepting his body. Loving everything. Each sensation winding her higher.

"Now!" The final thrust was brutal and pushed them both beyond the precipice.

TWENTY-THREE

DANIEL HELD THE BLOOD WINE IN HIS HAND, WATCHING IT swirl as he moved it around and around in the goblet.

"Are you going to keep playing with that, or drink it?" Samra's voice held an amused quality.

"I don't know." His mind still had to find some kind of equilibrium after the explosive session with Cressida. It wasn't so much that he regretted it. How could he? It was more that now he worried she might decide to move on, after he'd forced her to open up and face her demons.

"Just drink it, Daniel." Samra's frustration with his inner ruminations made him laugh.

"Oh well, I guess if I must." He tipped the cup to his mouth and let the life-giving liquid dribble down his throat.

He slid the goblet back to the table, considering what had to come next. Cressida had been adamant that he should be tutored in swordplay and Samra, as the best warrior in the house, had been nominated to spar with him. On any normal day he'd probably enjoy it, but not today, when he wasn't really working at full capacity. He grasped the grip of the rapier Samra had chosen for today's lesson, feeling the weight, while he familiarized himself with the weapon.

"En garde!" His head snapped up as Samra assumed her pose, sword ready. She wore black yoga pants with a matching black bandeau top and black cotton slippers, her hair scraped back into an untidy ponytail.

The first time he'd thought to fight her, she'd worn exactly the same thing. When he'd asked if she was worried she'd be injured, Samra had laughed off his concern. It had only taken a single session to learn why.

Now she waited, spinning her sword from hand to hand while she watched him. Her eyes focused on him, but he knew she was intensely aware of every move the metal made. Samra was a scary whirlwind of action.

"Come on, Daniel. I really am starting to become quite impatient."

He shook his head, trying to clear the fog that had invaded his brain. "Yeah."

He lifted the sword and it wobbled a little, and she laughed. "Oh you've got to be kidding me!" She dipped her sword to the floor and he lunged.

A quick sidestep by Samra and a single foot thrust out as he shot past her had him stumbling into a heap at her feet.

"Daniel? How many times have I told you not to telegraph your moves? That was so bad..." She shook her head and he reddened.

Even as he scrambled to his feet, she assumed a listening look, cocking her head to one side. "Bastards. Get your things, Daniel. It's time to put what you've learned into action."

Before he could grasp the importance of her words she was gone, running through the doorway. He hurried after her, coming upon scenes of contained chaos.

Across the hallway Cressida waved to him and he rushed in her direction. "One of our nests is under attack. *Quickly.*" He noted she already wore her customary red leathers as the house vampires flooded into the hallway.

"The cars are on their way. Prepare yourselves for battle." She stalked off and he trailed, her long legs eating up the distance.

"Which one?"

"The House Grimardi." The house his father had moved there after he'd left Javed's. Daniel's blood thudded slowly in his veins, as if the fluid had somehow thickened and become sluggish.

"My father..."

Cressida laid a soft hand on his shoulder. "I won't lie to you, Daniel. It's bad. If he's alive when we get there, you should find him immediately. If not, we'll need your help to battle them."

The urge to scream rose, but he knew it would serve no purpose. He locked his shoulders. "If they've..." He stopped, unable to say the words that gave finality to his father's life. "I'll make them pay."

She nodded, while through the link he could discern her fears and worry. For the nest, for his father and for him.

"I won't fail, Cressida." As he spoke, the cars drew up the path and the seething mass of vampiric warriors flowed down, finding cars and climbing within. They carried a variety of weapons, some swords, others whips, some chains, and attached to belts he noted the new ultraviolet pistols. Samra joined them in the lead vehicle, putting a tiny earpiece in.

Samra had insisted on the inclusion of these tools, claiming they would help with communications, and Cressida had agreed. 'Any advantage would be welcome', she'd said in their planning sessions.

The silence in the car was fraught as Daniel imagined the worst possible outcome. Nothing, however, prepared him for the sight as they crossed the threshold to the estate.

Smoke billowed through broken windows as combatants spilled out of the doors onto the lawn. Some battled on the grass while the gravel crunched beneath them as they moved in a macabre ballet.

Some vampires rushed from the vehicles, others glanced around to seek victims, and it was clear the rogues hoped to take control of the nest.

The noise, a mixture of clashing steel and screams, married with the ripe scent of blood. Daniel's teeth descended and his gaze narrowed. The pulsing of blood in his veins sharpened as the predator rose. With one task at the forefront of his mind, he moved, cutting his way through those fighting, shoving and pushing.

At the wooden front door, an unknown warrior blocked his path. "Move!" The guttural sound was unlike him. And when the warrior bared his teeth and lifted his sword, Daniel had no qualms.

"They are ours. We're no tame vampires. We take and we feed." Those were the last words the creature before him spoke as Daniel raised the blade and the arc of steel sliced the air. It buried itself in flesh, the sword slicing through bone and sinew as easily as a knife through soft butter.

From the defeated vampire's clumsy movements and inability to protect itself, he knew it had been untrained. The dead vampire crumpled in a heap at his feet. He stepped over it, uncaring now, as smoke continued to pour from the building.

Any humans within were in danger of death by vampire, fire or smoke inhalation... "Father!" He roared the words, but in this hell no answer could be heard. He moved to the stairs and headed up them, two and three at a time. Bodies were strewn everywhere. Children, women and men of all ages.

Anger churned deep in his gut. At his father's room he stopped, a sound within catching his attention. The soft wet *thud, thud...*

The door was locked and he pushed against it. Once. It jerked and bowed, but didn't give. Again he pushed and it sagged, but held.

Daniel made one more charge with a primal roar. The collision hard, then the hinges bent. The door fell to the ground and Daniel with it.

He found his father on the bed, a vampire holding him from behind in the parody of an embrace. Her mouth at his neck as the final *thud* sounded.

"Dan...iel." The whisper assaulted his senses as a glazed look descended on his father's face.

The woman pulled back, a laugh tinkling through the air as she carelessly wiped away the trickles of blood off her chin. "Hmm, you're a sexy one. Why not throw in your lot with us? The master isn't much fun, or good-looking."

Rage overwhelmed him and Daniel threw off any shred of humanity as he raised his sword. "I'll kill you."

The woman's face hardened. "Try it."

She leaped at his shoulder. He moved, sidestepping and whirling, as Samra had taught him. His blade cracked against bone and the vampire crumpled to the ground. The blood-red veil that invaded his senses demanded justice. A quick downward thrust pinned the woman to the floor.

"You'll never take another." He tugged the dirk from his belt and with it in hand, he took her head.

As he stood there, looking down, the last vestiges of endorphins leached away. Hate, despair and anger filled him. They were mainly directed at himself. He'd killed. In anger, in fury.

Dropping the head to the floor now seemed important. It took willpower to release his fingers. The head hit the wooden floorboards with a wet *thud* while his soul ached with grief.

He spun and stepped heavily in the direction of the bed. It was as he reached for his father that he heard the call. *Daniel!* It was more of a shriek.

"Cressida!" He roared, feeling her fear and something that froze him. Now he moved faster than ever before. The connection between them was dimming. *Hold on! I'm coming!*

Tearing down the steps became nearly impossible as the bottleneck of fighting warriors blocked the way. He jumped over the railing, thanking God it was only one story. The landing jarred, but he pushed himself up and kept moving.

The thread of their connection wavered but he followed it. She lay on the driveway, curled in a fetal ball, arms wrapped around her stomach. Blood soaked the pebbles below her while bodies littered the ground around the battle zone.

Three vampires, not yet dead, lay nearby, their bodies hacked and slashed. Clearly Cressida had put up a fight.

Even as he crouched down, thoughts of how to save Cressida's life came to the fore. Just as he raised his wrist, ready to slash at it, Samra arrived, lifted her gaze to Daniel and nodded. "Blood. That's what she needs."

Their gazes clashed, then he jerked his head in the direction of the engagement. "Finish it!" She gave a single nod before returning to the fray.

Daniel tugged Cressida's arms from the wound in her abdomen. It pulsed and he knew he had to feed her or she'd die. He used the dirk and made a single deep slice across his wrist. Blood fountained and he urged her lips open. *Drink, my love. Drink deep.*

She didn't and fear ate at him. "Drink, dammit." He thrust his wrist roughly against her mouth and watched as the blood seeped between her lips. Her body convulsed and she gagged, before latching onto the deep gouge. Teeth sliced through his flesh and she fed.

Her body was stiff and unresponsive until she'd taken several deep draws, then he felt the tension ebb away. Her breathing eased. When he looked down, it was to see the flow of blood had stopped.

Around him, the sounds of battle calmed. A pair of legs, black leather-covered, filled his view. *Samra.*

"It's done."

He nodded before glancing at Cressida. Having taken her fill, she now lay limp in his arms, her golden hair matted with blood and other matter he didn't want to consider.

Scooping her into his arms, he surveyed the damage. "We'll need a report. Secure the perimeter and arrange for any..." Now words escaped him. *Survivors?* How could there be any in this carnage?

Samra nodded as if she knew his thoughts. "I'll arrange billets for the survivors. Take care of Cressida."

HER BODY ACHED. EVERY MOVE REMINDED HER OF THE BATTLE they'd fought, and, according to Samra, had won. Daniel, however, was noticeable by his absence and she fretted.

The healer pushed another goblet of blood wine in her direction. "This should be sufficient to heal your wounds. They were extreme, and you lost a lot of blood." The man rose slowly.

"The others?"

He patted her hand. "The ones I can help will make a full recovery, my dear. Like you, it will take time. Your warriors have been...diminished."

She made a face at his words. He was right, and she'd now depleted the security of her nest. It was a beginner's mistake, and she conceded that she'd grown unused to battle readiness.

"The other nest?"

His face paled. "Very few survived. Some of the children holed up in the kitchen, climbing into the refrigeration system. Several show signs of hypothermia, but they too will recover from their physical injuries. The rest..." The doctor sighed. "Too many dead for these old bones to face, I'm afraid."

The next question trembled on her lips. "Daniel's father?" The man shook his head silently, and Cressida placed the drink on the bedside table before slumping backward.

Was that why he hadn't been in to see her? Or was it something else entirely?

Weariness weighed her down. She should be up and dealing with things, not hiding in her chamber like some helpless invalid. She started to straighten, to lever herself up, when the wooden walking stick of the healer found its way to her chest, pushing against her breastbone.

"You will rest, Cressida, otherwise that great lion outside will skin me alive, I have no doubt."

"What great lion?" Hope surged.

"Daniel. He's been pacing the hallway for the last however long since you were brought back. Now lie down, so I can send him in." As the doctor reached the door, he turned. "I mean it. You need rest, otherwise you'll relapse. Then he really will be out for my blood."

She sighed, wincing as her body reacted sluggishly. When the door opened though, all those thoughts fled. The man in the doorway was pale, his face and body streaked with blood and soot.

"He said I could come in now."

Cressida gave a tiny smile and he returned it, but she noticed it didn't reach his eyes. "I'm so sorry, Daniel. I honestly hoped..." She let the words trail away when he tensed.

"It's not your fault, Cressida. I should have moved him well before this. Petitioned for a place here."

He blamed himself, she realized. "Would he have moved?" She urgently needed him to understand it wasn't his fault. None of this was.

Daniel blinked slowly, and the ache she felt now wasn't anything to do with her body. "I..." He shrugged. "I could have made him."

"Daniel, a wise person, once told me that I can't fix what's been. I have to make the best of it. I'm passing that wise advice along to you now."

His dark hair flew around his face as he shook it. "No. It's not that simple."

"It is. It has to be. Otherwise you'll be like me. Bitter and cold. Trying to distance yourself from life. Don't push me away, Daniel." Frustration and fear filled her. Surely he wouldn't make the mistakes she had.

When he gulped she stood up and moved from the bed, then moaned as pain lanced her.

In that instant he was there, helping her back to the bed. "Oh God! I'm such an idiot. You're right. Of course you are." The grip of his hand on hers warmed her through, and he lifted the goblet to her mouth. "Drink this while I tug my head from between my cheeks."

She snickered at his unfamiliar comment. "So men do sometimes admit they're wrong?"

"Not often. So don't get used to it."

She drained her drink and raised a hand to his face. It was both dear to her and incredibly sexy. "You should shower, then rest. What time is it, anyway?"

"Nearly dawn. We have the last of the survivors billeted. The house is a write-off. There was a fire tonight and most of it is unsafe." He shrugged and she wanted to hug him close and tell him it was all right. But they both knew nothing would be all right until Attar was defeated. "There was another nest attacked."

When she rose, he pushed her back. "It was a ruse. A ploy to further weaken us."

"Daniel?" He shook his head and she sighed. "Go shower. I'll still be here when you're done."

When he left, she strained to hear the sounds of water running and imagined him washing the remnants of the night away. He reappeared in the doorway, wearing a pair of drawstring pants that rode low on his hips. In silence, he padded to the bed and sat down carefully. "If you don't want me here tonight..."

She reached out a hand, gripping his. "Stay. Hold me today and tonight we'll talk." When they finally settled down, she scooted into his embrace and thanked God for another day together. She lay like that until his breath evened and she knew he slept.

ATTAR STALKED FROM ONE END OF THE ROOM TO THE OTHER, seething as he tossed the plans that had failed over in his mind. Even so, he listened to the report from his second.

"How many did you lose?" He whirled suddenly, his gaze

focusing on the face of the shaking man in front of him. *Idiots!* They were all fools and he'd be better off without them! Except right now his numbers were once more depleted.

His second flinched at his anger, but Attar didn't care.

He needed rest, he needed sustenance, and he needed an army. This loss meant he'd have to make more vampires. It would take blood, time and resources, all of which were running low.

"Sire, I believe...we lost forty-seven warriors." Jastin bowed low, his greasy black hair nearly touched the floor, and lightning-quick, Attar struck. He flung Jastin back against the wall and the warrior hung there before slumping.

"You failed me! Now we must rebuild the army I created." The cramp in his stomach felt like a copper cord tightening in his gut, and his teeth ached to sink into human flesh.

"Sire..." Jastin crawled up to hands and knees. "I will fix this." The breathless promise filled Attar's mind. He wanted to roar that it could only be fixed with Jastin's death, but that wouldn't work. He needed warriors too much. Instead, he swung around once again. He'd already lost others. Those who'd run away like cowards and he seethed.

"Bring me the cattle to slake my thirst."

Jastin nodded quickly, his movements urgent, before he sped away. Within minutes he returned with a whimpering teen budding into womanhood.

"Please, don't hurt me. Please..." Her green eyes were round and the hair scraped back from her neck gave him an excellent view of her artery. It pulsed wildly as her blood pumped faster.

Fear always made feeding so much more pleasant, he conceded.

He tore the girl from Jastin's grip, ripping the skin of her upper arm, and the essence of the rich blood drove his hunger to higher peaks.

She struggled against him and he touched his fingers to her down-covered cheek, pleased with the feel of her. Maybe he should—

Before he could complete the thought, the stench of urine rose in the air, becoming stronger.

Anger coursed richly. "Take her away! I want no piss-covered wench to sate my hunger!"

The girl sobbed as Jastin dragged her back to the hastily erected holding cells, the sounds echoing in the empty building while his stomach continued the gnawing, roiling hunger that ate him from the inside out. This time when Jastin returned, he dragged an older man behind him.

Attar took one look, then lurched across the room. The paper-thin skin gave beneath his incisors. The blood tasted old, musty even, but Attar didn't say a word as he drank every drop.

The carcass slumped to the floor when he was done, and he looked down at it with distaste. "Next time, bring me something younger."

Jastin cowered against the wall. "That's... He and the girl were all that's left."

"The others? Where are they?" His harsh demand sent his second to shaking and avoiding his gaze.

"You've either... You've turned them or...fed."

"Bring me more!"

"But, sire... We have no extra warriors fit to hunt. Most who returned are injured."

Attar didn't care how dangerous their situation was. He didn't want to hear about the injured. He hungered.

"Let me make this clear to you, Jastin. *I hunger. You. Find. Sustenance.*"

Jastin bowed deeply. "Yes, sire. I will find sustenance for you. What about the girl?"

Attar flicked his hand. "She is soiled. Get rid of her."

His energy nearly spent, Attar slinked to the dais bed he'd had them prepare and laid his body down. Every inch of him ached, as had happened in the past when his hunger hadn't been fully allevi-ated. *How long until I have more food?*

He'd survived this kind of hunger before, and he could again. He'd simply twilight, so his body could rest.

The meditative steps—his mother had taught him in childhood—were easy to follow. First, relax the muscles, letting go of the pain. Next rest the mind so it is quiet.

In that state, he waited for Jastin to return.

TWENTY-FOUR

"You really don't have to hover over me, Daniel. It's not like I'm going to collapse." Cressida spoke softly, with more than a hint of amusement, and Daniel groaned, aware there was no escape from what lay ahead. He knew what he had to do, but the fear of leaving Cressida behind when Attar was still loose left his stomach in knots. He pushed away the fear.

"I thought I was being discreet." He shook his head. *I wonder what I did that tipped her off?*

"Oh. Well, if you hadn't been thinking so loud, I wouldn't have guessed."

He noted her grin and it lightened his heart a bit, before the emotion melted away, leaving him with the sadness that had dogged him for the last few days. "Maybe Samra could...?"

Cressida shook her head. "I really don't need a babysitter."

The memory of her lying there on the ground slammed into him. Ever since the battle at the nest, he'd fretted whenever she wasn't in his sight. "No. But I need to make sure you're safe."

The grin faded as she moved in his direction, her long blue dress wrapping around her legs. "I understand your concerns. But you have to realize, for hundreds of years I've taken care of myself. I've been a warrior for too long to be able to let down my guard."

"I know. It's just..."

"You have to go. I understand that, Daniel. We *both* have tasks to attend to. I need you to go attend to the burials and leave me to complete my work. Vincent will drive you there, wait with you, then you'll return. Of all of us, you're probably in the most danger." She laid a light kiss on his cheek, and as much as he wanted to turn his face so she kissed his lips, he knew now wasn't the time.

He had a meeting with the undertaker to attend to his father's interment and those of the other nestlings who'd lived at the estate.

Vampires take care of their own, he'd been told many times over the years, so he'd make sure they were memorialized appropriately. But, God, how he wished he could have handed this over to someone else. Someone who didn't feel the weight of grief that pounded into his brain, turning it to a morass of sludge he fought to rise above.

The trip was swift. Daniel chose to sit in the front seat with Vincent, uncomfortable with the partition between himself and the driver. Besides which, Vincent was fun most of the time. Today he was morose, like a lot of the vampires, no doubt thinking of the friends he'd lost.

At the ceremony the night before, the bonfire had been difficult. Cressida had officiated, though she really wasn't yet recovered.

The attack on the house had set everyone on edge.

"You good to do this, Dan?" He knew the driver was worried about him. The sense of not really being here was more than a little off-putting, but he guessed it was better than trying to tough it out while he lost the plot. Right now, he didn't have the time for that.

If Attar attacked again, well, there would be more dead.

Next time it could be Cressida, or Celina, or... He shied away from those thoughts. *Not now.*

"Yeah. But I could sure use a good friend to help me." Vincent locked the vehicle, setting the alerts the witches had placed on it, knowing that on their return it wouldn't be some kind of vehicular grave.

Entering the House of Restful Peace had Daniel shivering. The dead really weren't something he'd spent a lot of time around, and a cold shiver of unease skittered up his spine.

"Please take a seat, Mr....?" The man looked as uncomfortable as Daniel was, leaving him thinking the man might not have dealt with vampires or such large affairs before.

"Just Daniel is fine. Look, I'm here to arrange—"

"The funeral for your father. Can I get you a cup of tea?" The man stilled, turned pink and opened his mouth, no doubt to apologize at the gaffe of offering tea to a vampire.

"It's okay. Really. If we could..." He spread his hands, hoping to get this over and done with as soon as possible; the man nodded.

"Yes, of course."

He pulled out a pad and paper, wrote Daniel's name at the top, then started asking questions about his father. What age was he? Had he been a believer in the spiritual world? Daniel answered each one, thinking carefully before he spoke.

"No. My father was a very..." He searched for the appropriate term. "He was very earthy."

The undertaker nodded and made a careful notation.

"Will you be needing a priest for the others?"

He stared at the man, feeling lost. "I...uh..."

"It's common for the councilors to officiate in these circumstances." Vincent's murmur reminded Daniel that they had faced this kind of situation before.

"And the date?"

"Well, it would be best if we could have one large ceremony."

The man across the desk started. "Well, uh... As to that, I'm not sure we have enough caskets..."

"Order more then. We can wait until you do." For an instant a spear of anger surged.

"It's not really that simple. The cost alone..." The man was tugging off his glasses and a bubble of frustration popped inside Daniel.

He stood, angry with the man and the argument about money. "Do it!" He shook his head and subsided. "I apologize. It's just..."

Vincent spoke up. "The nests will cover whatever it costs. Please arrange it." Now that Vincent had spoken, he sat back, hating the lack of control he was experiencing.

His detachment grew, as if he was there but not really as he scanned brochures of flowers and caskets. In the end, he chose a dark wood, walnut the man said, with brass fittings and a white satin liner. Whatever specifications he had for his father would also be used for the others.

Finally, he settled on sprays of lilies and a sea of cyclamens to be planted in memory of everyone who'd died.

By the time he left the building, Daniel was sure the smell of death must have permeated every cell of his body.

"Heading back now, Daniel?"

He looked Vincent in the eye. "Yeah, I need to see Cressida." She would make him feel whole again. Somehow, she knew exactly what to do. The drive home was quick and by the time they'd pulled up outside the house he bounded from the vehicle.

The sound of raised voices filled the entryway and he moved fast, ready to protect Cressida with every ounce of his being. He shoved open the doors, surprising everyone within.

Eyes swiveled toward him. "What the hell is going on here?" His voice boomed and several goggled in his direction.

"I've informed them that someone is reporting to Attar. I want to know who."

He stepped into the room, watching as several cringed away.

Knowledge seeped into him—he could give her this. The magic jumped and jerked as if it urged him to use it. *I can make them tell you.*

Cressida's eyes opened wide as she absorbed the shock.

Can you? Really? Can you be sure it would be accurate, though?

He stopped for a moment, smiling. *Yeah.*

Then do it.

HE READ THEM. SHE COULD SEE IT ON HIS FACE AS HE strained, and she worried the whole time about the effects of his actions. Her choices. Clearly, they could feel the intrusion into their minds.

Cressida watched them all. In the corner, Gervaise cowered in his chair, eyes wide while rivulets of sweat poured down his face. His gaze darted to and fro as if seeking who was probing.

It's Gervaise. He doesn't realize though... He thinks that we...that he will be raised up and the rest of us cast aside.

Cressida heard the disgust in Daniel's thoughts and she shook her head. *How could he do this?*

It was simple, though.

He wants power.

Cressida stood. The movement was still slow and her body twinged, but she was on the road to recovery. Better than those poor warriors whose bodies had been ashes that day.

"Councilors, it's true that someone who holds the sacred trust of the nests is a traitor."

Fear rose, sharp and acrid in her nostrils. She'd already told them that, but reinforced her words with the anger that roiled in her gut. "Oh yes, someone here has sold us out. To Attar. They want power and position. And we have the power to know who it is." She glanced at him, imbuing knowledge in her words and gaze.

Gervaise slide farther down in his seat.

"Who?" Cressida demanded.

Another councilor rose to their feet. "*What? Gervaise?* Surely you wouldn't do that?"

"How could you? We took an oath!" Called a second.

The voices babbled accusations and Gervaise paled, cowering away from the anger that built in the room.

"I... He... I was bewitched!" Gervaise's screech took on a pleading tone. "It's not my fault. He made me do it!"

"But that's not true, Councilor." Daniel strode forward, his face a mask of fury. "You went to him. You approached Attar, back before the Slaughterhouse Rout. It was you all along!"

When Daniel would have engaged the man, Cressida held him back. "No, Daniel. That is not our way."

She turned back to the others gathered around the table. More than one showed the need for blood on their faces.

The time-honored tradition of *De Premiere Instance de la Justice* would be enacted.

"Friends, you know how we deal with traitors. He must be given the chance to prove himself at trial. Guards!" Samra and two others, who'd been guarding the doorway, entered the room, their eyes wide as they took in the scene. "Take Councilor Gervaise into custody. Make sure to use the cuffs, Samra. Note the number in the Book of Justice."

Samra bowed without a word and indicated to the men, who moved into position.

"No! Don't do this! I'll make reparation! I will repent!" He struggled against their hold as they dragged him from the room, and Cressida let go of the breath she'd held. The exhalation seemed to deflate her, and she dropped to her seat.

"Councilors?"

"You had no choice, Cressida. He has to pay. Tell us when you wish to convene, and we will be here. The Trial of Justice must be enacted and swiftly."

She nodded.

"But before we leave. You had Daniel scan him and all of us, didn't you?"

"Yes. It was the only way."

The councilor inclined his head. "Then I have another question. Why at the time of the attack on the nest didn't Daniel just..." He waved his hand in the air and Cressida's heart nearly stopped.

"I..." There really wasn't an answer, not unless he could somehow explain it for himself. She glanced at him, beseeching him to give an account.

"I didn't, because it didn't occur to me. I was focused on finding my father. Then Cressida was hurt. I'm not even sure I could have stopped it. I don't know how finite my powers are." The question had stunned and hurt Daniel, she noted. His chest moving rapidly and the pallor of his skin reinforcing that knowledge.

"I think that is something that needs to be investigated then. With all due respect, if Daniel is as strong as you give the impression he is, there must be some way we can protect those within the walls of any given house by using his skills."

Cressida nodded, gnawing at her lip. Celina had used the protection stone before, so surely there was some way Daniel could reinforce the nest using the same power? Then they could...

Too many. Too big. Could he even manage it?

"We'll reconvene tomorrow night at ten. I thank you for your attendance." She dismissed them. Now was the time to consider all the angles and prepare for the trial and possible subsequent replacement of Gervaise.

If they could survive the rest of the night, that was.

One by one the councilors stood and trooped through the door, a quiet bunch of elder vampires.

Then the room was silent, with only Cressida and Daniel present. "I messed up, didn't I?" His lost tone tore at her.

TWENTY-FIVE

DANIEL ROSE QUIETLY. CRESSIDA REMAINED ASLEEP, AND HE felt gratitude that the fates had been kind enough to give him time alone. Time to think over the mess he'd made of the situation.

He padded across the room, his feet clad in slippers, and scooped up the dressing gown that lay across the boudoir chair next to Cressida's side of the bed. Had his actions put the life he was building with Cressida in jeopardy?

The thoughts played in his mind and he carefully crept to the door and opened it. The hallway was empty and he headed downstairs to the kitchen where the cook stood at the big stove, stirring something. His stomach gurgled and he shrugged, reaching for the fridge.

"Master Daniel, can I get you a warm blood wine?" Dorothy's voice startled him and he jumped. He'd been sure she didn't know he was there.

"How did you...?"

"Well, let's just say it's all in your scent." She grinned, and for the first time he noted how long and sharp her teeth looked when she spoke. They were longer than any other vampire he knew.

Could she be…? His mind stuttered at the thought that she could be neither human nor vamp. Was she a *were?* "So, you're also not human?"

"Didn't your mama ever tell you it was rude to ask such questions?" she bantered playfully, but there was the hint of a bite beneath the surface. "No, I'm not human. Nor am I like those girls, I'm *were.*"

He hadn't realized Cressida had welcomed any within her nest. He'd always believed the Councilors nests were purely human and vampire. Something new to consider.

He opened the fridge door, looking for a bottle of blood wine, and spied instead a blood shake. The label caught his eye. *Maison de Sang.*

He laughed, his shoulders shaking, as he stood in front of the wide-open door.

"Shut that damned door before I make you, fang boy." Even Dorothy's terse comment couldn't stop him.

She stalked over, her long red hair tied back in an intricate braid, and slammed it, sealing the cold goods inside.

Tears ran down his face as he considered that his father would never know that the role he'd taken on—*Yeux Secondes*—had brought this beverage and the growth of his previous nest to near completion.

"Daniel?" Cressida was there. Somehow she'd found him when he needed her the most. Now he cried, uncaring that anyone was watching.

"He'll never know."

"No, he won't. But what he will know is that you cared enough to be there, to try to save him. He'll know you loved him." It wasn't enough, but it would have to do, because he couldn't change the past.

The wave of grief blindsided him, left him lost. How? He'd held himself so tightly! Cressida stepped up to him.

It was going to happen. It had to. You can't dam it up inside and think it won't escape. You have to grieve and accept that he's passed or you'll go mad.

Cressida wound her arms around his middle, her embrace telling him it was okay to cry. To express the feelings that welled.

How long they stood there he couldn't say, but finally the jagged emotions seeped away, leaving him hollow and tired. "I need..."

"I'll get you the blood wine. Go sit in the drawing room." She shooed him out with soft touches and he let her. He needed to be alone to think over his emotions. The cabinet was closed, but on a whim he opened it and turned on the television for the first time since his change.

The news reporter looked grim as he reported on the investigation in the House of Grimardi massacre.

"Sources have informed us that the massacre was linked to the current vampire war. The Attar faction instigated the attack, which left an entire nest dead, Frances."

"Thanks, Martin. We cross now to Elizabeth on the ground at the governor's mansion where tonight a candlelight vigil is being held. I see there are also protesters. Elizabeth, what can you tell us about that?"

"Well, Frances, Governor Sorvein has been meeting with officials from the Vampires Banishment League today. They are asking for the governor to overturn the Human Nestling Act of 2045, which allows vampires to have human nestlings living and working in their houses. They recommend that vampires should live only in specified locations, far enough removed from human habitation that it poses no threat to human society. They also contend that vampires should be restricted in ownership of properties, including residential complexes, economically important businesses, and those which are medically related."

"Will they be successful, do you think, Elizabeth?"

"I'm not sure anyone knows the answer to that at this stage, Frances. What I do know is that if the vampires are forced to relinquish these investments, then the price of these entities will drop, based on information I have received from the Realtors Association."

The camera panned the crowd, and he saw hundreds of protestors carrying placards. He'd seen it before, but never on this level. The numbers looked to be equal to those involved in the vigil. His stomach knotted again.

"They don't understand. If we remove our protection, then the humans will be in even greater danger."

Cressida took the seat beside him and he noted the lines on her face. "How do you deal with that? What they're saying is absurd and dangerous."

She shrugged slowly. "Because it's the price of coming out to the public. We will do what's needed to protect our own."

"Is there really that much anger against us?" He turned his head to look her squarely in the eye.

"Yes, there is."

She handed him a goblet and he drank deeply.

"So what do we do now?"

"We find and beat Attar. But before we do, there is some emergency damage control to be undertaken."

"What do you mean?" He had more than an inkling he wouldn't like what she was about to say.

"I need to meet with the governor and this Vampire Banishment League. See if I can't buy us some time."

"I really don't think—"

"No. This is something the head of the Council does. It's not up to you to think about it or not. It's my role." She touched her hand to his and the chill of her skin scared him, left his insides quivering and turning.

"Cressida, I don't want to lose you." He didn't want to give in to the fear that dogged him, but he also needed to make sure that she understood how deeply his emotions were involved. He'd not really had a chance to tell his father, and he bitterly regretted that. He wouldn't fail with her.

"You won't. I'll have Samra and a contingent of guards at my side the whole time. What could go wrong? Now drink your blood wine so I can dress."

"You already knew about this?" Disbelief colored his words.

"I did. I have to know what people are saying so I can take action quickly. That's what the head of my House and my *Yeux Secondes* does. You are no longer human, and no longer hold that title, but you understand the way the position works."

He did, of course, but it didn't make it easier to bear. "When?"

"I have an appointment in two hours. Given that, I should be home before you finish your training."

He only hoped it was that simple.

THE ROOM HUSHED AS SHE ENTERED IT. ROW UPON ROW OF seats were laid out, so others could attend the Trial of Justice for Gervaise. At the beginning of the procession was Gianna, who made her way down the hall. The regal manner in which she conducted herself never ceased to amaze Cressida.

A line of councilors rounded the corner and filed behind the long, scarred wooden table.

Cressida shivered a little as the chill of the dungeon-like room invaded her bones. Never before had she attended one of these ceremonies as councilor, let alone *Conseil Superieur*.

Scanning the sea of faces showed her that the most senior vampires, including the nest masters and mistresses, their consorts, seconds and even human *Yeux Secondes* were in attendance. She wasn't sure if it was a show of solidarity or something altogether different.

"The power of our unity is our strength." Cressida turned in Gianna's direction as the ceremony opened. "One of us has betrayed the trust we invested in them. They gave an oath of honor, loyalty and righteousness, but they have sullied that. They bring disrepute to the name Vampire. Tonight, we come together to test the truth. Let the *De Premiere Instance de la Justice* commence!"

Gianna took her seat and the vampires followed like a waving sea that subsided beneath her power. "As is our way, there is one who will make the final determination. We, who are flawed. We bring forth another, far removed from this place. They shall listen. They shall see and they shall determine." The room shook as Gianna spoke the words that would open the trial.

Samra escorted Gervaise to the dock. The wooden box was more like a cell, reinforced on the outside with copper bars, so even if he managed to tear it apart, he still couldn't escape.

He whimpered and shook. Cressida hardened her heart against the sliver of sympathy that raised its head. *He endangered all of us.*

"Gervaise, according to the rites of masterhood, you gave an oath. The pledge you made was the same as all who accept that role. As a counselor, you gave a further oath. *In all you do, the greater good of the nests shall override your own position. That you will give your life and immortality to ensure survival of vampire and innocent alike.* Remember you this oath?" Gianna leaned forward in her seat and Cressida heard the gasp that he gave. Gervaise cowered away, and the ripe scent of terror filled the air.

"I... My lady, I did give that oath." His face glowed bone white and he struggled with the words, but the tingle of magic in the air told her Gianna was forcing him to speak truthfully.

"You partook of the blood and underwent the test. Tell me then, are the charges against you truthful or no?"

Cressida clasped her hands. She knew the truth. Knew that he'd made that pact, but now they needed him to admit that he'd broken it. *How could there possibly be any question?*

"I...I..." He shook his head and closed his mouth. His only hope now was to refuse to answer. Then, the pact would hold, though be severely tested. Clearly that was the option he'd chosen. Gianna turned to Cressida as if to say 'it's your turn'.

"Make your case, Councilor."

Cressida rose, the scrape of the chair filling the almost silence. Only the sobbing of the man in the dock echoed. Cressida gnawed at her lip. *Where to begin?*

"I became aware of the anomaly several weeks ago, as I began working with a select and trusted team, hoping to uncover the identity of the one who conspired against us. The situation was precarious, but I had a feeling that information was being made available to Attar."

She stepped along the front of the seating area and gazed on Gervaise while pondering the reaction of those gathered. "This was before the massacre in New Orleans. I felt at the time that it would be unwise to send most of our warriors to the site, but it was appropriate to send enough of a force as was necessary. Not long after committing ourselves to this course of action, Attar made the decision to attack the House Grimardi. Of note is that it happened to be the one that sent the most warriors to New Orleans. These warriors were offering succor to our kin. It left their house exposed and vulnerable. This was known only to those of the Grimardi House and a select few, under orders from myself."

Anger suffused her, and she moved with a jerk in the direction of the dock.

"Who knew of this decision?"

Gianna's words stopped her. It was probably as well, as fury coursed. She'd probably rip Gervaise apart—limb from bloody limb.

"The councilors, the master of the nest and my own people." She shrugged and turned her eyes back to Gianna.

"You have said that information about the safe rooms in the New Orleans nest was divulged. You received a video message?"

The remembrance of that terrible message had her gut clenching. "Yes, that's true. I had known the second as we'd shared a nest before his elevation. I also knew the Master's *Yeux Secondes*, as he was one of my own nestlings. The master messaged me and asked me to care for the child. His only surviving issue, now."

She turned back to those watching the drama unfold.

Anger speared her again as she considered the situation of the child. "She's seven, a slight little thing with blonde hair and blue eyes. Now she's an orphan. A child who was only saved from death because a seer warned her father that for her safety she should be sent away. If not for that act, her bones would have been burned in the crematorium as the rest were." She whirled around, looking at Gervaise. "Like all the other children whose bodies lie in the morgue right now. The *innocents you swore to protect.*" Gervaise flinched but didn't make a sound.

"You used a resource?"

At that Cressida gulped and turned, her gaze seeking Daniel. He nodded.

"I did. One of the neophytes can read the thoughts of others." Now a ripple of sound wove its way around the room and back again. Eyes narrowed and vampires sat forward in their seats. "My life partner."

Murmurs slid through the crowd at those words, but they steadied her, now that she'd spoken them.

"What did they see?" Gianna spoke quietly now and Cressida sucked down a lungful of air.

Her diaphragm expanded. "A traitor."

The room erupted. Cries of "Death to the traitor" and "Let the deed be done" echoed as Cressida closed her eyes, gathering herself.

"Can you prove this?"

Cressida walked down the aisle, stopped before Daniel and watched as he gave a slight nod. "Yes, my lady. I would ask to you think of something. Keep it in your mind." He stood. "You are remembering the first time you met Councilor Cressida. In a field. She wore a pale pink gown."

Cressida squeezed his hand briefly before turning back to face the front and Gianna.

The overlord spread her hands to those present. "Then he speaks the truth. Let the decision be made."

"Wait! Mercy, Gianna! I ask for mercy!"

The room quieted and all eyes found their way to the dock where Gervaise cried out piteously.

"You seek mercy? After your actions?" Gianna tapped the tabletop. "Give me something worthy. A way to beat Attar and face the assembled masses. They will decide on that."

The vampire paled further. "But...I cannot! He will kill me and mine." He wiped a bead of sweat from his face and Cressida's stomach turned. He sought mercy, yet he'd shown none in allowing the innocent children to die.

"You deny us information, yet you shared it with Attar?" Gianna spoke quietly and Cressida's hair rose as magic filled the air, arcing and flashing.

"I..."

Gianna waved a hand in the air. "Cressida?"

"I have presented the facts as known. I've explained the process. The witness has had a chance to speak, but chooses not to. I will rest my case there." Cressida walked with slow, measured steps back to her seat.

The powerful cloaking spell that had hidden an elder vampire behind the box during the trial dropped away with a sharp crack. He stood, showing himself to the assembled witnesses.

"In the way of our people, the case has been prosecuted. The evidence has been laid out before us. The defendant has not proved himself innocent, but the prosecution has presented compelling evidence. Normally, the one in judgment would retire to consider the evidence, but it is clear to me. You conspired with Attar, causing the death of many hundreds of humans and vampires. You've passed on sensitive information. *Privileged information.*"

He stepped slowly, peering at those assembled with his pale blue eyes. The frisson of power surrounding him rose and swelled with every movement until he reached the center of the table where he turned to Gianna.

It was an act of a second to reach out and clasp hands with Gianna, and Cressida knew she was reading his decision. Gianna blinked rapidly, then gave a tiny nod. "He has been found guilty of conspiracy. The only allowable sentence is death. Let it be done and may the immortal God have pity on your soul, Gervaise."

The presiding vampire, now having passed judgement, strode from the room, no doubt to be transferred away, back to his own nest far from their location.

"The judgment is made. I will have the guilty transported to my stronghold and dealt with by my executioner. I thank the *Conseil Superieur*, her nest and the council for their honesty."

It was over.

Gianna rose and exited the chamber while her personal guard filed in to take control of the prisoner. The crowd remained silent, watching as Gervaise was removed from the dock and marched from the room.

As the room emptied before her, she had the impression it all happened in slow motion.

Javed stopped and turned in her direction. "Cressida, we will need to arrange for a new councilor."

"Yes. But I fear that may have to wait, my friends. Let us attend to the urgent matter of protecting ourselves first."

Now the need to leave the chamber swamped her, and she hurried from the room.

"We don't have to do this tonight, you know." Daniel reached for Cressida's hand. It was cold and he detested the distance she'd put between them since the trial had ended nearly a week ago. Even now, as he reached for her, she tugged away.

With every step forward, he seemed to take a step back.

"Tonight. I need to do something useful." Her voice echoed the exhaustion he'd seen on her face. But she was a stubborn woman, he'd learned. If she wanted to do something, she'd plow on, regardless.

He reined in the urge to sigh. After all, he could understand her mindset. A councilor, someone she'd known for a long time, in all likelihood, had betrayed her and the whole of the vampire species. Not to mention the nests.

With all the oaths, and their joint history, he'd still treated every benefit and connection he'd enjoyed with contempt and thrown away any hope of a future. At least, that was what he guessed she felt. She'd been too remote to share her emotions again tonight.

"Fine, then. I've spoken to Hope and Xavier as well as Celina and Javed. They will stay if I let them know."

"I told you earlier…"

"Yes, okay, Cressida. I get it." He didn't mean to sound testy. All he wanted was to give her a break, but she wouldn't let him. Instead, she pushed back as hard as she could.

Beside him, she stiffened, then shrugged. "They're on their way."

A bubble of frustration rose. "Why did you do that?"

"What?" She spat the word and he balled his fist.

"I said I would let them know. Every time…" He flung his hand in the air. "You have to do everything before I can. Sometimes, when you do things like that…" *You unman me.* He stopped before he could unload his grievances. This wasn't helping. They were all on edge, and the proceedings certainly hadn't helped.

"I…I didn't mean…" Her halting words told him of her inner turmoil. When she gazed at him, her eyes were full of regret. "I just… I want to make things easy for you."

He sighed this time, letting the sound float between them. "I know. But, Cressida, I'm a man." She opened her mouth and he raised his hand. "I know, I'm a vampire, but that doesn't make me any less who I am. Who I've been raised to be."

"I'm sorry." Her whisper gutted him and he lurched toward her, scooping her up into his arms.

"I'm sorry too. I know it's difficult. You've been alone for a long time and aren't used to someone hovering. I want to help carry your burdens. They're teething problems in a relationship like ours. We'll get there, in time." He inhaled her scent, her hair tickling his nose as she nestled into the embrace. "But I need to protect you. My woman. My lover." Dipping his head while she raised hers felt natural. When their lips met, tiny sparks of electricity played through his veins.

"Ahem. While I'm sure this is really romantic, I don't suppose we can start training?" Xavier's voice cut through the silence. Neither of them had heard the four vampires arrive.

"Besides which, I have an idea." Hope pushed her way into the center of the room and tugged out the amulet she wore around her neck. "I had a dream. I think...I know how these work."

Everyone spun in her direction. "How?" Cressida held the chain of her amulet tightly in her hand, and the action made Daniel grin.

'They're conduits, just like the Graces said. But while three of us can make them work, they're not as effective as it would be if all six of us are working together. See, they connect us. All of us."

"If that's so, then why are there three black and three silvery white?" Celina's musings made Hope laugh.

"Oh, that's so simple. Think of it. What were we when we each met our mates?"

Daniel couldn't help himself. "Alive?"

Hope and Celina snickered, then Hope shook her head. "You're much closer to the truth than you know, Daniel. See, if I'm right, the black corresponds to the dark. You've all been vampires longer than you were human, yes?"

The three vampires agreed.

"Good, and we've been human longer than vampires..." Hope arched her eyebrows and Daniel tapped his forehead.

"Day and Night. Black and White." So simple and yet... *It makes so much sense.*

"So how do we use them, Hope? You said you'd seen?"

"Sure. Our powers can be shared through them, but only to our partners. The biggest positive is that we can communicate widely between the six of us. Last time, when it hurt? That was two groups of three, not all six at once. We didn't realize that it's meant to be all of us, and so there was a kind of feedback."

"That's why it hurt? Hmm, so how do we...?" Cressida frowned.

"It's simple. If everyone grabs their amulet, I can initiate the contact."

"And you know this how?" Cressida's question rang out in the quiet room.

"Hope told me." Daniel started to close his eyes and heard a snicker.

"Hey, big brother, I don't think closing our eyes would be a great idea. I mean, if we're in the middle of a fight, it might make things worse."

He blushed a hot, deep red. Celina was right, of course. "I was only trying to make it easier."

Daniel? Can you hear me? This time the process didn't hurt, it just felt like a kind of molasses was being drizzled over him. It was tingly and not uncomfortable, but odd.

Okay then, I want Daniel to grab Cressida's hand and Celina to do the same to Javed. Xavier, you hold mine. We're the weakest link here, though.

They did as she asked, moving slightly apart from the other couples.

Now, you need to kind of push a bit of your power through the link to your partner. Don't worry about it going astray because you're connected to each other, just like the amulets link all six of us.

In his mind Daniel conjured an image of a flame, then shunted it to Cressida, who held out her hand. A flicker, a tiny whisper of light played over her palm. She smiled and cupped it. "Ow!"

The connection snapped back. "What happened?" His heart pounded wildly in his chest.

"It burned me."

He laughed at her startled tone. When she frowned at him, he cupped her soft cheek. "I'm sorry it did, but just think, it worked."

Wonder crept over her face.

TWENTY-SIX

The following evening, Cressida followed Daniel down the stairs. He twitched but stood apart by choice. The air about him of grief almost broke her heart.

"Daniel?"

He turned in her direction, his face so white it made his eyes looked like bright orbs.

I want you to know I'm going to support you.

He nodded and for a moment she saw a shimmer of moisture, then he blinked and it was gone.

I know.

The cars waited on the asphalt, ready to take them to the memorial center he'd chosen. The crunch of many feet on the gravel filled the air while the bite of cold nipped at him. He wore unrelieved black, as did she, only a red band at his arm. As she scanned those leaving for the service, he saw a sea of black with the red bands and shook his head. How unlike the memorial for the lost vampires, where everyone had worn bright colors.

Most humans wouldn't understand the band of red on their arms, but it was a tangible memory of the humans lost from their world, the red signifying the blood connection they'd shared.

Once within the vehicle, they settled themselves in the back and he took her hand.

Cressida didn't pull away as if she understood his grief, but struggled to understand that his need to grieve in a solitary fashion.

Daniel understood that she couldn't see that it wasn't that he didn't need her support. Life partners were meant to face the good and the bad together for eternity, but this was his father and he still was close to his 'human' life. It was only mere weeks ago.

So he looked out the window, watching as the cars made their way through the gathering gloom. As they swept into the drive at the crematorium, he shivered. It was always like this, visiting the structures humans erected to celebrate the dead.

The vehicle stopped and they clambered out, Daniel offered her his hand. He didn't say a word and dropped her hand once he was sure she was safely out.

"Daniel? Let me help you."

"I can't." The words were strangled, and this time he couldn't hide his misery and pain.

"I understand. I do."

He shuddered, breathing deeply, blinked and gazed upward. "I should have saved him." Then he slumped into himself, shoulders sagging, and shook his head. "I'm a bloody vampire and I couldn't save my own father. Why is that, Cressida? Why didn't I remember that I can use magic?" It was a cry, ripped from deep within him.

She touched his cheek, while others swarmed around and into the building. "I don't know, Daniel. Maybe...?" She didn't finish the thought, instead she gripped his hand tight. "I'll be right here beside you. Whatever, however. Take from me what you need."

He nodded with a jerk of his head and turned, taking her with him into the building, pulling his emotions deep, blanketing them so they couldn't break free.

Row upon row waited, humans and vampires side by side, the sound of weeping filling the air and the emotional cacophony battering at his psyche. Caskets lined the room, one after the other, and looking at them horrified him. Thankfully they'd managed to keep the location of the memorial quiet, otherwise there'd have been news crews camped out the front and trying to gain entrance. *They'd have a field day with this view.* His stomach lurched.

Slowly they took their place at the front pew, as did the survivors from the nest. The children who'd hidden themselves in the refrigeration system huddled at the end, and he wanted to reach out to them... *Cressida? Go to them.*

He knew Cressida warred with her emotions. The children needed as much support as he did. Maybe even more, and he was determined not to demand more from her than she had to give. In her eyes he read her indecisions, that she didn't want to abandon him in his time of need. But these innocents had to have everyone's support.

She stood and made her way over. The children raised their heads and he knew she saw grief, horror, and yet there was also stoicism on their young faces. Nestlings were far more aware of loss than their unhoused counterparts.

"Who are you here with?" Daniel heard her quiet question to the children gathered and sighed before joining Cressida. Whatever he was or felt, he would support her too.

The oldest girl, maybe fourteen or fifteen, pointed to Hope and Xavier. "Them." She cleared her throat. "Master Xavier and Hope, Councilor."

"Are you all staying there at the moment?"

"Yes, Councilor."

He glanced at the younger children and knew they ranged in age from four to fourteen and wondered how they were coping.

I need to talk to Xavier and Hope when the service is over.

"All of you have my deepest sympathies." What was there to say to these children who'd lost everything? They'd not just lost their families and their home, but also their carefree childhoods.

The older girl attempted a smile, but it was a grimace. "Yeah. Thanks," she croaked, and Daniel so badly wanted to embrace the girl, who was coping with unimaginable stress as she balanced at the cusp of adulthood. It was almost overwhelming for him, a fully grown man. How could these youngsters possibly not experience emotional scarring from their experiences? What would be the long-term ramifications of what they'd survived?

The music swelled, long and mournful, reminding him that they should return to their seats. The sounds of shuffling feet and sobbing people rose, then ebbed away.

The councilors had decided they'd conduct the service, and he was grateful for their support through this emotional ordeal.

Cressida gripped Daniel's hand as they welcomed everyone.

"They may be gone from our lives, but they will never be forgotten. They are the families that we lost, many of us long ago. It is our duty to honor them every day for the rest of our long-lived eternity." The councilors named the dead. The list felt like it went on forever, but she understood their thinking. It made every person's loss real to all gathered.

At the end of the pew, the children wailed as their family members were named and the appropriate caskets slid from sight. At one point the youngest child rose, sniffling, and started to shuffle forward. Daniel intercepted her and pulled her against his chest before kneeling and whispering to her. He cried for the child's pain.

"I want my mommy and daddy." The whimper died away as the casket slid from view.

"I know. I want my father too, little one," he muttered, eyes burning while his stomach clenched.

"Did your daddy...?"

"He was one of the lost." Daniel pointed to the casket nearest them and the child clutched him tighter.

The pain within him grew, blooming and sucking at his soul.

Cressida glanced at him, touched his arm. *He has to pay.*

He will pay, Cressida. Together we will dispense justice. For everyone. Xavier's thought centered her.

When it was finally done, Daniel kept his arms wound around the dozing child, rubbing his hand up and down her back. *She's finally relaxed into an exhausted stupor.*

If that had been our child... His eyes burned again as a tear wound its way over his cold cheek, as so many had in the last three-quarters of an hour. He wiped it away. No use weaving fairy stories, he told himself firmly.

We could take her home with us. Her mind touched his gently.

You're taking her with you? Xavier's mental tone held a question, and Cressida shrugged as Daniel watched.

He wondered if Cressida could feel his emotions billowing when he touched her arm. It was almost as if she understood but feared the gravity of this decision.

Does she have siblings? She's asleep right now, so rather than wake her...

No, Cressida. Her brother and parents all perished. If she's happy we'll leave her be for now. Take her home, and if she needs to return to us, we'll arrange it.

The crowd stood and left, while Cressida took Daniel's hand. He looked up, blinking owlishly. "We're all done?"

"We don't have to go if you aren't ready yet." She caressed his cheek with her thumb, wiping away a solitary tear, and the love and warmth she radiated kept the chill inside his chest at bay. "We can stay as long as you need."

He glanced at her, then to the front. "There's nothing left here. I want to go home."

Together they rose and the three of them left the building.

TWENTY-SEVEN

"Sire, I have news." The vampire advanced slowly into the room, and Attar lifted his head from the cadaver he was feeding on.

"Then I hope for your sake it's good."

The messenger blanched as Attar thrust him to the floor, where he lay still but alive—not for long, though, if the slow beat of his heart was anything to go by. "Your informant has been executed, sire. The whispers among the outcasts and rogues are that he was tried and found guilty."

Attar smiled; ribbons of scarlet blood dribbled over his chin. He could feel the drips but didn't care.

"Then find me another informant, worm!" He advanced on the vampire underling he'd flung to the floor.

"Uh, sire? I'm not sure it's going to be that simple. See, they are flocking to—"

His ire raised, Attar whirled and struck out with one hand, the thwack of flesh on flesh filling him with a savage glee. "You think...?" He mocked Jastin, who cowered once more against the wall. "I didn't give you leave to think, Jastin. I gave you an order." Now his voice dropped to a silky hiss while he jutted his head toward the one who had assumed the demeanor of prey. "Really, though, why don't I just...*replace* you?" The words took the tone of a threat and it was clear Jastin read the meaning on his face.

"Sire... I would serve you..."

"I will give you one last chance. Tonight. One of the bigger nests. Take control of the house. Kill them all. Leave no one alive this time, except the cattle you bring to me."

Jastin bowed low, his hair brushing the tiles. "Yes, sire. I will do that for you."

Then he slinked away as Attar eyed the human on the floor. *I so hate to waste a meal...*

HIS BODY ACHED AND HIS EYES BURNED. THE CHILD WAS settled into the bedroom next to his and Cressida's and he'd given instructions that they be called if she needed him.

The emotions that roiled within him were numerous and conflicting. Sadness and grief gnawed at him, but there was a new kind of tenderness too. Unlike anything he'd ever experienced, he felt a connection to the tiny child in the bed. The way she'd nestled against him, as if she sensed he could keep the demons at bay, filled him with joy and sadness.

It was heady.

It was also humbling and scary.

Daniel! There's been another attack. This time on Xavier's nest!

The call left shivers of ice trickling down his back. He cast a last look at the child on the bed before dashing into the hallway. *"Coming!"*

He ripped at his suit as he entered the dressing area and there she was already. This time he imagined himself dressed, black leather pants and jacket covering him. He reached for his belt as he looked down. His magic was certainly improving.

Cressida? I want to try something different. Are you ready?

As if catching the thought in his mind, she smiled. "Oh yes. Let's do it."

"Ready?"

She tugged at her zip, then placed her hand in his outstretched one. "Yeah."

He closed his eyes, imagined the estate and the old house. Them —both of them—on the lawn.

The clash of swords and snarls told him he had done it even before he opened his eyes.

Everywhere he saw the writhing mass and he snarled.

"Daniel, can you protect the humans?" Cressida spoke quickly, and he felt a moment of panic at the thought of leaving her unprotected.

"Cressida?"

"It's not like last time and we don't have time to argue. You need to get to the humans."

"I honestly don't think it's that simple. They're scattered." He glanced in her direction and caught sight of her gnawing her lip.

"Fine then. Protect the children. Their needs come first. I'll find Hope and Xavier and..." She waved a hand and he understood.

They both sprinted off in differing directions. He to the house, blanking his mind to the memories of the last time she'd gone into battle without him. He had to focus on the children. Finding them. Protecting them.

He cast his mind outward, seeking their essences, and found them at the top of the house. Horror filled him as he tasted their terror.

He latched onto the mind of one child and saw through her eyes. They were surrounded by slavering beasts, hungry for their blood.

He blinked and imagined himself standing in front of them. It didn't work.

Daniel had no time to reconsider his actions. He ran, taking the stairs two and three treads at a time, up higher and higher while his blood pumped through his veins at a rapid clip.

At the attic he stopped only long enough to orient himself, then sped down the long hall. A door stood ajar, and the scene before him was enough to freeze his blood.

What looked to be the three oldest of the massed children gripped long, twining candelabra and used them to keep the vampires at bay.

For a second Daniel allowed himself a grin before the predator deep within him rose.

"So Attar's army can't even beat children?" Slow and steady steps brought him level to the one he was sure led the warriors' actions.

"First, we'll kill you and bathe in your blood, then we'll suck these children dry." The creature before him laughed and the other two joined in, their voices scratchy as if disused.

"You can try." He braced himself, knowing he could use magic, but the tactician inside him whispered that he should keep that hidden unless he absolutely had to show his hand.

When the leader lunged in his direction, Daniel feinted to the left and the vampire hissed its displeasure. He wanted to laugh, but the caution Samra had drummed into him had him settling. Instead, he stifled the sound before it rose and studied the vampires before him objectively.

The other two vampires hovered around the edge and for a moment Daniel thought of television and movie fights where they would only engage one at a time.

The urge to roll his eyes came and went in a flash as he refocused on his foe.

Daniel reached down and wrapped his hands around his sword. It hissed as it dragged free of the scabbard. Deliberately, he held it at an odd angle while advancing before the children, hoping to shield them.

The first vampire leaped and again Daniel moved at the right time, landing on the balls of his feet, facing the direction in which his assailant moved.

"Is that the best you can do?" He couldn't help the taunt, and this time his opponent reacted with a growl before dropping a shoulder and charging.

It hit him hard and Daniel gave an *oomph* as wind rushed from his lungs.

It wasn't enough to stop him, though, and as planned Daniel grabbed the vampire just as it made to sink its long incisors into his shoulder.

They wrestled, bodies straining and arms exerting pressure against each other as they turned in a parody of a dance, gyrating as they struggled for superiority.

The creature threatened him, describing vile acts, from drinking his blood to the variety of ways he would use his body; Daniel blocked it out. The children cried and whimpered in the background, but he couldn't protect them from this depravity. All he could do right now was save their lives.

A blow to Daniels shoulder made him redouble his efforts and he dug deep, growled and gave one massive heave. The creature sailed through the air.

Glass smashed as his opponent fell through the window and Daniel turned to face the other two watching.

"So what'll it be, boys?" He gave one step then another and they looked to each other, eyes feral and wide. They both jumped in his direction, arms flying and giving the impression of bad karate movements.

He flicked one vampire over his shoulder, his body moving like a well-oiled fighting machine. The other he grabbed with his hand and tugged. He hit the floor with a thud. "Don't look, children." He stomped down with one foot, reached for the vampire's hair, and with a crunch tore him apart. His eerie scream cut off sharply.

The second vampire watched, shaking as if recognizing an alpha warrior.

With a snarl he hurled, "No quarter will be given."

Daniel had found his inner protector and embraced it. The children would be saved, no matter the cost. Any shred of humanity sank beneath the surface of his primal instincts.

The last vampire turned as if to run, but Daniel caught it. "You'll do nicely, little one. Now let me see what you know?"

He dug deep into the flesh, squeezing. The vampire arced and squirmed, looking for a way to escape. "Nothing! I don't know..." The shrieks were heartfelt as Daniel brought him closer.

The smell of rot assaulted his nostrils, as if the creature had rolled in old meat.

He'd prepared to strike again when a mental voice impinged on him. *Don't kill him. We've taken several prisoners and the fight is done...for now, anyway. Bring him downstairs.*

Adrenaline coursed in his veins. *I want the kill. I need it as surely as I need the marrow in my bones.* He fought the primal instincts down. Cressida needed this one more.

The rate of his pulsing heart settled, fell back into its normal pattern, slowing moment by moment, but he didn't release his grip as his prisoner shuddered in his grasp.

Daniel? The children?

They're safe. I'll bring this vampire down in a minute.

There was silence for a full minute. *Send the children to the kitchen. I'll see you in the hall with your captive.*

Now he turned back to the whimpering watchers. "Children, go downstairs. Someone waits for you in the kitchen." To the oldest he glanced and instructed, "Don't stop, no matter what you hear. Get all of them down there."

Without a word, they shuffled past and he tugged his captive closer. "You'll regret the day you came near this house and those children."

The vampire whimpered and moaned as he dragged him down the hall and the steps. With every move he became a heavier weight on Daniel's arm. The moaning of "I'm sorry," and "he made me do it," irritated, but it didn't stop him. At the hall, he tugged the vampire over to Cressida.

She scanned him up and down before the tightness of her mouth eased. "Samra! Take the prisoner. Get whatever information you need."

Samra looked every inch the amazon in her tight buckskin pants and close-fitted top, her hair tugged back into a long ponytail. "Hmm, Cressida says you did good." After tossing the words over her shoulder, she took the man away and Daniel shrugged.

"Well, that was different."

"She's not big on compliments, but when deserved she gives decent praise." Without a word of warning, she rose on tiptoe and fitted her mouth against his. "I'm pleased you did good too. We saved the kids and managed to do a better than creditable job at defending the nest."

"That's a good thing. I don't think I could manage another funeral like today." The sadness he'd been ignoring settled around him like a cloak once more. "When does this end?"

Her eyes filled with understanding. "It takes time, Daniel. But you controlled the hunger. In fact, you did better than good. That trick of yours gives us an advantage. We just need to work out how many you can move."

His gaze narrowed. "You know, if you can shadow my power..."

She grinned. "Perhaps. We might be able to move the six of us at once."

"Holy shit!" *Move the six of us?* That would give them such an advantage. Now if only they could pinpoint Attar's location.

"I know. Pretty heady stuff, right?"

He cleared the excitement that now buzzed in his veins.

"Come on. We've still got work to do before we can go home." She clasped his hand, gave a tug and he nodded.

TWENTY-EIGHT

Cressida watched, her emotions banished for the moment as Daniel extracted every drop of intelligence from the creature.

"I... He's in a warehouse near the Brooklyn Expressway. That's all I know. It's big. Used to have clothing, and it's got a brick exterior."

Samra closed in on the man. "That's the best you can do?"

Exhaustion and his injuries had left the man with a gray tinge to his skin. "That'll do, Samra and Daniel. I'm sure we can find him from there. Lock him in the cells."

Kharisma appeared at her shoulder. "Excuse me, Councilor. May I have a word with you?"

"Yeah." She watched as Samra unfastened the lock on her prisoner and he attempted to pull away. Samra merely clucked her tongue and tripped him. *Tu es stultior quam asinus.*

Cressida rolled her eyes and glanced back to Kharisma. "What's up?"

"I have a theory. But I need access to the prisoners to prove it."

Kharisma now had her whole attention. She leaned in. "And that would be?"

"None of these have been chosen to see how well they can assimilate the vampire DNA. I'm of the opinion that Attar's connection to them is weaker, as the virus hasn't embedded itself optimally."

A grin spread over Cressida's face. Not an optimal transmission? Yet another chink in Attar's armor, hopefully.

"Fine, Kharisma. Take what you need and put a hurry on the bloods."

"Oh, I've done better than that, Councilor. Xavier himself will take the samples and await the results."

Cressida grinned. "I love it when we can all work together. *Do it*. Let me know the results as soon as you have them."

"I will. I'm looking forward to it almost as much as you are."

A quick glance at the clock reminded her that dawn was less than an hour away, so she gave the order for the vampires to return to their homes. They had done what they could to see the nest through the day. A quick glance in the direction of the sealed quarters showed her they hadn't been breached. The remaining humans were prepared to guard the prisoners with their ultraviolet guns.

Finally satisfied, she and Daniel climbed into the last vehicle and headed for home.

They'd barely entered the hall and shut the door behind them when the first rays of daylight shone down.

Together they climbed the stairs, weary to the bone but triumphantly so. "It's a shame we didn't have time to find the nest."

"Tonight, Daniel. We need to plan this carefully and our own vampires are tired, both emotionally and physically. We can at least celebrate that we didn't lose any today."

Daniel was silent for a while. Even as the door to their suite opened, he was immersed in some kind of silent battle with himself and she let him be. More concerned at this point with considering what they'd learned.

So Attar has a nest in the warehouse district. We'll have to organize a team, but if I don't miss my guess, it will be too late. He'll realize he's lost quite a few warriors and we'll be tracking him back. It won't matter whether he knows what abilities and trackers we have, he'll be on the move. It makes tactical sense.

They couldn't send in humans, as they'd be slaughtered if Attar still had a sizable army up his sleeve.

Tonight was the break they'd been looking for. All they had to do was run him to ground.

She scoffed at her own thoughts. Bring him to ground, indeed. He was a formidable foe, not some half-trained fool. He was dangerous and wily. They'd have to be careful and take in their best.

"Cressida?" His voice was carefully neutral and her hackles rose.

"What?"

"Your baby. Tell me about her." His words gave her pause.

"You want to know about my baby?"

"Yes."

"Why?"

"Humor me. What was her name?"

"Her name?" She stared at him, wondering where this had come from.

"Yeah, her name." She turned away as feels swamped her.

"Eleanore. Eleanore Rose. Why?"

"Did you see her? After she was born?"

The jagged edges of her memory caught at her, tearing her soul once again.

"Yes."

"What did she...? What did she look like?" He held himself aloof, tense and wary.

"She was perfect. She had a tuft of white-gold hair. I never saw her eyes though. I always regretted that." And she did. In her mind, she'd always thought they'd be blue. China blue and sparkling in the sunlight.

"The girl in the room next door? Her name is Samantha. She's four."

Totally lost now, Cressida scrunched her face into a frown.

"What does this have to do—"

"She's an orphan. Like Marian, Rachel, and Lucy. No family. No home."

She couldn't divine his thoughts much as she wanted to. He'd erected a barrier and that confused and hurt her.

"Why? Why are you telling me this?" Her mouth dried as she waited for his answer.

"We could be her family. The daughter you wanted. The daughter neither of us can have. We too can have a family like Javed and Celina."

Her breath caught as her imagination ran madly ahead. A child. Their child.

"I don't know. I mean, we live in dangerous times—"

"We'll always live in dangerous times until humans and vampires can coexist peacefully. But we don't have to decide now. She's safe here for the moment. I just, it occurred to me that she has no family and no home..."

The seed was already sown. It took root, digging deep into her heart and her psyche. The clawing need for family filled her with warmth and lightness.

He backed away with a tiny smile. "Before we do anything else I need a shower and a drink. We can talk later—in bed?" As if realizing the emotional Pandora's box he'd opened, Daniel gave a mock leer, lightening the atmosphere.

Her laugh broke the strained air between them. "You're such a man! Go on. I'll follow you in."

For a moment she let her imagination carry her away. Pudgy arms around her neck, tiny baby kisses on her cheek. A single tear dribbled down her face and she wiped it away. It seemed in such a short time he'd learned to read her so well. How had that happened? He was caring, loving. The perfect partner. "How did I get so lucky?"

"I heard that!" he bellowed from the dressing room, and Cressida smiled.

She raised her hands and, without conscious thought, stripped off the layers of her battle suit as she moved toward the bathroom.

Lover boy? Are you naked?

She felt his shock and smiled. Now this was something she'd never tried before. She opened her senses wide, so he could see inside her mind. *Maybe what you need, my love, is me. Wet and naked in your arms. And making love to you. What about you imagine my mouth...*

The rumbled laugh from the bathroom sounded carefree. "I've heard of phone sex, but telepathic sex? That puts a whole new spin on things."

She rounded the corner and walked into the shower stall behind him. "I can think of better sex. Like when I do this." She slid her hands around his waist, sighing against his skin as his muscles tensed.

"Or this..." Her hand slid down his soapy front to find his erection and grasp it firmly. "Or even this." The last words were little more than a whisper, her mouth grazing his shoulder and she let her incisors drop into place then pierced him gently. He hissed as his body convulsed in orgasmic pleasure.

He locked his knees and she smiled.

Now it was her turn to need and burn, she thought as her sex pulsed. She moved and he made a sound of regret. "We've only just started, lover boy. Now come on, help me shower, then we can find the bed."

Only instead of helping her bathe, he lifted her into his arms and kissed her. It was hard and hot, and every inch of her body felt molten by the end. Lost in the sensual haze, Cressida gasped for air, and when he carried her to the bedroom, leaving the water running, she could only hold on while he embraced her.

Her damp skin chilled ever so slightly in the air, and she shivered. "I'll warm you up."

Now her body skittered with sexual delight, while her mind replayed scenes of their previous lovemaking sessions.

The satin sheets beneath her skin molded around her, a soft cloud shrouding them. When he kneaded her breast, she arched with a cry, desperate for more.

Cressida keened, head thrown back, exposing the long line of her neck.

Her nipples peaked, hot sensitive buds of desire jutting against his touch, and every movement excited her further.

"Daniel!"

His breath warmed her, left her nerve endings singing, and the touch of his mouth and tongue on her body had her writhing.

Hurry!

He laughed at her demand, the rumble setting off tiny explosions as nerves quivered beneath her skin.

"There's no rush, my love. We have all day."

You wouldn't!

His laughter echoed through the almost silent room.

Well... Maybe not all day. But you know... His eyebrows jerked up and down and she snickered until the intensity settled over his features once more, dragging her back within the web of desire.

He slowly dipped his lips to hers and she was sure she'd expire before the kiss began. The whisper of his breath had fanned her face and her eyelids drooped heavily.

Her awareness was consumed by him. She gazed over his body, taking in the strength of his shoulders and the breadth of his chest. His scent was spicy and wholly male. He felt hot and hard, yet his skin was silky soft.

The maleness he exuded made her feel feminine and desired. It left her constantly aroused, but never more so than now.

Once again she shifted, hoping and waiting for him to touch her. The urgency built, the need twisting tighter in her belly.

Please!

The kiss was barely a glancing brush of his lips against hers, even though she opened wide to welcome him and his erotic caress. Instead, he dusted her jawline and down her neck.

She arched, giving him access to the vein at her throat, then he stilled as her breath caught. She knew he would break the skin in the most intimate and carnal act of their kind.

Not yet.

Her body jerked as the tug of desperation nipped at her. *Now!*

He merely settled himself closer, the heat from his skin scorching her, fanning the flames of desire to greater levels. She let her emotions dance in the conflagration while her hands shook wildly, clutching at his shoulders. She curved her fingernails over his flesh and pulled at him.

His soft touches, the act of him running his hands over her body, wasn't enough. Not nearly.

The moan was torn from her throat, a vocal echo of her anticipation.

When he found the flesh of her belly, his hands splayed. *Womanly. Curved. Just as I like you to be.*

His mind relayed what he saw—soft white flesh, blonde curls peeking at the junction of her thighs.

He moved his fingers, inching them lower, and she shuddered.

So soft. So beautiful.

Kiss me!

He did; hard and forceful.

He used lips and tongue to splinter her mind while he played with her body, caressing each dip and hollow, filling the emptiness that had nearly devoured her.

With his fingers, he finally parted her swollen flesh, finding it slick and damp.

Ready. For me.

He slid a finger deep within and she panted as her orgasm loomed.

Not...not yet... Come to me!

Then he moved and she blew apart, mind blanking as the waves crashed over her senses.

The sensations ebbed away slowly and her body gloried in the feeling of him, the way he kissed her deeply, tongue thrust deep within her mouth. His hand... Oh God! How it pleasured her.

The determined moves were a pale imitation of the true sexual act. She gasped as he drew away and he shifted, this time splaying her legs to find space to settle his body.

Wait! Let me touch you...

The laugh was choked. "If you do... I doubt I'll last." She scanned the hard planes of his face. His eyelids were drooping and the redness of his skin betrayed his arousal as much as the distended veins in his neck and the jut of his cock. They all told her just how ready he was.

When she glanced down, he hissed and his penis jerked before her fascinated gaze.

Sauce for the goose is the same for the gander.

Even as she moved to encircle the flesh, he gripped her hand tight. "Next. Time."

He seated himself at the entry to her body and she gulped, ready for the dance to begin again. In her mind she knew no one else would ever satisfy her, fill her totally the way he did.

As he slid deep, she told him with her hands and mouth. Her mind continued the litany.

Forever mine. The only one who will ever really see me and fill me completely. Heart, mind, and body.

His movements were controlled, rocking back and forth while they shuddered, fingers gripping flesh.

Her heart rate was like a freight train careering out of control. She panted and hummed. Needing more...

When he bit her neck, incisors sliding deep, she reciprocated. The rush of blood, hot and rich, pushed her while their bodies undulated wildly. Nothing to restrain them as ecstasy crashed down upon them.

TWENTY-NINE

When he woke, he turned slowly, not wanting to wake Cressida. Her skin glowed in the dim light and he reached out, lightly touching the soft flesh he'd caressed the night before.

She was an amazing woman, soft and sensual in bed, but an amazon in battle. Her mind reminded him of a steel trap, deep and sharp. She was quick as well.

She'd make a great mother, if everything worked in his favor. *If only...* He banished the what-ifs.

They were vampires. Much as he wished she could carry his child, that wasn't in their future. Not biologically, anyway.

He cupped her breast, loving the way it filled his palm. Perfectly sized, with a nipple the color of ripe berries. It tightened beneath his hand and he sighed, not wishing to wake her, but unable to contain the sounds of satisfaction.

"You should, you know." Amusement filled her voice and he grinned, relishing the playfulness he heard.

"How long have you been awake?"

"Enough to hear the echo of your thoughts." He frowned as she continued, "Daniel, I can't change..."

A thread of anxiety slid through him. "I'd never ask you to. I love you. All that completes me is you."

She turned on a sigh. "Do you really think...?"

He saw the question in her mind and wanted to say yes. That absolutely the child sleeping next door would be theirs.

His mind told him that would be cruel. He would never abuse this woman's trust, making rash claims he couldn't keep. "We'll inquire. If the stars align, she'll be ours. If not, I know another option will raise its head someday. We have time, Cressida." He leaned in, resting his forehead against hers. The tension in her frame ebbed away and the worry and concern that filled him settled.

"We do. But right now, time's wasting. We should be downstairs. I need to gather the warriors."

He glanced at the clock beside the bed. "It's not yet four. We have another hour..."

She laughed. "Much as I can't think of anything I'd like more, we need to plan and prepare. So come on, lazy head. Time to get up."

They dressed in what had quickly become his regular attire of leather.

"It suits you, you know?"

Strapping on his belt, he glanced at her, watching as she gathered her hair to fasten at the nape of her neck. Then, together, without a backward glance, they made their way downstairs.

At the bottom, one of the nestlings was carrying the little girl, Samantha. She looked up fearfully, her face screwed tight, before sticking her thumb into her mouth.

"Mistress, Master, I was about to take her upstairs to change."

"That's all right, Sarah. Leave her with us for a while." Daniel smiled at the girl.

Cressida raised an eyebrow. She knew Sarah had been working with the child during the day. She'd spoken about the child's lack of understanding of her situation. She and Daniel had discussed her future and he'd suggested he should talk to Sarah, so when he began Cressida didn't countermand his words. Daniel reached over and plucked her from the woman's hold. "Hello, little one. Have you had dinner yet?"

She popped the thumb from her mouth and shook her head. "S'ra said after bath time."

"Sarah, can you bring her dinner through to us, and our wines?"

Sarah gave a tiny nod. "If you'd like, Master." She shuffled away as Daniel settled the girl at his hip. They walked slowly across the hall and Cressida opened the door to her private sanctum.

He considered the desk, discarding that as a location in favor of the more casual meeting area. The deep chairs and small table would suit their needs better right now, he thought.

"I want my mommy."

His heart constricted at her words.

"Sweetie, do you remember what happened at the house?"

She shook her head, her hair flying around like a soft, cloudy halo. "Jenn'fer took us to the kitchen and put us in the fridge. It was cold. Then I sleeped."

Daniel? How do we tell her? Cressida's eyes shone and the band that constricted his lungs dug a little deeper.

She's a nestling. While she may understand they've gone away, she'll learn quickly and young. All we can do is offer support right now. He turned back to the little girl. "Honey, do you remember when the bad ones came?"

She nodded. "Jenn'fer said they'd hurt us. That's why we hid."

He took a deep breath, ready to say the words that would change the little girl's world forever. "Your mommy died, Samantha. Your daddy too. The bad ones hurt her and now they're with the angels."

"S'ra said they gone. When are they coming back?"

Daniel's eyes burned and he glanced at Cressida. Tears shook on the tips of her eyelashes.

"They can't, baby. Once you go to see the angels, you can't ever come back." Daniel spoke gently.

In his arms, the little girl shuddered. "But I want my mommy! I want daddy!"

He tugged her closer, hard against his heart. "I know, baby. I know."

Just as he was sure she would erupt into hysteria, Sarah entered the office with a tray.

Daniel gathered the child back into his arms, then dropped into the seat. The plate was colorful, with sliced chicken, carrots cut like flowers, a tiny mound of corn and artfully gathered beans.

The little girl squirmed and he tugged the nearest chair over after depositing her in it.

"Where's your dinner?"

The squeaky voice made him laugh, as did the lightning change of emotions.

"We'll..." He cleared his throat. "We eat after you go to bed."

It was common practice for the young to be shielded from the realities of the vampiric life—many nests would only introduce the truth once the child understood certain abstract concepts. It made it easier when the children were introduced to newly turned vampires.

He watched as she grabbed the food in her chubby fist.

You handled that much better than I could. You've experience with young children, then?

Living in nests where there are always children, you can't help but get experience. Come sit down, Cressida, and drink. She'll be more comfortable.

She did, lifting the goblet and slowly draining it.

By the time Samantha had finished her meal, she was yawning and Cressida glanced in his direction. "The others should be down by now."

"Sarah?" He turned and noted the nestling waiting in the open doorway. "You should take her upstairs."

The woman nodded. "Take care this evening." Then she hefted the tired child into her arms and left the room.

Cressida strode into the room, gazing over those who'd gathered in silence.

"Last night we faced Attar's men. As you know, he refuses to meet us face-to-face. Instead, he hides and uses others to do his dirty work. He's weak and he's running out of time and options. But tonight we have discovered, with assistance from one of his own, the location of his stronghold, and we'll take the battle to him. Whether we'll find him there remains to be seen. Personally, I wouldn't be surprised to find he's fled, because he's a coward, sending those he's created as disposable warriors, hoping to weaken our strength." She dug deep, seeking the words to galvanize those gathered in the room. "If he's fled, we'll find traps set for us. That's how he works. He relies on sneaky, underhanded tactics because he doesn't have the strength or ability to tackle us head-on."

She dragged a deep breath in, expanding her lungs as she looked to those before her. *How many won't see the end of the night?* That thought was self-destructive, so she banished it.

"Take all precautions, team up with another who will watch your back at all times. Keep your mind on where you are, what you are doing. I want you all to return here in one piece. We've mourned the loss of enough in the battle with Attar. We must defeat him, here and now, because failure not only leaves us exposed after centuries of battling for the right to be seen, but it leaves o—our nests and those who serve us unprotected. That goes against everything we've fought for and given oaths for."

Grunts and nods met her steady gaze.

These were seasoned warriors for the most part. She'd instituted a mentoring system for the newer ones since taking the office of councilor, but although no one would go in unprotected, there were many who'd had minimal experience of battle. She personally knew of several dozen who'd only participated in the most recent, since Hope's change. That made them easier targets.

When Daniel touched her hand she blinked, letting go of the insidious cloud of fear that had gripped her.

"You have your assignments. Take your time and stay safe! Dismissed."

They trooped out in silence and she watched them leave.

She had confidence in them, but every time she sent warriors into battle it was with the knowledge that it was her decision.

My command.

Those who died did so under her direction. That knowledge was sobering.

With a shake of her head she stretched upward, clearing her mind. The battle that lay ahead would be fierce, of that there was no doubt, particularly if they did happen upon Attar.

He and his abilities couldn't be taken lightly.

She needed to be highly focused.

"We should go." She flicked a look in Daniel's direction. "Come on."

He followed her, his attention on her a palpable and living thing. Settling into the car, the schematics she'd had her human staff gather, fixed in her mind as she checked everything she'd done, every plan she'd made.

The entry was short with a potential bottleneck. The hallway then opened onto a variety of rooms and down into a dungeon. If the layout was as she expected, that was where they'd find his waiting room, suite of personal rooms and training area.

They traveled in silence, a short trip, and she noted the human government had made good on clearing the area of people. No need for more carnage, she'd argued, and they'd agreed hastily, well aware of the losses suffered to date.

She gnawed at her lip, thinking of the traps they might find.

The building itself was squat, red-bricked and utilitarian. Old shutters banged in the cool breeze as she called Daniel forward to scan it with a heat-seeking device.

Warriors armed with whips, UV guns and swords surrounded it. *Samra, what's the ETA for Xavier, Javed, Hope and Celina?*

Any minute now. They weren't far behind us.

"Ready, Daniel? Remember to stay with me. We don't want to be separated. I know your magic is…" She waved her hands as the adrenaline started pumping.

He grunted. "I know. Same back. Remember, none of us have exactly nutted this out yet."

The reminder of how little experience they had using the amulets and sharing power twisted her gut. They really weren't ready for this. God help them if he was still here.

As two more cars disgorged their passengers, she gave the alert and suddenly noise filled the air. Urgent and angry sounds swelled, her mind blocking the extraneous noises automatically as the four others wearing amulets reached them.

"Ready?" Cressida didn't wait for their agreement before she strode forward into the heart of the melee.

Doors crashed open, feet thudded.

A blinding light shone and they shielded their eyes as a boom sounded. Dust followed, chased by coughs and splutters.

Nothing. Where is he? Hiding? In her heart, though, she accepted that this was likely too little too late.

The stairs, old rickety wood, lay ahead in the heart of the building and she hurried down them.

"Samra? Report!"

The warrior bounded up, her leathers stained and her face tight. "I'd say he's gone. But he did leave you a present."

That piqued her interest and she followed the woman, feet thudding on the uneven cobbles. At a doorway, Samra turned back in her direction and stepped out of the way.

A body. A vampire Daniel had battled at Samantha's home but who'd escaped, she realized, remembering his face from the vision Daniel had shared after the battle. His body sprawled in a pool of congealing blood.

She stepped forward carefully and sank to her haunches beside the creature. His eyes were open, staring at a fixed spot, a look of terror the death mask on his face.

Cressida reached out, detecting a faint hint of heat. "He's not been dead long. We've not missed them by much." She grunted in anger. "Damn him."

She rose slowly and turned. She saw her team gathered by the door.

"Bloody hell!" Celina shook her head. "He's a cunning bastard, isn't he?"

Cressida bit back the epithet that rose to mind. "We'll get him. He's running scared." She wasn't necessarily sure she believed that herself, but it would have to do for now.

Javed reached into a pocket. "Kharisma requested you get this as soon as possible."

Cressida took the paper without a word.

"What is it?"

She gazed at Hope. "This information will hopefully clear up a thought I've had for the last little while." The sheet of paper crackled as she unfolded it.

Cressida,

We were right. The DNA traces that we've run have indicated that the receptors to the viral infection are of a lower percentile than is considered optimal for changing. There were two speci-mens that rated in the minimal rating and may have survived the change, but the rest would not have made a full transition. It appears that Attar is changing humans without considering the risks. From what we've been able to ascertain, most of his vampires will not be tightly bonded to him and won't be subject to his will.

K

The news stole her strength for a moment. It was one thing to guess at this kind of information, but to have it confirmed meant the tightly guarded bonding of vampire to sire would give them an edge over Attar.

"So? What does it say? Is it good news?" Hope crowded forward.

"Yeah, it's the best news I've received since Attar woke.

THIRTY

ATTAR STALKED ACROSS THE SMALL ROOM, HIS BODY QUIVERING
with anger. Once more they'd brought him low. To a position where
he'd had to run and find a new and decidedly less-than-perfect nest.

Now his forces were in disarray. He had no second and he was
here, in a building that didn't meet his particular needs.

No subterranean sleeping zone, safe from the dangerous sunlight.
"You, girl! Come here."

Her eyes were wide with fright and she shook. He felt the need to
feed, but he had no one to provide sustenance. He could drink her
dry. That had been his plan initially, but then he'd have to send his
warriors in search of sustenance and supplies.

His army was weakened.

He advanced, teeth descending, and she scurried in the direction
of the window, squeaking loudly. Hearing her cries filled him with
pleasure while the scent of her distress filled the air.

Even now he looked forward to the taste of her blood, fresh and
unsullied.

In her haste she tugged open the curtains, and for the first time he
noticed how they billowed in the cool air. The girl too realized there

was no barrier to escape and slipped out, barely taking a second to look over her shoulder. Off she scurried, like a frightened rabbit.

He could go after her, but he was king! Instead, he'd send one of his warriors. They were the ones to hunt and chase like dogs through the countryside and warrens.

Attar roared and a number of his blood-bound fighters ran into the room. One look at their blank gazes simply fed the bubbling cauldron of fury inside him.

"Go after her, you fools!" He flung an imperious hand toward the window and they peered into the gloom.

One leaped through the opening while the others scurried through the door. He used his mind, hoping to follow them somehow, but the link was weak.

Not for the first time, he cursed the loss of Jelani. He may have been foolish, but he'd been aware of his master's needs before his own. He'd have ensured Attar fed well and had another bolt hole.

Time passed as he scowled and paced, waiting for the triumphant return of those he'd sent to find the woman. When they did return, it wasn't with the happy boasts of the successful. Behind them they dragged another woman, old and pockmarked, her face marred with the cosmetics many used to enhance themselves. She smelled of stale sex and other, even less savory chemicals.

"What is this?" His furious bellow caused them to flinch.

"Sire, she escaped, but we brought you this instead." The warrior tugged the woman forward.

She didn't protest her treatment, instead she whined, "What about my money? I need my fix."

The mixture of the stink and the sight of the marks on her arms when he tore the shirt from her filled him with distaste.

"Hey! Watch the shirt. I had to give a BJ to get that!"

"Silence, cow." He sneered at her as he pulled her close. The sour scent of her breath almost turned his stomach, but he required sustenance. Once he'd fed, then so would his army.

As he sank his incisors into her flesh the muddy blood fountained, and he flung her away before turning to retch on the floor.

The warriors slinked from the room before he could catch them up, but the bellow of anger he gave shook the building to its foundations.

Cressida looked out over the garden. The sight and smell of the plantings didn't soothe her spirit. Attar was wily and cunning, managing to escape them yet again.

"Samra, you're sure they have no further information about the new location?" She didn't turn around. She already knew the answer, but even so it was a bitter blow to realize that for every step forward there was another step back.

The beep of the phone broke her introspection and she frowned, picking it up.

"Cressida." She spoke even though glancing at the caller information screen told her it wasn't a number she knew.

"Councilor? I was... Uh, it was suggested that we should contact you."

A woman babbled and Cressida quirked an eyebrow while cradling the earpiece. She caught Samra's eye and her second bowed before leaving her alone. Cressida retreated to her desk and lowered herself into the plush chair.

"And you are?"

"Oh, apologies... I've never spoken to a vampire Mistress before. I mean, a Councilor..."

She grinned at the words.

"Well, now you have. How may I help you?"

She heard the hiss clearly over the lines as the caller obviously attempted to control her fear and excitement.

"I'm Officer Fernly with the NYPD Liaison Service and we currently have a woman here claiming she was attacked by a vampire.

Except, he doesn't sound like any kind of vampire we've ever heard of. We were wondering if...? I mean, given the circumstances..."

Gripping the receiver, she hoped that maybe this was the break they needed.

"Indeed, you need us to talk to her? To try and find out who and where?" She carefully traced circles as she spoke, harnessing the thrill that rose.

"Yes. We think she may be another one of Attar's survivors. We can bring her to you, as we know about the situation with the creature."

"Of course, officer. When should we expect you?"

The door to the office opened and she raised a hand, stopping whoever it was from interrupting, and closed her eyes while she listened to the woman, blocking out sounds from beyond the doorway.

"It'll maybe take us an hour or so, but that means—"

"We can shelter her here until tomorrow, or if she fears our kind, I can arrange for her to be transported to one of the other residential facilities while we rest along with our human staff." She waited while the human conferred with others in the background.

"That would... Uh, if you could."

"Perfect, we will be awaiting your arrival."

She opened her eyes, replaced the receiver and looked up. Samra and Daniel waited on the other side of the desk.

"Well? Is it a lead?" Daniel brushed his hand over her shoulder.

She smiled. "It could be."

"So?" Samra leaned over her desk. Cressida rose out of her seat, well used to Samra's tactics. As she slowly made her way around the desk, Samra's gaze followed her.

"You'll have to wait and see, Samra. Now, we're expecting guests soon. There will be a human who will require accommodations. I'm not yet certain whether here or in one of the residential facilities. Please ensure they are prepared." Thus dismissed, Samra left them, muttering imprecations under her breath. As Daniel turned to leave, she stopped him with a hand on his shoulder. "Daniel, I need you here for this, and I will need the others as well. Can you arrange that?"

"Sure."

Then he too left her alone with her thoughts.

By the time the officer, and she was unsurprised to note she'd seen her previously, and young woman arrived, Cressida had made preparations for the discussions and the cleanup that would come afterward. The six of them had settled into the casual seating area.

The young woman was bedraggled and eyed them cautiously, her hand twisting in the policewoman's grasp.

"Do I have to do this?"

The woman patted her on the hand. "I'll stay, Emily. I promised, didn't I?"

"But they're vamps...like he was."

When Xavier made to rise, Cressida sent a quiet command to wait and he subsided once more.

"Emily? Will you come and sit down? We'd like to ask you some questions about the vampire who attacked you."

The woman started and looked at her with horror. "What do you...they know. They probably want to..."

"No, Emily. Officer Fern...?" She looked at the woman, then to the officer whose name she couldn't remember.

"Fernly, Councilor. Genny Fernly."

"Officer Fernly explained that you'd been accosted by a vampire. Emily, we are searching for one. I need to ask you some questions. To work out if it's our quarry. If it is, then you will be helping us to..." She racked her mind, seeking the best term that wouldn't scare the woman further.

"He's been killing humans and vampires alike, Emily. You trust the police, don't you?"

Cressida watched as Daniel took the initiative. She'd noticed how he put people at ease before, and Emily nodded at him.

"Good. Think of us like the police for vampires. It's our role to bring him to justice. Make him accountable for the crimes he's committed. But to do that, we need your help."

"W-what do you need me to do?" She still sounded hesitant, but Cressida saw the white of the officer's knuckles had returned to a healthy pink.

"Good girl. It's important that we know what he looked like and where he is."

"I can...I can do that."

By the time Officer Fernly left, Emily was tucked up in the human wing of the house, fast asleep, and a patrol had been placed around the location Emily had given them.

Their human allies would ensure no one went in or out while the vampires slept.

DANIEL RUBBED HIS HAND OVER THE BACK OF HIS HEAD. THE constant inactivity with brief periods of intensity was wearing them all down.

After Officer Fernly had left, Hope and Celina had herded them down to the training room on the pretext that they'd been thinking over the use of the amulets they all wore.

The ability to share power had grown easier to command, and he was amazed at how much smoother it was to communicate between themselves without words now.

When they'd concluded, it had been far too late for the couples to leave, and though Daniel had offered to transport them to their own homes, they all agreed it was better to stay the night. Besides, his ability to transport more than one still wasn't as strong as he'd hoped.

"Daniel, stop wearing a groove in the floor. Just stand here while we wait for the warriors. As my consort, it's important that you and I look calm and collected. That we share our resolve in this matter."

He scanned her and read the doubts and fears that shook her core.

"You're not as calm as you appear to be."

"No, Daniel. If this goes wrong..." She gulped and he took her hand. "We could lose a lot more than a single nest or warrior. Massing our warriors," she shook her head, "that's a big risk. By only leaving a skeleton force at each house, we risk the devastating outcome of an attack here, or at any nest, if we're wrong."

"According to Officer Fernly, the patrols haven't seen anything." He cupped her face and she rested against him as if absorbing his strength.

"We can't rely on that. We don't really know how strong he is, what powers he holds."

Just then the door boomed open and the three witches entered. "Oh, we can tell you, his powers are few and weak, we can sense that with ease. They've lessened over the years. Being the first born, he was the most powerful, but power is imbued in the witch, not the vampire. What he has was inherited from their mother, but over the years his skills have decayed. He might be the ultimate vampire now, but any magical powers he'd once possessed are almost non existent."

The two couples that they'd been working with made their way down the steps, their chatter ceasing as they saw the three women facing Cressida and Daniel.

"What do you mean?"

Jemima smiled. "Well, the vampire virus? There are genes carried by certain families that make them and us susceptible to mutations. You see, our sister, Attar's mother, was only a half-sibling to us. Through the line of our father. Attar's mother took many lovers and—"

"Hang on." Daniel shook his head. "What do you mean she took many lovers? Were they all the same crazed killers?"

"No. Attar had other brothers and a sister, as you have already learned. When our kind came into being, it was because certain strains of the virus and our gene pool mutated. You already know that from Hope and the pathogens she carried. Later on, there were further changes, resulting in the *weres* and suchlike. Witches are a human variation of the vampire strain, but the virus factor transforming in the blood of those with certain DNA factors are, shall we say, alien to your DNA?" Danicka frowned. "I think that's all of it, now."

"No, wait." Selena raised her hand. "Gianna. She is our grandniece, as you know. Even though Attar killed his sister, Arumi and his brothers, he, like many of their kind have limited knowledge of gestation. We believe he didn't know Arumi had already delivered Gianna, so his retribution came too late to destroy the line. The children of our sister's kind leave and have no further contact with parents and so on, once they achieve maturation. Now, Daniel, David, Hope and Celina are all distantly related through Gianna's daughter. And she's not really aware either about our connection." The witch blinked and nodded. "Anyway, the one born before she embraced her change to vampire and as such are also susceptible to the change."

"You've been drip feeding us all along. Why didn't you tell us all this originally? It would have made things so much easier." Daniel balled his fists as anger coursed through him.

"We never promised any of this would be easy, Daniel. While we knew some, we also had to dig for information. It wasn't just handed to us on a platter, dear. All we promised was that we would right our sister's wrong when the time was right. That's exactly what we are doing. Righting the wrong." Selena's response didn't enthuse him.

"So what you're saying is—"

"That we will help you defeat him. While he slept, there was no need to be concerned about him." Hope opened her mouth, but Selena shook her head. "Estersham was a problem, it's true, but you were able to deal with him. We knew that. That's why we didn't interfere, only simply watched over you and your kind, but Attar waking? That changed the whole game. You need help to defeat him, and that's our role."

Cressida turned turbulent eyes on the three women. "When this is done, we need to talk." They'd kept back so much information. What else had they kept secret and hidden?

Jemima nodded. "Yes, we do. There is much to be finalized. Now, have you everything in place?"

"The warriors will be massing here..."—the rumble of vehicle engines rose, as the cars drove up the lane—"about now."

"And your plan?" This time it was Gianna who demanded the answer, and surprise filled Cressida as their Overlord sauntered into the room.

"It is as complete as we can make it, Liege."

Gianna smiled at Daniel. *Does that include your magic?*

Cressida grinned as Daniel responded to the assembled group. "It does, Liege."

In response, Gianna merely smiled.

Daniel was hunched over the laptop in the back of the car. He'd called in a favor owed and now accessed satellite images of the house they would soon storm.

Around the rear, a small laneway ran by the house, and on their command the movement of vehicles was minimal—covert government agents in plain clothes and ordinary cars. The rest of the neighborhood had been quietly evacuated, down to the last cat and dog.

Patching into the military satellite system allowed them to get a real-time view of the surrounding area, and that told them there was no movement outside. A small mercy right now.

He hummed, then pointed out a spot on the screen to Cressida. "Here's the lane where we've got the majority of the guards. The police finalized the last of the evacuation ten minutes ago. I've been watching since we arrived and no one has gone in or come out."

Cressida leaned over his shoulder. She pointed to a spot. "What's that?"

"That is the command post for the SWAT team and vampire-human relations officers."

"What are they doing there?"

He felt the emotions that she couldn't totally hide, a mixture of frustration and anger, and noted the way she tapped her fingernails on the arm of the car seat.

He smiled at her. She'd avoided a lot of the more modern behaviors society had acquired, yet somehow she'd cultivated more than a mere distaste for bureaucracy. He stifled the snort that rose before sobering.

"Sadly, that's because there's human involvement. It's their job to ensure none of the humans get...eaten."

She groaned and rolled her eyes. "What do they think we're going to do? Pretend they're takeout?"

He snorted a laugh, but the sour look on her face remained.

"Come on, Cressida. We don't have to like it, just work with it."

She sighed and turned back to the screen. "No movement?"

He shook his head, rubbed at the back of his neck, and computed the information before him.

"But what?"

"It doesn't feel right." He groped for his pocket and withdrew a mobile phone. "Let me make a call."

The call connected and ran directly to voicemail. He swore and Cressida raised her eyebrow.

"Well, that didn't work quite the way you expected."

He could see she was making an effort to soothe him, but the prickle of apprehension continued.

"I'm just... It doesn't feel right, Cressida. I can't explain why..." He shrugged and she laid her hand on the knee he'd been jiggling up and down.

"I understand what you're saying, Daniel. But unless there is something more than a sense, we're committed to this course of action. Attar must be defeated."

"I know. It's something I can't put my finger on. I wish..." But what exactly did he wish for? That it was over? He sure did want the battle concluded. That they could go back to some kind of normality? That wasn't going to happen—not like before, anyway.

After all, now he was a vampire. He wanted them to have a chance to make a life together, though. Free from the threat of Attar.

"There will always be something, Daniel. No matter the time, place or circumstances." Cressida's quiet words made him jump. She was obviously reading his emotions.

You can, can't you? Is it one of the perks of masterhood and being a councilor?

She smiled enigmatically as the car drew to a stop, then her mirth died away like dew in the morning sun.

Attar sent his minions out as soon as the sun dropped below the horizon. His rest had been disturbed by noises and banging, hushed though it had been. At first he'd thought it part of the normal day-to-day routine of human life, but as the day wore on, his mood had deteriorated.

Jastin made the mistake of creeping into the small dark room at that moment, interrupting his thoughts, and Attar tore out his throat, fangs flashing like razors. The only sensation he felt when it was done was hunger. Jastin had failed him miserably and the need for a new second clawed at his mind. More vampires followed Jastin into the room, and he growled his displeasure.

Hunger ground in his belly, as if stretching the muscles then contracting them as thin as possible. The one woman his warriors had brought to him overnight had left him feeling ill after a few sips. Now the sun had set, and he stalked the length of the room.

"Bring me sustenance!"

Two of his warriors, a tall female and a short, wiry male, nodded and left. He was able to follow them part of the way until the contact halted abruptly.

The sudden disconnection was odd and he growled, trying to grasp what had happened. A younger woman, one of his newer warriors, padded her way across the room. "Master?" She cocked her head to the side, her gaze direct and clear. "Tell me what you need."

Ahh! Here is one with spark! He could send her out and should she be successful, maybe she would be able to fulfill his need as second. He almost rubbed his hands together with glee. She might allow him to watch his enemies scurry like ants.

"Go find them. See why they are no longer in my mind."

She was looking at him as if calculating his reactions before nodding.

"Indeed, sire." Before he could speak again she was gone, rounding the doorway and out of sight. He tried to follow her, but as he'd found with so many others, he couldn't.

Within minutes she'd returned. "Sire, I bring news. Humans and vampires have encamped outside. They seem to be waiting for others. As to the ones you sent out, they are lying in the nearby streets, not dead, but unconscious. I feel... There is imminent danger ahead and we should leave."

"I forbid any warrior to leave this building." His voice boomed. *So they think to capture me, do they?*

The nasty smile he gave left the vampires who'd gathered in the room with him blanching.

He'd beaten his opponents every other time and he would again.

This time they would have the benefits of a nest. Once he'd built up protections... The others would need to breach the perimeter. Never in the millennia preceding had anywhere he'd fortified been violated. It would be the same here. It was an advantage he'd deny them.

His mind turned over ideas and stratagems he could employ. "Cease your noise and assemble."

As the warriors scrambled to follow his bidding, he watched. What they didn't possess in training they had in strength of numbers. He'd crush those who defied his will.

I am a god! They will bow before me.

With that in mind, he started to give orders for the defense of their position, and when it was done, he reclined once more on the bed, watching as his warriors scurried off.

Yes. He would grind these foes into dust before he glutted once more on sweet human blood.

THIRTY-ONE

"Can I help you, ma'am?" A young man, possibly in his late twenties, strode toward Cressida as they made their way toward the Black Zone, the vampiric code name they'd chosen for Attar's nest. It would make it easier to call, should they need to name their location to others.

"I don't think so." Cressida would have pushed on, but the man sidestepped in front of her.

"Ma'am, I'm sorry, but this is a restricted zone. You'll have to go back beyond the cordon." She read the name *Davies* on his shirt.

Her eyes widened before she started to grin. *Aha, so he likely doesn't know who I am, do you think, Daniel?*

"Ma'am? I'm going to have to insist..."

An older gentleman, one she hadn't spied before but knew well, stepped up to the young staffer.

"Uh, Davies? That's Councilor Cressida. You'll want to let her and her entourage through." There was a brief hint of amusement in the older man's tone before the young man stepped back out of the way.

"I thank you, Captain Usain. *Young* Davies here hadn't recognized me, so I'm glad you were able to clear the identity issue."

Daniel winced at her comment about young Davies, but it didn't hurt to put youngsters like that through their paces, she thought. After all, in thirty years' time he might be in Usain's position. And Usain had learned much from the few times she'd sat him on his backside as well. *Nothing like a ploy that works, generation after generation.*

Now she sashayed her way in the direction of the planning tent. Computer analysts and strategists gathered around, pens in hand and maps on the table, while the large halogen lights shone down, as hot as the days of summer.

Her people took their places around the tent, consciously assuming the positions of guards. The humans had done their job well during the daytime hours, but the night belonged to the vampires.

"Ladies and gentlemen, we thank you for your assistance, but I'd like to confer with Captain Usain once you've cleared the area."

There were gasps of surprise, and more than one of the staffers indicated their displeasure with being removed from their position.

Usain stalked in her direction. "With all due respect, Councilor—"

"Usain, trust me. I'll explain everything soon. But if you value the lives of these men and women," she gestured to those watching, "you will clear the area. I cannot be responsible for your losses otherwise. And there will be losses."

Why are you bothering with the male human, Cressida? You should take command.

With all due respect, Gianna, things are different now. Times have changed and they aren't afraid of us. We work side-by-side—

Nonsense, Cressida. They are human. They do our bidding.

Over the years Cressida had become aware that Gianna had lost touch with humanity. Dealing only with the upper echelons of vampiric society had left her social capabilities blunted.

Gianna marched into the light, her red hair forming a nimbus around her head. "Who's the human in charge?" Power echoed and the lights flickered and dimmed a little as she spoke.

"I am. And you would be...?"

She grinned at Usain, and Cressida had the impression she was weighing up the burly, dark-skinned man. "I am the Overlord. You, however, may call me Gianna."

Usain looked as bemused as many did when meeting the Overlord for the first time. Cressida swept her arms in the direction of the humans still watching. "We need to clear them out before we can set our teams in motion."

Gianna smiled, and before she knew it, the humans were rising and walking away into the dark.

"What did you do to my people?" Usain leaned away, his hands gripping the table as if it were all that was keeping him there.

"A simple compulsion. They are tired and ready for home. But not you, so why is that?"

Usain watched her, his face a mask of concern. "You just made them leave?"

"Something like that. Now let's get down to business." Gianna took the seat nearest to her. "Cressida, it's your plan. Explain it to this human here."

Cressida cleared her mind. "Our foe is Attar. He's the one that's been attacking the nests. Last night he took a human—a girl—but to her credit, she managed to escape. The police brought her to us in the early hours. We've since received the information that he has a makeshift nest in this location."

Usain sat heavily in the seat opposite, pale with worry. Not for the first time, she wanted to apologize for the lack of information, but that wasn't the way it worked in vampire and human relations.

"You see, the attack from two nights ago led us to a nest he'd abandoned probably half an hour beforehand. It was too late to give chase, so when we were given the gift of this girl..." Usain stiffened at the word gift.

"You mean you *fed* from her?" Usain's face mirrored the horror her words had evoked.

For a moment Cressida ground her teeth together. Sometimes it was hard to explain what she meant. Humans didn't always understand the meanings of statements when it came to vampires. This was one of those times.

"No, we didn't. Not at all. In fact, she's safe with the humans in the council nest. But she gave us the information we needed. That's why the humans, reinforced by *weres,* were keeping an eye on this location." The shuffle of feet joined with movement in the shadows and the human gulped.

"Just what do you mean by *weres*?" His voice wavered slightly and she had to control her grin.

Cressida sighed. "Well, it's not really my secret to tell—"

A slender and dark-haired man slunk out of the darkness. Cressida was, as always, surprised by his piercing and otherworldly ice-blue eyes. He was dressed in faded jeans and boots, but wore no shirt. Even in the glow of artificial light, it was clear he was broad-shouldered and with superb definition in his muscular upper body. "No, it isn't your place to tell of us. But Attar made it necessary when he attempted to change Jelani. Our mythology warned us that there was a vampire-*were* hybrid, but no one saw it. Or at least, no one that survived. But the rumors continued to circulate."

He settled into a chair with a grunt.

Cressida acknowledged the male *were* who joined them at the table. "I greet you, Lord of Lycans." His gaze narrowed as he scanned her face, then the stiffness in him leached away and he grinned.

"Cressida, you haven't changed in over fifty years. You're still the same sexy, smooth talker you always were." Simon and she had been friends for more than two centuries, and at one time she'd even considered a dalliance, but the timing and situation had never been quite right.

Now she understood it was because Daniel was the only man for her, and the one she'd waited for.

Daniel, however, didn't know that and tensed beside her, and a shaft of pain tackled her, right beneath her ribs. It was a shadow of his emotions, but right now they didn't have time to deal with the niceties of his or her bruised feelings. "Daniel, I would introduce you to—"

"The Lord of the Lycans? Yeah, gotcha."

Simon glanced at her quickly, his gaze assessing. "This is your consort, I take it?"

She took a single deep breath before answering. "He is also my life partner."

Simon reared back. "Well now..."

"I can also talk for myself." Daniel's face was dark and closed.

He doesn't mean anything to me.

I hope not, Cressida. You've publicly announced we are life partners and I intend on keeping you to that.

If ever there was a time for her to roll her eyes at his possessiveness, now wasn't it, but they'd be talking about all this and so much more if they survived the night.

"Fine, now that we've all been introduced, it's time to get to the planning and strategy bit of the meeting. Before it's too late." If there was a certain dryness about her words, she couldn't help it.

Too much was at stake.

"So, here are the others of my force. Hope, Javed, Celina and Xavier are going to help us..." In turn she indicated each member, who either shook his hand or inclined their heads. Information was imparted quickly as they considered issues and problems at lightning speed.

Within minutes, Usain was agreeing with them as the plans were laid out. "I'll make sure the humans are kept well back, then."

"Good. And Usain? Stay safe. I'm not ready to break in your replacement yet."

The man laughed at her words as she rose.

THIRTY-TWO

They waited in the dark, having crept up the alley. The building beyond was shadowed and Daniel frowned. Do they know we are here, he wondered. He wanted to test the boundaries, but as he gathered his magic, Cressida stilled him.

"He knows we're here. I would be shocked if he didn't."

Hope settled back against the wall, looking to drop into a light doze, just as they'd agreed. A chill, biting and quick, flicked up the narrow way. "Ready?"

Hope's words were almost inaudible, but Cressida nonetheless quieted her. "Shhh… They'll hear you."

During their planning, the group had agreed they needed the most up-to-date information as well as to ascertain the layout of the building. Daniel's stomach flip-flopped, though, at what else she might see. Who they might lose.

Celina tugged a tiny shard of the protection stone, one she'd used before, from her pocket. "Are we ready?"

Daniel slid his hand over his half-sister's shoulder. He would lay in place another layer of enchantment as she began her incantation.

While Attar and his minions might hear hers, they wouldn't be able to detect Daniel's.

They'd discussed their strengths over the last few days, and this was the single greatest advantage they had—their ability to work cohesively as a team.

He wove his magic through her words, seeking to not only block them from sight and their words from hearing but also to create a null zone. A place where no one could read them. Only the six of them would know what had been found.

Hope fell into the stupor and they waited, hoping this would give them the information they required—information that had remained veiled and hidden from view. Perhaps with that additional knowledge of his location, they might be able to glean his plan.

Hope's eyes opened, and for a moment the shock of anguish and fear on her face plowed into Daniel's psyche. Then Hope gasped. "Don't let the others in. Cressida, whatever you do, we need shielding before anyone enters the building."

It was too late. The first team had already advanced and started to enter. Now all they could do was watch and listen, their hearts shattering as the screams of terror and pain began slicing through the night.

Hope fisted her hands in Daniel's jacket, tugging at him. "You have to stop them!"

"I'll do what I can." Daniel closed his eyes, casting a net of security while seeking those he knew. Maybe he could tug them from the building they'd just stormed... But his magic was blocked. *Shielding?* He gripped the amulet. "Help me." His grunt was met with the rest of the team giving him what they could. It wasn't enough.

"The witches said he had no magic! How can this be?" He growled and the night air rippled with repressed fury.

We never said he had no power. Just that it's dim. A faint version of the power you share. He could hear their thoughts, but they were hidden from his view. He couldn't even follow the thread of their magic to whatever location they had taken up.

"Goddamn it!" He hurled a flash of power outward. It lit the night, showing him the wrestling bodies that lay beyond the dim glow that now illuminated the building from within.

"We should—" Even as he rose, Cressida held out her hand, barring him.

"Stick to the plan. Daniel. You will weaken us if you leave now." He heard the words she didn't say, deep in his brain and his heart. *If something happens to you, we cannot fight... And I won't have the strength to continue without you.*

Her thoughts stopped him cold.

On one level, he understood why he should accept her ruling. She'd been a warrior for so long that she knew what needed to be done and said. He was new and green. On the other, the screams of pain went on and on, jarring his mind but also leaving his soul aching at the punishment the warriors were taking.

"How many, Hope?" He turned to her, but she had her hands over her ears as moisture tracked down her face. Xavier wrapped his arm around her, his face tight as if he too could hardly bear the sounds.

Huddled against the wall, it felt like hours. Daniel's hands grew numb, clenched into fists, before the final sounds died away.

Celina had slumped into a crouch on the ground during the noise and she rose to her feet. "We can stop the second wave. I have an idea." Celina was already muttering something, her lips and hands moving swiftly through the dark night. He knew she was running through her magic spell inventory in her head.

Daniel gripped his amulet in his hand and dropped himself into her mind, searching for her thoughts. For a moment he was confused by her plan, then, as understanding filled him, he grinned. "Oh, Celina, that's magic." He blinked as the words he used to praise her echoed in his skull.

She giggled, breaking the air of despair that had settled over them. "I know. That's why it will work."

"Cressida, compel them to line up before us. Celina thinks if we run a simple spell, not a love spell, but an attraction one, we can stop them long enough for the warriors to gain entrance. They'll be too interested in each other to have any interest in our warriors."

"Won't she need...?" Javed frowned. Daniel knew why she didn't have any of her normal implements. He didn't have time to tell him that this time he was acting as the magical conduit, but if it made the fight easier, then he'd find the precious minutes to explain.

"Normally. But you see, this is where I can help by melding our magic to make it happen. While she talks through the spell, I can imbue it with my peculiar kind of magic, so she won't need the normal items..."

"I will need something though, a way to spread a compulsion among the warriors. Like a spray bottle filled with water."

Daniel nodded and brought one to mind, concentrating on his palm. Then it was there, the small bottle Cressida used to tame her hair before braiding it.

He laid his hands over Celina's. She worked on the spell that had formed in her mind, and he wove his magic through it. In his mind he conjured the sight of individual threads of purple and yellow, twining around each other in a tight band.

When it was done, the water in the bottle sparkled as if tiny confetti flakes filled it. He turned to Cressida. "The second wave warriors will need to be prepared. Have them file by us so we can... vaccinate them." He frowned, unable to think of a better choice of words and no time to consider the problem.

Cressida gave the order. The vampires formed a line and one by one they squirted the liquid on their hands.

Cressida watched..."How long?"

"Maybe ten minutes. It's weak, but we only need to slow them down. Nothing more."

She nodded and watched as the end of the line marched before Daniel and the final warrior extended his hands. Kharisma winked at him from the front of the line of thirty or so warriors. "Hope this is good stuff."

"It better be."

Then Kharisma straightened to her full height, unhooking her favorite blade from her belt. "No quarter!" As they watched, the warriors charged into the night while Daniel and the others shuddered in the cold night. Anxiety rippling between them.

Silence filled the air as the warriors entered the building and disappeared from sight.

Then Cressida turned on her heels to look upon them, and her face held a cold distance. The warrior woman had returned. "Shall we?"

THIRTY-THREE

The noise levels in the complex ran high, and as the spell wore off the warriors from the combined nests were hoping to bring the majority of the newly turned to holding facilities they'd set up around the neighborhood. It had occurred to them that some might actually be helped, once Attar was defeated.

Making their way up the stairs resembled the climbing of a mountain, mounded high with the bodies of those who'd been unsuccessful in the first attempt to gain entrance. The clang of feet on the metal steps rang out, although there was already a raucous melee in action.

Beyond the door, wherever Cressida looked, she saw wrestling figures as the seasoned fighters faced off against the rabid creatures Attar had spawned. Fury settled over her like a mantle, heavy and cloying.

If these newly turned could be rehabilitated, then they'd do so. If not, they would be humanely destroyed. It was all that could be done. Cressida comforted herself with the knowledge that her people would find the ones in whom the shreds of humanity lurked beneath the blood hunger.

The band of six stopped at the top of the first flight of stairs. While the building wasn't as large as many residential complexes in the area, there were still moving bodies and they couldn't afford to be scattered. After a quick scan, Daniel shook his head. Before they could continue, they flattened themselves against the walls avoiding the battling vampires who erupted in a frenzy around them. Blades shone in the night, flashing here and there. Up another flight of stairs they fought, ducking and weaving to avoid injury on their way toward their destination.

The bangs of opening doors and clanging metal echoed through Cressida's skull, briefly disorienting her.

"This way." Daniel gestured, a magical representation of the schematics of the building blazing in hand. They had used the information gleaned from the girl, realizing it was necessary to move to the center of the structure, understanding it was the easiest to fortify, when a *boom* shook the walls and floor. The building shuddered and Cressida instinctively reached for Daniel's hand and the magical construct disappeared.

Masonry rained down upon them and they covered their heads as billows of particles filled the air. Cressida choked and waved her hand at the mist.

"What the hell was that?" Celina coughed, gripping the edges of the door.

"I don't know. But I think we'd better find Attar...and quickly!"

Daniel grunted and suddenly the way cleared.

With care they pushed their way through a doorway at the end of a corridor, and there before them waited a band of vampires, brandishing knives and even power cords that had obviously been torn from electrical equipment.

"*What the hell is this?*" Xavier stilled them, his hand flung out.

"Don't underestimate them. We have no idea what kind of training they have." Cressida caught Daniel's gaze, her concern plain. "Just do what you can." The blade in her hand wavered for an instant.

. . .

They moved, each targeting a specific vampire. Even as they advanced, Daniel kept an eye on Cressida. They were confined to a small hallway, with a crush of waiting combatants behind them. This wasn't a good area for an attack, he was sure. *It's all we have.* He caught Xavier's eye and nodded.

Daniel flicked his gaze to the side, hunting for an alternative so they could spread out, but there wasn't one. He tugged the small blade from his belt and lunged at the man who came at him, jaws wide open, incisors razor sharp and bloody.

The claws on the vampire's hand nicked him, merely a scratch, but it annoyed Daniel, who pivoted to follow through his defense, momentum carrying his action forward, and he finished with a brutal kick of his leg. Now he thanked all the hours of practice Samra had demanded of him as the creature attempted to capture him around the waist. It tried to sink long fangs into his shoulder. He twisted again, muscles screamed, but he loosened the hold the warrior had on him. Then he struck, the blade sliding home between two ribs with a sucking noise. A harsh yell split the air.

Daniel?

All good, Cressida. The glance in her direction was automatic, but he spied another attacker, its face wreathed in smiles as it aimed at her. *Watch your back!* He slid in behind her, meeting the next opponent squarely, once more moving as he had practiced in those long hours with Samra.

Clangs and grunts filled the air. Movement, whirring and flashing arms and blades. Blood spurted and spilled onto the ground, the skirmish brief but fearsome, and by the end they all panted and leaned against the walls, wheezing and chests bellowing in the aftermath of the bout. Daniel gazed at them, amazed that they carried nothing more than the odd bite or cut. "Amazing."

Xavier clapped his shoulder. "You did well. But this is only the beginning. I would expect it will grow fiercer the closer to Attar we get."

Xavier's words didn't make Daniel feel any better, but he shrugged them off. After all, this was what they'd been training for.

"This isn't a good battleground, Cressida. We need space to be able to wield our weapons." Javed wiped at a trickle of sweat on his brow.

"I know. But there isn't likely to be a room with more space." She shrugged. "He probably chose this chamber because it's easier to defend."

Daniel straightened at Cressida's words, accepting the truth.

"Cressida!" The cry came from beyond them and they surged forward.

The door was shut and she laid her fingers on the silver knob. Who knew what lay within?

Cressida?

Her nerves jangled as she slid the knob a little to the left. The door squeaked in protest and she pushed it forward.

"Welcome, little one. Bring your friends in too." She stood and scanned the view before her. For a second, she blanked. This was a face she knew, and it occurred to her in an instant—

"You!" She advanced only to stop when he tugged a woman, sobbing wildly, against his chest. A human. An innocent. One of those she'd sworn to protect.

How to proceed?

The grin on his face was obscene and cold. "Oh yes, my dear. Had you forgotten me?"

How could she? This was the face that had dogged her dreams for centuries—the vampire who had caused the death of her child and her husband.

Here was her sire. The one she'd vowed so many years ago, to hunt and defeat.

Deep inside she might quake, but she knew if she showed any chink in her armor, he'd take advantage of it. He'd kill her and the others with her. Not to mention the humans. This was a creature with no sense of remorse.

Cressida forced her mind to concentrate. *Do not engage him until I've had a chance to secure the freedom of the humans.*

Cressida? Is this...?

She cut Daniel's query off with a sharp hand motion. She couldn't splinter her thoughts any more than they were already. To do so would mean death for more than them.

"So...Attar? Strange, you never called yourself that before."

He leered. "Well, my dear, I wear many faces and answer to many, many names. Yet, it seems to me, you were one of my greatest creations. Just look, you leading a... What would you call this?"

She ignored the question and indicated the humans, tied together hand and foot. "Do you really need to subject them to this? Not afraid of us and that we might beat you, are you?"

"Afraid? Of what...you?" He laughed and the sound scraped across her raw nerves. "My dear, you may be one of my best creations, but you'll never come close to what I am. I *am* a God!" He spread his hands wide.

"And why, Attar, is that?"

The smile this time displayed yellowed but razor-sharp teeth. "Because, I'm a god! I've always been one and will be forever."

She couldn't control the gasp that slipped from her mouth.

Cressida? He's not a god, he's a butcher.

Daniel's correction made her smile and Attar, seeing her reaction, frowned. "Well, Attar, it occurs to me, if you're a god, you really don't need them." She pointed to the humans who cowered nearby.

The cunning look he'd displayed earlier returned. "True. I don't, but..." Something in his manner telegraphed his next action and she lunged, hoping to tug the human away. He bared long incisors and struck. A stream of red blood spouted before he drew deep, and the rich scent muddied her senses as adrenaline coursed.

Behind her, Daniel groaned and the hunger he'd begun to learn to control flared. It took on its own life, echoing through the link between them. She grabbed his hand, digging her claws deep into the flesh of his palm, forcefully dragging him back from the precipice of hunger-induced thrall.

Control, Daniel. We need control if we are to save them. His grasp was tenuous, she knew, but he held on as if she were the only thing keeping him sane.

Her body coiled like a spring and she made to leap, to tug another human away, but a body careered into her.

"Drop her." Gianna had entered the room, and Attar shoved the human to one side. She lived still. Her heart continued to beat, but it was sluggish.

Daniel pivoted and grabbed the human up before Attar could move to stop him. A smear of red betrayed the severity of the woman's injury and, lightning quick, Daniel sliced at the rope bonds. "Get her out of here. Go through there." He thrust the injured woman to another released captive.

Cressida's gaze was drawn to the window behind the injured woman, but the scent of blood enticed her again to the look at the site of the injury. It had been years since she'd fed directly from the vein except to undertake the change of neophytes. It wouldn't take much, and it always felt so good...

"Take it, Cressida. Feed." Attar's words, so insidious and mesmeric, tugged at her while the hunger nipped at her on a primal level.

The pulsing vein at the injured woman's neck was so close... Her tongue flicked out as if tasting the air.

"Cressida." Xavier's growl dragged her back from the edge.

Before the captives could clamber out of the window, a woman appeared, her face a mask of hatred.

Watch out, Daniel!

He started, his focus snapping from helping the prisoners escape. The warrior woman grabbed the injured human and pulled toward her face then inhaled deeply while Cressida grimaced. It was obvious she was testing the scent of her prey.

"Ours! We will feed on them!"

She turned in the direction of Attar, who gave a grin. "Yes, my dear. Ours to feed upon!"

Her strike was fast, and Cressida knew she couldn't have saved the woman. The attack was brutal and the cry of the injured ended abruptly as the warrior slaked her thirst.

Cries of fright and revulsion filled the air, and Cressida thought fast. How to engage Attar and this creature? How to ensure that the remaining humans survived?

Before a plan could be formulated, Xavier surged forward and the female warrior threw the body of the now deceased captive to the floor. "Oh look! Up for some fun, are we?" she snarled.

Daniel took the opportunity to push the others through the window. "Go!" Then he turned back, muscles tensed as he lurched before Cressida.

Attar jerked, his face a mask of fury as chaos descended. Amid the noise and confusion, the door flung open. Attar stopped in his tracks and a cackle erupted. Several more of the voracious newly turned creatures entered the room and Hope, Celina, Xavier and Javed engaged them. The clang of knives and swords filled the air. Gianna surged toward Attar and Cressida helped Daniel. Muscles bunched and moves little more than jerks as flesh connected against flesh. The woman who was Attar's guard was well trained, and there were times that Cressida feared she and Daniel would both perish as she hunched over, avoiding yet another blow.

Thrust. Parry. Retreat. Engage. Forward. It was a hideously deadly waltz, dangerous at all times but imbued with lethal grace.

The woman drove them back to the center of the room, hands and legs flying. Cressida struggled to maintain an effective telepathic communication while engaged in battle, her eyes moving, watching the combatant the entire time as her hands blocked yet another punch that rattled her teeth. *Let. Me. I have. An. Idea.*

Cressida took up the slack, engaging her foe while Daniel's eyes flashed. He raised his hands and the woman stilled, her mouth open as the sharp teeth arched toward Cressida.

"I can't...hold her...long."

She could only guess at what it was costing him while he sweated, the strain clear in the cording of his shoulders, and face turned red as the female vampire fought against the magical bindings. The veins in his neck bulged. "Do. It."

Cressida swooped quickly, realizing that this woman wouldn't give up. It was rare for one with a taste for blood like this to be rehabilitated, and she doubted there was any interest.

The flashing hate decided her and Cressida gripped her, one hand reaching for the hair almost at the scalp while the other dug deep into a fleshy shoulder. She grunted, heaved, and a crack sounded. Silence descended for a second as head separated from body.

A yell caught her attention and a magic wave carried a crashing surge of power erupted, washed over her. It stole her breath and thoughts. Cressida followed it, spun around, and horror filled her.

Gianna lay in Attar's arms, eyes wide open and focused on nothing.

Attar grinned with satisfaction while dark rivulets of blood dribbled down his chin. "She is gone. Nothing more than a shell."

Cressida reached out, fingertips only inches from her Overlord's body. "Gianna?" She whispered the words, unable to believe what she was seeing.

Gianna.

Dead.

Her head lay at an unnatural angle while the pulse of her heart faded from their hearing. Her face was pale.

"You killed her!" The accusation was the only sound, and they watched the creature before them smile as the words died away.

"Now then. Make your bow to me. I reign supreme and my duty to my sister is done. The scourge has been removed."

Cressida absorbed the words. *He thinks he's won? There is no victory for him, because I'd die rather than let him reign over them.*

If that happened, it would be blood servitude forever. The innocents would be slain.

Cressida? Daniel's voice echoed in her mind.

Intention warred with madness. Cressida squared her shoulders. *We will fight him, my friends. We took a solemn oath to protect the innocents. We must not fail.* With a shaking hand, Cressida corrected her grip on the sword.

The slow bubble of anger and horror died away, leaving the spewing hot lava of fury pumping through her veins. Adrenaline surged and she stalked toward him, her face tight and cold. "You failed, Attar! You lost! We—" she encompassed all of them in her action, "we are all her issue. Generations of us exist. Generations, Attar! The blood lives on!"

He paled. "No. It cannot be." He stumbled, flinging an arm out as if seeking support. There wasn't any. His army was gone.

"It is." She advanced, uncaring of the danger, wanting only to rip and tear the abomination in front of her limb from limb, while energy and magic surged. "You may have killed Gianna, but the fight lives on. Just like her the others moved too, so they stood, a wall of justice, shoulder to shoulder.

He reached out, trying to grab her, and arcs of light filled the air. Cressida moved, motions so fast they were simply whirls of action, too fast for the eye to see. She panted and Daniel took her hand, reaching out. "You may defeat us, but there will never be an end to this battle. Not until you are dead."

I will kill you. My mother's will shall be done. There will be no humans whose blood is mixed with mine. It was forbidden, and I will reclaim the purity of our bloodline! The words echoed in her mind. He'd used the blood connection between them to thrust them deep into her psyche. She brushed it aside, as if it were a mere cobweb of insubstantial thought.

Cressida laughed, but there was no mirth, only coldness.

This time it was Attar who retreated.

They advanced, knowing here was the place and the time.

Ready, my friends?

"Ready." All of them spoke as one, as they reached instinctively for the amulets.

DANIEL OPENED HIS MIND WIDE, AND THE OTHERS DID THE same, their thoughts and feelings mixing in a whirl.

Cressida? Let us move to either side. We'll use the fire as we planned. Javed? You and Celina take the rear. Hold him in place while Hope and Xavier take the front line. It's just us. We can do this, but we must stick together.

May our will prevail. Cressida added the thought like a benediction. Then they took their places.

Hope stood sentinel by the door, her whip curled in her hand, while Xavier held the long sword he favored. As they expected, another magic wave washed toward them. Battered them. The strain telling in white lines bracketing lips.

"Ready?" Cressida looked at Daniel, determination settled on his face.

"Yep."

Daniel created a tiny flicker as they'd agreed and set it free, the orb the focus for Attar, so he wouldn't be aware of the circles of magic being crafted behind him. Cressida stepped closer to her quarry, holding the cold hard steel up so Attar wouldn't pounce on Daniel. His eyes glittered in the half light, mesmerizing but frozen.

Attar cackled. "Is that the best you can do, boy?" He created a fire ball and flung it.

Cressida batted it back with the flat of her sword, sneering as Attar growled primitively.

. . .

Telepathically, Daniel heard Celina chanting and he sensed the flow of power to Javed as he flung the tiny little flame at Attar. As expected, he batted it away as Cressida had done with Attar's.

Once again he crafted a flame in his mind, shoving the power to Cressida this time, while they both held onto the amulets. When the flicker hovered in her hand, Attar's face tightened with disbelief. "No! You cannot!" Before they could strike out, the circle Celina and Javed had crafted together settled around Attar.

The chalk they all held flew to Daniel, who dropped the tiny light ball in his hands. Now, instead, he used the chalk marking six circles on the floor, once more using his powers to impel the chalk to move, whilst linking individually to one of their group at a time. Two circles ran close to Attar while the other four were for the protection of innocent lives and the building. Attar fought the bonds that enveloped him. "I will not submit!"

Frigid sweat poured down Daniel's back. He ignored it. A misstep now and they'd all be lost. This magic was complex, and they'd all agreed he'd be the apex. Every ounce of concentration was needed.

The roar filled the room, shaking the foundations of the building, and Daniel lost his footing, almost fell to the floor as Attar hacked at the dancing circle of blue-pink magic surrounding him.

"You cannot hold me!" He fought the glowing wards. The weaker one, Javed's, was in the middle. They'd planned that the smaller and weaker magic should be the one used first, giving the strongest among them a chance to reinforce their work.

As a body, the six surged forward, linking hands, now assured they'd be safe from Attar as they worked together.

Daniel poured his magic into the flame, willed it to grow brighter and hotter. It licked and wavered, seeking fuel for the conflagration. Sparks of purple and gold shot up. Cressida muttered under her breath, eyes half closed as they'd practiced, her own brand of magic sliding into the melding of wills.

The fire danced and swayed, as they each added their individual strains of power while Attar jerked this way and that, trying to avoid the licking tongues of the hungry flame.

The larger the flame grew, the more brittle their control became, until it was close to raging wild. Attar could fight the conflagration if it wasn't threaded together just right, Daniel knew. They had to finish the spell before the circle was breached.

"Clear the building." His voice boomed, imbued with the essence of the six. They couldn't check. There was no way to release the spell now until it was completed.

Beside him, he felt that Cressida was as nervous and tense as were the others. The ability to feel each other's urgency transmitted through the amulets.

The magic of the first ring snapped and for a moment Daniel's control wavered again. He hauled on the magic, anchored it, and reformed the flame in his mind.

"I will slay you. Drink your blood and feed your entrails to the masses." Attar screeched and raged, while the fires licked at the circle between him and the now wild flames.

Daniel? Are you ready? Celina's mental tone was a thready whisper, and it was time.

Let it go...now!

They only had an instant as the ward dropped and encircled Attar in the flames. This was one opponent Attar couldn't slay, though he tried.

The sights and sounds, the unmistakable stench of burning flesh, assaulted their senses as Attar burned.

"No! I'm a god! You...can't..." His final shriek, unfinished and wild, loosened a backlash of power so strong that it knocked them from their feet. They flew through the air, the walls connected with their bodies and he oompahed and the impact jarred Daniel. He looked in Cressida's direction. She too lay on the floor, her gaze dazed.

Attar's remains, a pile of ash littered the floor as the fire traced its way in their direction. The circles having cracked in that last moment.

Javed was there, tugging at him. "We've got to leave now."

The conflagration crept closer to the wall with a *whoosh* as they hurried out. Warriors streamed down steps and along the hall, footsteps muffled by the carpet beneath their feet. More than one carried a fellow fighter, and Daniel wondered how many casualties they'd suffered that night.

A cloud of smoke billowed now from broken windows as the roar of a fire, out of control, echoed in the dying building. The flames of orange and white swallowing whatever lay in its path.

Daniel stumbled down the shallow steps to the road as he heaved in the fresh oxygen and, like so many others, he slumped to the ground. At some time during their flight down the hall Cressida had taken his hand and now he pulled her against his chest.

Trails of silvery tears chased down her cheeks. "We lost so many."

He nodded, the lump in his throat clogging his words.

"Daniel?" Her voice broke and he tugged her close, feeling the echoes of pain and grief.

"It's done, Cressida. He's gone. The evil who stole so much from you."

In that instant she broke, sobs tearing at her. He held her close, knowing this was part of any healing process—hundreds of years overdue. She'd lost her husband and her child. Her humanity and had fought so others wouldn't pay the same high price she had.

"I never..." Her sobs died away and she snuffled, swiped shaking hands over her cheeks and her eyes glinted. "When I lost everything, I never thought I'd find such a gift again. I loved my husband, but now, it seems like that was a different person. Not me. The one who fills my night with joy is you, Daniel. You gave me a chance to be again. Not just a councilor, but also a woman." She moved up, and kissed him on the mouth, her taste salty with her tears.

Before he could speak, a tremendous bang echoed in the night, as the roof collapsed into the structure and the sound of sirens wailed above the noise.

He held Cressida close against him, aware that their hearts beat in synchrony, and turned to the others. "We did it."

They walked slowly toward a bedraggled and more than slightly secondhand-looking army of vampires.

At the command post, Usain hovered, his gaze softening when their party came into view.

"And...?"

"The deed is done. Send in the trucks." Usain gave a slight nod and Daniel smiled as Cressida clutched his hands.

"Oh and, Simon? I think there's some cleaning up. Could you...?" Cressida coughed and Daniel tugged her closer.

"Time to go home, I think."

She made to argue, but he stood firm and she gave in with a tiny sigh. "Fine. I'm going home. Contact me..."

Usain grinned. "Cressida, if we need you, we'll be in touch. But to be honest, I think a wind would knock you over right now. But before you leave? I have a question."

Cressida swayed as she turned to Usain and Daniel reached out, bolstering her. "What?"

"If fire could do that, why didn't you use it before?"

Daniel cleared his throat. "It wasn't normal fire. We'd found an obscure hint last night, it let us to believe that in history, someone had tried to kill him with normal fire which didn't work, but they'd used this kind of magic to deal with the remains of the sister and brothers. It was a conjured fire, a magical wildfire, if you will. The spell was garbled and we weren't sure it would work. We had to re-write it and hope for the best. Unlike real fire, it destroys magic without any other damage. Or so we thought." He looked back at the building, vast jets of water streaming into it from the firetrucks as they tried to save the buildings either side.

"Oh." Usain clearly didn't know how to take that so instead he simply shrugged and turned away.

They piled into the waiting cars, each heading to their own nests. There was still much to do before the sun rose in the sky. They needed to count their dead, attend to their injured.

And Gianna...

How would that be handled? He would ask Cressida... But later once she'd rested and he'd attended to her wounds.

"The witches knew more than they told us." She croaked into the darkness, as if she could read what was on his mind.

"Yeah. They certainly did. We'll need to talk to them." He pulled her close, savoring the warmth of her body. His fingers found a tear in the shoulder of her leather jacket and he burrowed within, seeking her flesh. Then he rubbed gently, with only a fingertip, reinforcing his feeling of togetherness and life.

As the gates loomed, one witch appeared, opening the wards for their entry, and the big car crunched its way up the graveled drive to the house.

Before she could climb out, he held her for a second longer, gazing into her eyes. "I will always be beside you."

Her hands cupped his cheeks. "As will I."

They shared a gentle kiss, a brushing of lip against lip, sealing their vows to each other.

THIRTY-FOUR

Tiredness seeped through Cressida's system. Her body had been working on pure adrenaline for the last hour or so, but now even that was petering out.

Daniel was hunched over a computer, inputting the data they'd managed to scrape together, including the names of their lost.

He looked up, saw her watching him, and closed the lid of the laptop. "Come on. Time for bed."

Their clothes still stank of fire and blood. For a moment she wondered if they were too tired...then she dismissed the thought. Waking up tomorrow, she'd feel even worse.

"A shower first, I think."

His bleary eyes still, amazingly, carried a glint of amusement. "Need someone to wash your back?" He leered, though it was only a shadow.

For the first time in hours, she laughed. "I think I'm too tired for that kind of carrying-on."

He sobered also, winding his arm around her waist. Together they shuffled to the stairs. Each step jarred her aching body, and it was clear from his hisses that Daniel felt the same.

They stopped at the door nearest the stairs and cracked it open. Sarah turned in their direction, her eyes gleaming in the light.

"She sleeps deeply."

Daniel reached out, then stopped, as if he thought better of his actions.

Cressida nodded. Tomorrow would be soon enough to embrace Samantha. So they pushed the door closed and stumbled toward their suite.

Once the bedroom door was closed, they shucked their clothes, letting them form a pile by the door. "I think I'll burn them."

He nodded. "I'm in agreement. I don't think I can ever look at any of these again. Christ, I've never seen anything like it." His hoarse voice tugged at her heart.

"Not on that level. I'd honestly thought we'd never have to battle like that again. That in these civilized times..." She shrugged.

Together they padded to the bathroom and the water, once they stepped beneath it, washed away the soot and grime. The blood that stained their skin melted underneath the spray and she leaned close, his scent surrounding her.

Her body, as battered and bruised as it was, reacted the instant their skin touched.

He laughed, sliding his hand over her cheek. "Maybe we could manage this..."

The deep kiss left flickering fires streaking through her, and he gripped her hips before hauling her up.

Without thought, she wound her legs around his waist and he plunged within her body, sheathing himself deeply.

The orgasm crashed down, filling her senses, and she screamed her pleasure while he jerked and shook, fingers digging into her sensitive flesh. Daniel groaned his release as he held tight, and the echoes of their cries filled the small room.

Inch by inch she slid down until her unsteady feet found the floor of the stall.

"Well, that was..."

Her mind was still fogged and she couldn't think of the words to complete her thought.

"Amazing?" He wiggled his eyebrows and she laughed in spite of her exhaustion.

"Something like that."

She shivered as they entered the cool bedroom. Even though they were wound in the soft towels Daniel had snatched, the air remained chilled and they shook.

The thoughtful and caring act still had the power to reduce her to a melted puddle, she realized.

Together they headed for the bed and lay down. Daniel snuggled against her and touched the amulet still hanging around her neck. *"Will we have to give these back, do you think?"*

"I don't know. Maybe. I suppose it really depends on what the witches decree."

The fog of sleep advanced on her as he whispered, "Forever, my love. The three of us."

The idea of the three of them was the last thought until they woke the next night.

His eyes opened. Nighttime. His body didn't ache, although it had only been the night before that they'd battled and beaten Attar. It wasn't a dream or some kind of nightmare that filled one with terror. Cressida lay beside him and by the light of the small lamp the outlines of bruises still showed on her face.

Javed? Xavier?

They grunted in his mind. *We're here. What's up?* He had the impression of crumpled sheets and warm bodies, and he shook his head. Not really what he wanted to know.

We need to get hold of the witches as soon as possible so we can put this behind us. They needed to get the information from them, the things that had been missed, so they could make firm decisions for the future.

Shouldn't it be Cressida calling the shots, Daniel? Javed's dry tone nearly made him laugh.

Maybe, but she's exhausted and I don't want to add to her pressure. I think we also need a debrief. How soon do you think you could round up your troops?

Unlike you, Celina and I have kids now. Give us at least an hour to catch up, dress... A stray thought had Daniel snickering.

Cressida snored a little and rolled toward him. Maybe that wasn't such a bad thought.

Hey, lover boy, stop broadcasting! Xavier's tone brought him back to earth with a thud.

Well, I'm still learning how to control this. I'll see you in an hour.

They broke off as Cressida opened her eyes. "Everything okay?" She spoke low, her voice still fogged with sleep, as were her eyes.

He brushed a stray lock of golden hair from her face, wondering for the first time how he'd come to find such an amazing woman. "Perfect. Just perfect."

As he hauled her into his arms, a knock came at the door.

"It's Samra." Cressida groaned, pulling on the wrap from the seat beside the bed. "What?"

"There's a little girl waiting to see you. So if you could, uh, you know, let us in."

They scrambled from the bed and raced to the closet. "Give us a moment!" They dragged out the first sets of clothes they could find. For her it was formal pants and a camisole. Long boots. She reached for the matching jacket.

"Here, put this over your top." Daniel threw her a jumper of white wool.

"I can't..."

"Sure. We've got a daughter now. Suits are only for formal occasions. Besides, we need to go shopping and buy you some more casual things."

She gurgled as he tugged on jeans, boots and a lightweight shirt. Teamed with a jumper, it felt right for the first day of what he knew would be the rest of his life.

"Come in!"

Cressida looked at him, horrified, as she was dealing with her hair, but the door squeaked open and a little girl came dashing toward them.

"Cress'da! Dan'el. Samra has a pony!" Her face glowed as Daniel scooped her up in his arms, feeling the chubby small child weight of her. He popped a kiss on her forehead and passed the girl to Cressida, where she snuggled in.

They left the bedroom and headed down the stairs. Hopefully they would receive the news he was waiting for.

In her office, he lifted the lid of the laptop and checked his emails. It hummed and message after message dropped into the inbox.

"Are you waiting for anything in particular, Daniel?"

Samra smiled as he frowned. "No... Not really." Of course it wasn't true. He was waiting on an email confirmation of news he'd requested on the night of the funerals. It seemed like long ago, yet only three days had passed.

No use hanging around, he thought. He called for a meal for Samantha, and he and Cressida sat with her while she ate and chatted. She told them how she'd filled her day, helping in the kitchen and playing in the small sandpit they'd had hastily purchased. He reminded himself they'd need to take her shopping for more clothes and toys. Perhaps they could also see if anyone had photos of her biological family, so she'd have something of them with her forever.

A ding in the inbox echoed and he rose, passing the child back to Cressida. While he was sure that there wouldn't yet be an answer, his heart filled with hope.

A single message caught his eye.

Request for Nest Guardianship.

Daniel,

After investigation, the Nestling Advocacy Association has taken your petition for full guardianship of the minor Samantha Rose DeLund to the appropriate government agency.

An interim order has been granted, but I believe, in the circumstances, that your permanent application for adoption of the minor will be granted. You will be required to attend at least a single meeting with an appropriately trained supervisor, but given the circumstances, we see no impediments.

We would advise you to make any and all necessary preparations for this interview with all speed. We will place ourselves at your disposal.

Should you have any queries, please do not hesitate...

"Daniel? Is everything okay?" She'd risen and advanced in his direction. Daniel slumped to the seat, unable for a moment to frame a comprehensible answer to Cressida's concerned query.

"The NAA are going to help us." Joy filled him. He and Cressida might just become parents after all.

"What? When did you contact them?"

"I contacted them immediately after I had the idea. I wanted to find out before I spoke to you. I didn't want to get your hopes up."

They both looked at the little girl, now busy eating ice cream, a hint of chocolate smeared on her face as she grinned.

In their haze of joy, they didn't hear the door open and four adults enter the room.

"Is everything okay?" Hope stopped at the threshold.

"Everything is just damned fine." He couldn't wipe the smile from his face. "Nothing could be better."

EPILOGUE

"We call the Council to order, including the following three new members—Daniel, Life Partner of Cressida, Javed of the House al bin Habbad and Xavier of the Tudor House."

Daniel rose, pushing the heavy weight of his cape aside. He felt no hesitation in accepting the role he'd been offered, as had Javed and Xavier.

Samra had been offered the third vacancy, but she'd declined. *'I prefer to follow rules and enforce them rather than to make them. Choose Daniel. He's earned it already'*.

Cressida argued hard to assure the other councilors that although he was only a neophyte, he already had the experience to make tough decisions. And that he was dedicated to their way of life.

It hadn't taken a lot of arguing for them to accept him.

He took the chair amid cheers from those watching. Cressida stood close by.

"By the power invested in the vampire council, I must ask you to take your oaths." They did so, swearing to protect the innocents, to make just decisions and to protect their brethren from all harm.

Once the ceremony was concluded, they mingled with the

crowd. Daniel made a beeline for Cressida and their daughter, Samantha. The little girl flung her arms around his neck and he pulled her close. As always, he enjoyed the innocent smell of her. "You smell of baby powder. Have you been rolling in it again?"

She gave a big giggle and he tickled her.

Cressida grinned up at him. "So now you're a councilor."

"So now you're the Overlord."

She grimaced at his words. "I never expected—"

He kissed her, a hard, quick smack. "I think that's why they chose you. You never did expect anything." His gaze softened. "But you earned it and I'm proud of you." He ran his fingers through Samantha's silky hair. "Both my girls are so clever." Samantha chortled and he joggled her up and down while she shrieked with pleasure.

He knew more than one vampire looked in his direction, their glances full of censure, but he ignored the looks while enjoying the time with his family.

Cressida grabbed his hand, "Come with us." She tugged him from the room.

In the courtyard, milling among the flowers, were the others from their now close-knit group. Xavier and Hope, Javed and Celina, together with Marian, Lucy and Rachel.

David stood in the corner, a young woman by his side. "It's good to see he's finally found someone who is interested in him."

Daniel grunted, thinking back to the last time he'd seen her, helping the young woman who'd been attacked. Now Officer Fernly, Genevieve as they'd learned was her full name, had taken to spending time with the new *Yeux Secondes* of the al bin Habbad nest.

Xavier had chosen a woman as David's replacement, and Daniel remembered the discussion they'd had afterward. *'Everyone is much happier now. We're a little less correct and upright'.*

"So? Now we're here, it's time to make some announcements." Hope joined the banter with a ready grin.

"We already know most of it." Javed had also unbent enough to show his cheeky side.

"Not everything." David strode forward, towing his partner into the circle. "Tonight I asked Genevieve to court, and she agreed." A round of kisses and hugs, back slapping and congratulations flowed.

Lucy stepped forward. "Since everyone is making announcements, I guess we should share what we plan to do."

The girls looked among themselves and nodded. "You do it, Lucy. You're better at this." Rachel gripped Marian's hands as they waited.

"Well, okay. See? We've been talking. Now that we remember who and what we are, we have a choice. We can either look for any of our families, or stay with Javed and Celina. We've talked a lot about our options."

For the first time since he'd met his half-sister, Celina looked stricken. Before he could reach for her, Lucy took her hand. "We want to stay. Celina and Javed? You're our parents now. You love us, care for us, and we just..." She stopped and gulped loudly.

"Unless you send us away, you're stuck with us, is what Lucy is trying to say." Rachel spoke quietly, though her words carried deep emotions.

As one, they flung their arms around the couple and held on tight.

Now there were very few with dry eyes in the gathering.

From the gloom emerged three women. Their iridescent gowns shone by the light of the torches and their hair was gathered up in elaborate sweeps. "Good, we're just in time."

"You!" Cressida took a step, then stopped.

"Cressida, forgive us for not telling all previously. You see, we couldn't. It wasn't our place." Selena spoke quietly, and Daniel saw more than one frown on the faces of those gathered.

Marian raised her head from Celina's skirts. "They can't. They're the Graces and they can only help to resolve matters. Not give the full answers."

Daniel frowned. "And how do you know that?"

"The young one speaks true. She's touched, you know. Maybe one day, she too might be a Grace, if she chooses. But for now, she is a child. Bright and clever with the knack of seeing." Selena spread her arm. "But now, we have come to say our goodbyes. Our task here is complete and we wish and long for rest. And home."

The other two witches nodded.

"What? You plan to leave?" Cressida leaned in and the three witches gave tired grins.

"Oh we'll leave soon enough. But first we wish to grant you all something special. If any among you wish to be freed of the curse of the vampire..."

"What?" Hope squeaked the word, which echoed.

Daniel watched as gazes met and clung. Hope and Xavier were the first to shake their heads.

"For all there have been secrets passed in the blood, I wouldn't change who and what I am now." Hope grinned.

"Nor would I. It brought me Hope and friendships that will last for eternity."

Celina grinned. "I have my family and Javed. I don't need to change anything else."

Javed's arm still encircled Celina, but he tugged her a little closer. "And I've learned of real love, friendship and family."

Daniel heard and felt the unsteady breath Cressida sucked in. She'd battled for so long with her past. What would she decide? "I too have a family and a love that I couldn't ever relinquish. Not even to death. Daniel?"

Her gaze was warm and loving, and he smiled. "And I will love my Cressida forever. Together with Samantha, we truly have everything we could ever ask for."

David coughed, and all gazes settled on him. "Well, Genny and I — she has so many things hidden from her. Secrets. She's my one. I know that, unlike before with Alexa. We've been talking... We want children in the future. We've only just found each other and need time to build what we have, but... I want her to know what is hidden from her."

Genny Fernly gripped his hands. "David?"

"Think of this as my gift to you, my love." He kissed her cheek tenderly.

"Perhaps, David. It's something you can both explore when you're ready." Cressida reached out and squeezed his hand.

The Graces turned to the woman and Jemima reached out her hand, the welling of power tangible. "Well then, when you're ready my dear, the answers shall become apparent. And with that, we bid you farewell." The witches rose and gifted the assembled vampires and humans with hugs.

Hand in hand, the three witches walked into the night without looking back. "I don't think we'll see them again." Cressida spoke quietly as she watched for a second longer, then turned back to the family waiting for her.

THE BLOOD BRIDE BY IMOGENE NIX

Hope just wants to be an ordinary nestling. She went to college and escaped, but now she's back and there's a secret everyone is keeping from her.

Xavier is the new master of the nest, ready to welcome home the daughter of the house who he has never met. He's unprepared for the woman who steals his breath and enchants him.

Now Hope and Xavier must fight for lives and those of the innocents. After all, it is only by overcoming the rogues that they will have a chance of a timeless future together. But will it be in time?

PROLOGUE

As silence descended on the house, the shadows grew—dark grays and blacks that bled into each other. First one figure then another broke away, making a run toward the house. Silent as the grave, they moved swiftly over dew-slicked grass. Then they stopped still. Waiting. Not a movement betrayed them until a signal propelled them back into action and they started crawling upwards. The walls damp coating no barrier to the intruders that ascended in the darkness.

The sound of each window breaking shattered the quiet—the figures were inside. Screams echoed through the night. Yet, in this area of large estates, heavy with noise-absorbing shrubbery, no one could hear those within. The blood-curdling screams went on and on before finally dying away.

Just one sound echoed through the night: The sobbing of a child.

The front door opened and figures trooped out—ghostly specters against an inky night sky, broken by a single outline. A child in white, carried at the center of the pack.

No sound broke the silence as they moved toward the trees surrounded the house.

Flames now licked at the manor: A deathly glow of oily smoke rising.

All that remained was a single person—wrapped in a cape of midnight blue beyond the house—watching them melt away.

Jemima moved toward the burning structure, breaking into a run as she breached the threshold. Vainly she attempted to enter, but the heat drove her back.

Now dashing tears from her face, she raced across the graveled driveway toward the gates, where the guardhouse was located. No sign of life existed within the building and some instinct of survival slowed her pace to a careful creep. Out of breath and heaving from exertion, she nervously checked within.

Small puffs of white vapor colored the glass. She darted from one window to another. Her cloak drawn tightly around her body, hoping it would camouflage her from sight.

Satisfied, Jemima entered through the heavy, wooden front door and moved toward the phone she spied on the floor. Her eyes darting here and there she dialed, listening to the rotary motor as it returned to the proper position. Time was short and if *they* came back, she needed to have shared the message.

The phone rang once. Twice. With a brrping sound it connected.

"Hello?" A male answered and she felt a warm flush of relief at the voice. A voice she knew well.

"The manor has been breached. The girl child taken." The words erupted and her hand trembled.

"On our way." The click of the receiver being replaced echoed loudly in the stillness of the room.

Copper. She smelled copper.

Her stomach soured, knowing it meant more deaths. Jemima looked around for the gun—a gun with deadly, holy water-infused copper bullets—she knew was hidden somewhere in the room. A gun she couldn't find. *No divine intervention exists here,* she thought.

Hopefully *they* didn't remain. Feeding. If they were still here, that's what they would be doing. She found a corner and scrunched down, hiding from sight.

Crouched low, she tried to stay as still as possible, listening for sounds of the vehicles she knew would be coming. She dug her fingers into the flesh of her arms; remaining aware enough to stop before drawing blood. That would surely bring them out. Jemima dragged the cloak around her to capture the warmth, yet there was little to be found.

The sounds of engines roused her from the corner of the room. Jemima inched toward the window, the lead of the old glass distorting her view, hearing raised voices she knew Mistress Cressida had arrived.

Jemima retreated. Remained hidden from the woman because if she knew, all may well be lost. From the shadowed room she listened to the conversation...

"It smells like Estersham." The Mistress' eyes closed. "If it is, we have a problem." She turned once more, her face set and eyes now glacial in intensity. "James?"

The man nodded as if he knew what was to come.

"If I take those steps, I cannot return. Another must stand in my place." Her voice hardened while her eyes glittered in the dim light, piercing in their intensity.

Then the Mistress' voice called out in the near silence. "You and yours have been my loyal servants for so many years. I took an oath to protect you long ago. I renewed it with marriage and births, over and over. Now, my home and yours have been breached and this child taken from us. The girl child, who will be the hope and salvation of our kind, was ripped from the bosom of our nest. I will repay your loyalty and I will get her back." The words of power rippled in the night and licked at Jemima's skin.

Available in Ebook
books2read.com/BloodBride-Nix

Direct Autographed Copy
https://bit.ly/TBB-Nix

When Cupid—otherwise known as Diocail— is banished from his home on a remote Scottish Island, he's set a series of tasks by the great god Lugh, who also happens to be his father.

In ***Blame The Wine***, he must bring two lovers together... BBW Cara and James, the man she's lusted over from afar who happens to be a super geek and head Veha Industries.

In ***A Stranger's Embrace***, Diocail is driven to help an

emotionally fragile Jane and Davis, a famous author. The task is more complicated, with the existence of Carstairs her could-be ex-husband and teenage daughter, Frannie.

In **_Revenge on Cupid_**, Diocail must take the ultimate chance and find his own happily ever after with Simone. Sometimes the past gets in the way and HEA's don't come cheap though.

The dusty, dingy little diner was full, even with its current state of cleanliness—or lack thereof. People from the surrounding offices didn't care about anything except the incredible, well-prepared food at a reasonable cost. They flooded in, like waves to the shore. As one tide left, another swept in.

"Honestly, Simone. I'm going to try getting his attention one more time. If that doesn't work, I'm out of there. I mean, how long can I keep trying?" Cara picked at the caramel tart she hadn't been able to resist with the cheap metal fork and flicked the blob of fresh cream that sat on top to the side of the plate.

"You've said that tons of times before. Besides, what are you going to do to get his attention? Hmm? Walk naked through the typing pool?" Simone bobbed the straw in her smoothie as she eyed her friend with a frown. "It's been what? Eighteen months since you saw him, and you've mooned over him from a distance ever since you met him. You need to move on, Cara. That is, unless there's something you haven't shared?"

The query was arch. Cara shivered even as she shook her head. "No."

Simone quirked an eyebrow, obviously unconvinced with the answer. Cara let out a deep sigh of frustration. "There's a position...it's only temporary, for a PA reporting directly to him." She speared a forkful of tart, chewed quickly and swallowed, before continuing. "In his office, full-time for the period of the engagement. I saw the memo yesterday. I mean, I have the skills, right? I can type, answer phones, make coffee, file, greet people. What's more, I can probably do it better than all those size eights in the typing pool that

Ms. Jackman seems to prefer." She nodded thoughtfully. "All I have to do is get past the ogre in Human Resources."

Simone stared at her, disbelief clear on her face. "Girl, I so remember that woman. If you think you can get past her, you're doing better than I ever did. That's why I left Veha Industries, remember? Maybe it's time to haul out your resumé and consider some other options. Look for something better." Simone shook her head and billows of her crimson hair swirled through the still air.

Cara understood Simone only had her best interests at heart. But this time she knew the outcome would be different. Hell, she could feel it in the air. The tingle of expectation.

"Cara, the HR ogre will hang you out for breakfast before she offers you anything like a position in that office. Remember her mantra? Good looks and good work make for a positive workplace!"

Simone didn't sugar-coat anything. It was another great reason for their long- term friendship. Honesty. But Cara didn't want to hear the truth in the statement. Even if it was exactly as her friend said.

Cara nodded quickly. "Yeah, I know, but if I don't try, then I won't know how close I can get to him, right? And the only way to catch his attention is to get past *her* and see him in person." Cara quaked a little at the information she needed to share. The favor she needed to ask. "Anyway, I tidied up my resumé and dropped the application into a memo envelope yesterday, so it's too late to back out now. I mean, fortune favors the brave. Doesn't it? If I don't snag an interview, I'm going to visit the career advisor across the street and register with them." She shrugged. "I'll look for temp work until something more long-term shows up. I can see what they have on offer and well...who knows? Maybe a job with the right boss is just waiting for me. But I'd rather this worked out, to be honest." Her voice trailed off into a whisper. "I really wish he would notice me."

Simone took a long slurp of her banana drink, and Cara noticed her questioning gaze even as she squirmed. Finally, Simone nodded. "It's your funeral. So anyway, you'd better show me this memo if you want me to be a referee for you. I'm guessing that's what you need, right? I'll have to know what I'm supposed to say about you before they ring."

Cara smiled. "Thanks, Simone. I knew I could count on you." She slipped a piece of paper out of her handbag and handed it over. "Sorry it's a bit creased. It was in the bottom of my bag, I stashed it so none of the others from the pool would see. You know how it is."

Available from Love Books Publishing
books2read.com/CelticCupid

Direct Autographed Copy
http://bit.ly/2vs7wtS

ALSO BY IMOGENE NIX

Warriors of the Elector

- Star of Ishtar
- Starline
- Starfire
- Star of the Fleet
- Starburst
- The Star of Eternity

The Star of Ishtar & Starline - Print

Starfire & Star of the Fleet - Print

Starburst & The Star of Eternity - Print

Blood Secrets

- The Blood Bride
- The Illuminated Witch
- The Sorcerer's Touch

The Search Duology

- Miss Elspeth's Desire
- Miss Isabelle's Craving

Reunion Trilogy

- War's End
- The Assassin
- Executing Justice

The Reunion Trilogy in Paperback

Sex Love & Aliens

- Tangled Webs
- False Webs (Sex Love & Aliens Vol 1)
- Covert Webs (Sex Love & Aliens Vol 2)

21st Testing Protocol

- Cyborg: Redux
- Children Of A Greater Evil
- When Evil Came To Stay (Forthcoming)
- Finis: The War To End All Wars (Forthcoming)

Celtic Cupid Trilogy

- Blame The Wine
- A Stranger's Embrace
- Revenge On Cupid

The Celtic Cupid Trilogy in Paperback

Zombieology

- The Reset (2018 - Love At The End of The World)
- I Dream of Zombies
- The Six Million Dollar Zombie

Knights of Pleasure

- Silken Knights (Not Yet Released)

Single Titles

The Chocolate Affair (also in Print)

Falling In Love Again (Previously A Sapphire For Karina)

BioCybe (also in Print)

Hesparia's Tears (also in Print)

Tomorrow's Promise

A Bar In Paris (also in Print)

Inheritance Of The Blood (also in Print)

The Plan

Loving Memories (also in Print)

Hero of Heartbreak Hill (also in Print)

My One & Only

Curse Bound

Raspberry Dreams (Not Yet Released)

Non Fiction

Self Publishing: Absolute Beginners Guide (With Suzi Love)

Written as Ciara Cave

25 Curated Ways To Get Rid Of Telemarketers

Book Signings for Absolute Beginners

ABOUT THE AUTHOR

Imogene is published in a range of romance genres including Paranormal, Science Fiction and Contemporary. She is mainly published in the UK and USA.

In 2010, Imogene Nix (the pen name not Imogene herself) was born. Imogene sat down and worked tirelessly for 3 months culminating in the book Starline, which became the first in a trilogy titled, "Warriors of the Elector." Since then she's had over 30 titles published and is now focusing on hybridising herself - with a mixture of traditionally published and self-published works.

In fact, she's taking control of many of her back catalogue books, which are slowly re-releasing as self-published titles.

Imogene is a member of a range of professional organisations world wide, and believes in the mantra of mentoring and paying it forward and is actively involved in mentorship (through NaNoWrimo and her vlog: In The Chair With Imogene Nix) and tutoring of new and upcoming authors.

In her spare time she loves to drink coffee, wine & eat chocolate and is parenting her spoiled dog and a ferocious cat along with her husband and 2 human daughters and looks forward to weekends away with her husband in their caravan "The Seven Year Hitch!" Do look forward to her caravan romance at some point!

Want to interact? There's lots of ways, but why not pop along and join the reader group? http://bit.ly/MakeFakeNix